TO THE RIM OF CHAOS

In dark blue vest with golden disk, his scar flaming beneath the blaze, Captain Lorq Von Ray left the line of people. The voice was big.

"All right, which one of you wants a hand-hold halfway to the night's rim? Are you sand-footed, or star steppers? What's the matter? Are you afraid to leave this little well of gravity funneling out into that half-pint sun?" He jerked his chin toward the high-lighted mountains. "Who's coming with us where night means forever and morning's a recollection?"

"Where we for running are?" Sebastian asked. The creature on his shoulders stepped from one foot to the other, flapping to balance. Its wingspan was nearly seven feet. "What out there, Captain, is?"

"We're hunting a nova," Von Ray said. "We have to go to the rim of chaos and bring back a handful of fire, with as few stops as possible on the way. Where we're going, all law has broken down. . . ."

Bantam Books by Samuel R. Delany
Ask your bookseller for the books you have missed

NOVA

Samuel R. Delany

BANTAM BOOKS
TORONTO • NEW YORK • LONDON • SYDNEY • AUCKLAND

This low-priced Bantam Book
has been completely reset in a type face
designed for easy reading, and was printed
from new plates. It contains the complete
text of the original hard-cover edition.
NOT ONE WORD HAS BEEN OMITTED.

NOVA
A Bantam Spectra Book / published by arrangement with
Doubleday & Company, Inc.

PRINTING HISTORY
Doubleday edition published August 1968

Science Fiction Book Club selection May 1969

Bantam edition / November 1969

2nd printing . . . . . . June 1973	8th printing . . February 1979
3rd printing . . . . . . June 1973	9th printing . September 1979
4th printing . . . . October 1973	10th printing . . . October 1980
5th printing . . . . August 1976	11th printing . . . January 1982
6th printing . . September 1976	12th printing . . . . . May 1983
7th printing . . . . . . May 1977	13th printing . . . January 1986

All rights reserved.
Copyright © 1968 by Samuel R. Delany.
Cover art copyright © 1985 by Graphic Associates.
This book may not be reproduced in whole or in part, by
mimeograph or any other means, without permission.
For information address: Doubleday & Company, Inc.,
245 Park Avenue, New York, N.Y. 10167.

ISBN 0-553-23621-0

Published simultaneously in the United States and Canada

Bantam Books are published by Bantam Books, Inc. Its trademark, consisting of the words "Bantam Books" and the por-
trayal of a rooster, is Registered in U.S. Patent and Trademark
Office and in other countries. Marca Registrada. Bantam
Books, Inc., 666 Fifth Avenue, New York, New York 10103.

PRINTED IN THE UNITED STATES OF AMERICA

H   22 21 20 19 18 17 16 15 14 13

To
Bernard and Iva Kay

ACKNOWLEDGMENT

The author gratefully acknowledges the invaluable aid of Helen Adam and Russell FitzGerald with problems of Grail and Tarot lore. Without their help NOVA would cast much dimmer light.

Chapter One

"Hey, Mouse! Play us something," one of the mechanics called from the bar.

"Didn't get signed on no ship yet?" chided the other. "Your spinal socket'll rust up. Come on, give us a number."

The Mouse stopped running his finger around the rim of his glass. Wanting to say "no" he began a "yes." Then he frowned.

The mechanics frowned too:

He was an old man.

He was a strong man.

As the Mouse pulled his hand to the edge of the table, the derelict lurched forward. Hip banged the counter. Long toes struck a chair leg: the chair danced on the flags.

Old. Strong. The third thing the Mouse saw: blind.

He swayed before the Mouse's table. His hand swung up; yellow nails hit the Mouse's cheek. (Spider's feet?) "You, boy ..."

The Mouse stared at the pearls behind rough, blinking lids.

"You, boy. Do you know what it was like?"

Must be blind, the Mouse thought. Moves like blind. Head sits forward so on his neck. And his eyes—

The codger flapped out his hand, caught a chair, and yanked it to him. It rasped as he fell on the seat. "Do you *know* what it looked like, felt like, smelt like—do you?"

The Mouse shook his head; the fingers tapped his cheek.

"We were moving out, boy, with the three hundred suns of the Pleiades glittering like a puddle of jeweled milk on our

1

left, and all blackness wrapped around our right. The ship was me; I was the ship. With these sockets—" he tapped the insets in his wrists against the table: *click* "—I was plugged into my vane-projector. Then—" the stubble on his jaw rose and fell with the words "—centered on the dark, a light! It reached out, grabbed our eyes as we lay in the projection chambers and wouldn't let them go. It was like the universe was torn and all day raging through. I wouldn't go off sensory input. I wouldn't look away. All the colors you could think of were there, blotting the night. And finally the shock waves: the walls sang! Magnetic inductance oscillated over our ship, nearly rattled us apart. But then it was too late. I was blind." He sat back in his chair. "I'm blind, boy. But with a funny kind of blindness; I can see you. I'm deaf; but if you talked to me, I could understand most of what you said. Olfactory endings all dead, and the taste buds over my tongue." His hand went flat on the Mouse's cheek. "I can't feel the texture of your face. Most of the tactile nerve endings were killed too. Are you smooth, or are you bristly and gristly as I am?" He laughed on yellow teeth in red, red gums. "Dan is blind in a funny way." His hand slipped down the Mouse's vest, catching the laces. "A funny way, yes. Most people go blind in blackness. I have a fire in my eyes. I have that whole collapsing sun in my head. The light lashed the rods and cones of my retina to constant stimulation, balled up a rainbow and stuffed each socket full. That's what I'm seeing now. Then you, outlined here, highlighted there, a solarized ghost across hell from me. Who are you?"

"Pontichos," the Mouse offered. His voice sounded like wool with sand, grinding. "Pontichos Provechi."

Dan's face twisted. "Your name is ... What did you say? It's shaking my head apart. There's a choir crouched in my ears, shouting down into my skull twenty-six hours a day. The nerve ends, they're sending out static, the death rattle that sun's been dying ever since. Over that, I can just hear your voice, like an echo of something shouted a hundred yards off." Dan coughed and sat back, hard. "Where are you from?" He wiped his mouth.

"Here in Draco," the Mouse said. "Earth."

"Earth? Where? America? You come from a little white house on a tree-lined street, with a bicycle in the garage?"

Oh yes, the Mouse thought. Blind, and deaf too. The

Mouse's speech was good, but he'd never even tried to correct his accent.

"Me. I'm from Australia. From a white house. I lived just outside Melbourne. Trees. I had a bicycle. But that was a long time ago. A long time, wasn't it, boy? You know Australia, on Earth?"

"Been through." The Mouse squirmed in his chair and wondered how to get away.

"Yes. That's how it was. But you don't know, boy! You can't know what it's like to stagger through the rest of your life with a nova dug into your brain, remembering Melbourne, remembering the bicycle. What did you say your name was?"

The Mouse looked left at the window, right at the door.

"I can't remember it. The sound of that sun blots out everything."

The mechanics, who had been listening till now, turned to the bar.

"Can't remember a thing any more!"

At another table a black-haired woman fell back to her card game with her blond companion.

"Oh, I've been sent to doctors! They say if they cut out the nerves, optic and aural, slice them off at the brain, the roaring, the light—it might stop! *Might?*" He raised his hands to his face. "And the shadows of the world that come in, they'd stop too. Your name? What's your name?"

The Mouse got the words ready in his mouth, along with, excuse me, huh? I gotta go.

But Dan coughed, clutched at his ears.

"Ahhh! That was a pig trip, a dog trip, a trip for flies! The ship was the *Roc* and I was a cyborg stud for Captain Lorq Von Ray. He took us"—Dan leaned across the table—"this close"—his thumb brushed his forefinger—"this *close* to hell. And brought us back. You can damn him, and damn Illyrion for that, boy, whoever you are. Wherever you're from!" Dan barked, flung back his head; his hands jumped on the table.

The bartender glanced over. Somebody signaled for a drink. The bartender's lips tightened, but he turned off, shaking his head.

"Pain," Dan's chin came down, "after you've lived with it long enough, isn't pain any more. It's something else. Lorq Von Ray is mad! He took us as near the edge of dying as he

could. Now he's abandoned me, nine tenths a corpse, here at
the rim of the Solar System. And where's he gone—" Dan
breathed hard. Something flapped in his lungs. "Where's blind
Dan going to go now?"

Suddenly he grabbed the sides of the table.

"Where is Dan going to go!"

The Mouse's glass tumbled, smashed on the stone.

"You tell me!"

He shook the table again.

The bartender was coming over.

Dan stood, overturning his chair, and rubbed his knuckles
on his eyes. He took two staggering steps through the sunburst
that rayed the floor. Two more. The last left long maroon
prints.

The black-haired woman caught her breath. The blond
man closed the cards.

One mechanic started forward, but the other touched his
arm.

Dan's fists struck the swinging doors. He was gone.

The Mouse looked around. Glass on stone again, but
softer. The bartender had plugged the sweeper into his wrist
and the machine hissed over dirt and bloody fragments. "You
want another drink?"

"No," the Mouse's voice whispered from his ruined larynx.
"No. I was finished. Who was that?"

"Used to be a cyborg stud on the *Roc*. He's been making
trouble around here for a week. Lots of places throw him
out soon as he comes in the door. How come you been
having such a hard time getting signed on?"

"I've never been on a star-run before," came the Mouse's
rough whisper. "I just got my certificate two years back.
Since then I've been plugged in with a small freight company
working around inside the Solar System on the triangle run."

"I could give you all kinds of advice." The bartender
unplugged the sweeper from the socket on his wrist. "But I'll
restrain myself. Ashton Clark go with you." He grinned and
went back behind the bar.

The Mouse felt uncomfortable. He hooked a dark thumb
beneath the leather strap over his shoulder, got up and
started for the door.

"Eh, Mouse, come on. Play something for us—"

The door closed behind him.

The shrunken sun lay jagged gold on the mountains. Neptune, huge in the sky, dropped mottled light on the plain. The star-ships hulked in the repair pits half a mile away.

The Mouse started down the strip of bars, cheap hotels, and eating places. Unemployed and despondent, he had bummed in most of them, playing for board, sleeping in the corner of somebody's room when he was pulled in to entertain at an all-night party. That wasn't what his certificate said he should be doing. That wasn't what he wanted.

He turned down the boardwalk that edged Hell^3.

To make the satellite's surface habitable, Draco Commission had planted Illyrion furnaces to melt the moon's core. With surface temperature at mild autumn, atmosphere generated spontaneously from the rocks. An artificial ionosphere kept it in. The other manifestations of the newly molten core were Hells^1 to ^{52}, volcanic cracks that had opened in the crust of the moon. Hell^3 was almost a hundred yards wide, twice as deep (a flaming worm broiled on its bottom), and seven miles long. The cañon flickered and fumed under pale night.

As the Mouse walked by the abyss, hot air caressed his cheek. He was thinking about blind Dan. He was thinking about the night beyond Pluto, beyond the edge of the stars called Draco. And was afraid. He fingered the leather sack against his side.

When the Mouse was ten years old, he stole that sack. It held what he was to love most.

Terrified, he fled from the music stalls beneath white vaults, down between the stinking booths of suede. He clutched the sack to his belly, jumped over a carton of meerschaum pipes that had broken open, spilling across the dusty stone, passed under another arch, and for twenty meters darted through the crowds roaming the Golden Alley where velvet display windows were alive with light and gold. He side-stepped a boy treading the heels of his shoes and swinging a three-handled tray of tea glasses and coffee cups. As the Mouse dodged, the tray went up and over; tea and coffee shook, but nothing spilled. The Mouse fled on.

Another turn took him past a mountain of embroidered slippers.

Mud splattered the next time his canvas shoes hit the broken flooring. He stopped, panting, looked up.

No vaults. Light rain drifted between the buildings. He held the sack tighter, smeared his damp face with the back of his hand, and started up the curving street.

The Burnt Tower of Constantine, rotten, ribbed, and black, jutted from the parking lot. As he reached the main street, people hurried about him, splashing in the thin slip covering the stones. The leather had grown sweaty on his skin.

Good weather? He would have romped down the back-street shortcut. But this: he kept to the main way, taking some protection from the monorail. He pushed his way among the businessmen, the students, the porters.

A sledge rumbled on the cobbles. The Mouse took a chance and swung up on the yellow running board. The driver grinned—gold-flecked crescent in a brown face—and let him stay.

Ten minutes later, heart still hammering, the Mouse swung off and ducked through the courtyard of New Mosque. In the drizzle a few men washed their feet in the stone troughs at the wall. Two women came from the flapping door at the entrance, retrieved their shoes, and started down the gleaming steps, hastening in the rain.

Once, the Mouse had asked Leo just when New Mosque was built. The fisherman from the Pleiades Federation—who always walked with one foot bare—had scratched his thick, blond hair as they gazed at the smoky walls rising to the domes and spiking minarets. "About a thousand years ago, was. But that only a guess is."

The Mouse was looking for Leo now.

He ran out the courtyard and dodged between the trucks, cars, dolmushes, and trollies crowding the entrance of the bridge. On the crosswalk, under a street-lamp, he turned through an iron gate and hurried down the steps. Small boats clacked together in the sludge. Beyond the dinghies, the mustard water of the Golden Horn heaved about the pilings and the hydrofoil docks. Beyond the Horn's mouth, across the Bosphorus, the clouds had torn.

Beams slanted through and struck the wake of a ferry plowing toward another continent. The Mouse paused on the steps to stare over the glittering strait as more and more light fell through.

Windows in foggy Asia flashed on sand-colored walls. It was the beginning of the effect that had caused the Greeks, two thousand years before, to call the Asian side of the city Chrysopolis—Gold City. Today it was Uskudar.

"Hey, Mouse!" Leo hailed him from the red, doffing deck. Leo had built an awning over his boat, set up wooden tables, and placed barrels around for chairs. Black oil boiled in a vat, heated by an ancient generator caked with grease. Beside it, on a yellow slicker, was a heap of fish. The gills had been hooked around the lower jaws so that each fish had a crimson flower at its head. "Hey, Mouse, what you got?"

In better weather fishermen, dock workers, and porters lunched here. The Mouse climbed over the rail as Leo threw in two fish. The oil erupted yellow foam.

"I got what . . . what you were talking about. I got it . . . I mean I think it's the thing you told me about." The words rushed, breathy, hesitant, breathy again.

Leo, whose name, hair, and chunky body had been given him by German grandparents (and whose speech pattern had been lent by his childhood on a fishing coast of a world whose nights held ten times as many stars as Earth's), looked confused. Confusion became wonder as the Mouse held out the leather sack.

Leo took it with freckled hands. "You sure, are? Where you—"

Two workmen stepped on the boat. Leo saw alarm cross the Mouse's face and switched from Turkish to Greek. "Where did you this find?" The sentence pattern stayed the same in all languages.

"I stole it." Even though the words came with gushes of air through ill-anchored vocal cords, at ten the orphaned gypsy spoke some half dozen of the languages bordering the Mediterranean much more facilely than people like Leo who had learned his tongues under a hypno-teacher.

The construction men, grimy from their power shovels (and hopefully limited to Turkish) sat down at the table, massaging their wrists and rubbing their spinal sockets on the smalls of their backs where the great machines had been plugged into their bodies. They called for fish.

Leo bent and tossed. Silver flicked the air, and the oil roared.

Leo leaned against the railing and opened the draw string. "Yes." He spoke slowly. "None on Earth, much less here, I didn't know was. Where it from is?"

"I got it from the bazaar," the Mouse explained. "If it can be found on Earth, it can be found in the Grand Bazaar." He quoted the adage that had brought millions on millions to the Queen of Cities.

"So I'd heard," Leo said. Then in Turkish again: "These gentlemen their lunch you give."

The Mouse took up the ladle and scooped the fish into plastic plates. What had gone in silver came out gold. The men pulled chunks of bread from the baskets under the table and ate with their hands.

He hunted the two other fish from the oil and brought them to Leo who was still sitting on the rail, smiling into the sack. "Coherent image out of this thing, can I get? Don't know. Since fishing for methane squid in the Outer Colonies, I was, not in my hands one of these is. Back then, pretty well this I could play." The sack fell away and Leo sucked his breath between his teeth. "It pretty is!"

On his lap in crumpled leather, it might have been a harp, it might have been a computer. With inductance surfaces like a theremin, with frets like a guitar, down one side were short drones as on a sitar. On the other were the extended bass drones of a guitarina. Parts were carved from rosewood. Parts were cast from stainless steel. It had insets of black plastic, and was cushioned with plush.

Leo turned it.

The clouds had torn even further.

Sunlight ran the polished grain, flashed in the steel.

At the table the workmen tapped their coins, then squinted. Leo nodded to them. They put the money on the greasy boards and, puzzled, left the boat.

Leo did something with the controls. There was a clear ringing; the air shivered; and cutting out the olid odor of wet rope and tar was the scent of . . . orchids? A long time ago, perhaps at five or six, the Mouse had smelled them wild in the fields edging a road. (Then, there had been a big woman in a print skirt who may have been Mama, and three barefoot, heavily mustachioed men, one of whom he had been told to call Papa; but that was in some other country . . .) Yes, orchids.

Leo's hand moved; shivering became shimmering. Brightness fell from the air, coalesced in blue light whose source was somewhere between them. The odor moistened to roses.

"It works!" rasped the Mouse.

Leo nodded. "Better than the one I used to have. The Illyrion battery almost brand-new is. Those things I on the boat used to play, can still play, I wonder." His face furrowed. "Not too good going to be is. Out of practice am." Embarrassment rearranged Leo's features into an expression the Mouse had never seen. Leo's hand closed to the tuning haft.

Where light had filled the air, illumination shaped to her, till she turned and stared at them over her shoulder.

The Mouse blinked.

She was translucent; yet so much realer by the concentration he needed to define her chin, her shoulder, her foot, her face, till she spun, laughing, and tossed surprising flowers at him. Under the petals the Mouse ducked and closed his eyes. He'd been breathing naturally, but on this inhalation, he just didn't stop. He opened his mouth to the odors, prolonging the breath till his diaphragm stretched sharply from the bottom of his ribs. Then pain arched beneath his sternum and he had to let the breath out. Fast. Then began the slow return—

He opened his eyes.

Oil, the yellow water of the Horn, sludge; but the air was empty of blossoms. Leo, his single boot on the bottom rung of the rail, was fiddling with a knob.

She was gone.

"But . . ." The Mouse took a step, stopped, balancing on his toes, his throat working. "How . . . ?"

Leo looked up. "Rusty, I am! I once pretty good was. But it a long time is. Long time. Once, once, this thing I truly could play."

"Leo . . . could you . . . ? I mean you said you . . . I didn't know . . . I didn't think . . ."

"What?"

"Teach! Could you teach . . . me?"

Leo looked at the dumbfounded gypsy boy whom he had befriended here on the docks with tales of his wanderings through the oceans and ports of a dozen worlds. He was puzzled.

The Mouse's fingers twitched. "Show me, Leo! Now you've

got to show me!" The Mouse's mind tumbled from Alexandrian to Berber Arabic and ended up in Italian as he searched for the word. "Bellissimo, Leo! Bellissimo!"

"Well—" Leo felt what might have been fear at the boy's avidity, had Leo been more used to fear.

The Mouse looked at the stolen thing with awe and terror. "Can you show me how to play it?" Then he did something brave. He took it, gently, from Leo's lap. And fear was an emotion that the Mouse had lived with all his short, shattered life.

Reaching, however, he began the intricate process of becoming himself. Wondering, the Mouse turned the sensorysyrynx around and around.

At the head of a muddy street that wound on a hill behind an iron gate, the Mouse had a night job carrying trays of coffee and salep from the tea house through the herds of men who roamed back and forth by the narrow glass doors, crouching to stare at the women passing inside.

Now the Mouse came to work later and later. He stayed on the boat as long as possible. The harbor lights winked down the mile-long docks, and Asia flickered through the fog while Leo showed him where each projectable odor, color, shape, texture, and movement hid in the polished syrynx. The Mouse's eyes and hands began to open.

Two years later, when Leo announced that he had sold his boat and was thinking of going to the other side of Draco, perhaps to New Mars to fish for dust skates, the Mouse could already surpass the tawdry illusion that Leo had first shown him.

A month later the Mouse himself left Istanbul, waiting beneath the dripping stones of the Edernakapi till a truck offered him a ride toward the border town of Ipsala. He walked across the border into Greece, joined a red wagon full of gypsies, and for the duration of the trip fell back into Romany, the tongue of his birth. He'd been in Turkey three years. On leaving, all he had taken besides the clothes he wore was a thick silver puzzle ring too big for any of his fingers—and the syrynx.

Two and a half years later when he left Greece, he still had the ring. He had grown one little fingernail three quarters of an inch long, as did the other boys who worked the dirty streets behind the Monasteraiki flea market, selling rugs, brass gewgaws, or whatever tourists would buy, just outside the edge of the geodesic dome that covered the square mile of Athenas Market; and he took the syrynx.

The cruise boat on which he was a deck hand left Piraeus for Port Said, sailed through the canal and on toward its home port in Melbourne.

When he sailed back, this time to Bombay, it was as an entertainer in the ship's night club: Pontichos Provechi, re-creating great works of art, musical and graphic, for your pleasure, with perfumed accompaniment. In Bombay he quit, got very drunk (he was sixteen now), and stalked the dirty pier by moonlight, quivering and ill. He swore he would never play purely for money again ("Come on, kid! Give us the mosaics on the San Sophia ceiling again before you do the Parthenon frieze—and make 'em swing!"). When he returned to Australia, it was as a deck hand. He came ashore with the puzzle ring, his long nail, and a gold earring in his left ear. Sailors who crossed the equator on the Indian Ocean had been entitled to that earring for fifteen hundred years. The steward had pierced his earlobe with ice and a canvas needle. He still had the syrynx.

In Melbourne again, he played on the street. He spent a lot of time in a coffee shop frequented by kids from the Cooper Astronautics Academy. A twenty-year-old girl he was living with suggested he sit in on some classes.

"Come on, get yourself some plugs. You'll get them eventually somewhere, and you might as well get some education on how to use them for something other than a factory job. You like to travel. Might as well run the stars as operate a garbage unit."

When he finally broke up with the girl, and left Australia, he had his certificate as a cyborg stud for any inter-and intra-system ship. He still had his gold earring, his little fingernail, his puzzle ring—and the syrynx.

Even with a certificate, it was hard to sign onto a star-run straight from Earth. For a couple of years he plugged into a small commercial line that ran the Shifting Triangle run: Earth to Mars, Mars to Ganymede, Ganymede to Earth. But by now his black eyes were a-glitter with stars. A few days after his eighteenth birthday (at least it was the day the girl and he had agreed would be his birthday back in Melbourne), the Mouse hitched out to the second moon of

Neptune, from which the big commercial lines left for worlds all over Draco, for the Pleiades Federation, and even the Outer Colonies. The puzzle ring fit him now.

The Mouse walked beside Hell³, his boot heel clicking, his bare foot silent (as in another city on another world, Leo had walked). This was his latest travel acquisition. Those who worked under free-fall in the ships that went between planets developed the agility of at least one set of toes, sometimes both, till it rivaled world-lubbers' hands, and ever after kept that foot free. The commercial interstellar freighters had artificial gravity, which discouraged such development.

As he ambled beneath a plane tree, the leaves roared in the warm wind. Then his shoulder struck something. He staggered, was caught, was whirled around.

"You clumsy, rat-faced little—"

A hand clamped his shoulder and jammed him out to arm's length. The Mouse looked up at the man blinking down.

Someone had tried to hack the face open. The scar zagged from the chin, neared the cusp of heavy lips, rose through the cheek muscles—the yellow eye was miraculously alive—and cut the left brow; where it disappeared into red, Negro hair, a blaze of silkier yellow flamed. The flesh pulled into the scar like beaten copper to a vein of bronze.

"Where do you think you're going, boy?"

"Sorry—"

The man's vest bore the gold disk of an officer.

"Guess I wasn't looking—"

A lot of muscles in the forehead shifted. The back of the jaw got thicker. Sound started behind the face, spilled. It was laughter, full and contemptuous.

The Mouse smiled, hating it. "I guess I wasn't looking where I was going."

"I guess you weren't." The hand fell twice again on his shoulder. The captain shook his head and strode off.

Embarrassed and alert, the Mouse started walking again.

Then he stopped and looked back. The gold disk on the left shoulder of the captain's vest had been bossed with the name Lorq Von Ray. The Mouse's hand moved on the sack under his arm.

He flung back black hair that had fallen down his forehead, looked about, then climbed to the railing. He hooked
boot and foot behind the lower rung, and took out the
syrynx.

His vest was half laced, and he braced the instrument
against the small, defined muscles of his chest. The Mouse's
face lowered; long lashes closed. His hand, ringed and bladed, fell toward the inductance surfaces.

The air was filled with shocked images—

Chapter Two

Katin, long and brilliant, shambled toward Hell[3], eyes on the ground, mind on moons aloft.

"You, boy!"

"Huh?"

The unshaven derelict leaned on the fence, clutching the rail with scaly hands.

"Where you from?" The derelict's eyes were fogged.

"Luna," Katin said.

"From a little white house on a tree-lined street, with a bicycle in the garage? I had a bicycle."

"My house was green," Katin said. "And under an air dome. I had a bicycle, though."

The derelict swayed by the rail. "You don't know, boy. You don't know."

One must listen to madmen, Katin thought. They are becoming increasingly rare. And remembered to make a note.

"So long ago . . . so long!" The old man lurched away.

Katin shook his head and started walking again.

He was gawky and absurdly tall; nearly six foot nine. He'd shot to that height at sixteen. Never really believing he was so big, ten years later he still tended to hunch his shoulders. His huge hands were shoved beneath the belt of his shorts. He strode with elbows flapping.

And his mind went back to moons.

Katin, born on *the* moon, loved moons. He had always lived on moons, save for the time he had convinced his parents, stenographers for the Draco court on Luna, to let him take his university education on Earth at that center of learning for the mysterious and inscrutable West, Harvard, still a haven for the rich, the eccentric, and the brilliant—the last two of which he was.

The changes that vary a planet's surface, Himalayan heights to gentle, blistering Sahara dunes, he knew only by report. The freezing lichen forests of the Martian polar caps or the raging dust rivers at the red planet's equator; or Mercurian night versus Mercurian day—these he had experienced only through psychorama travelogs.

These were not what Katin knew, what Katin loved.

Moons?

Moons are small. A moon's beauty is in variations of sameness. From Harvard, Katin had returned to Luna, and from there gone to Phobos Station where he'd plugged in to a battery of recording units, low-capacity computers, and addressographs—a glorified file clerk. On time off, in tractor suit with polarized lenses, he explored Phobos, while Demos, a bright hunk of rock ten miles wide, swung by the unnervingly close horizon. He finally got up a party to land on Demos and explored the tiny moon as only a worldlet can be explored. Then he transferred to the moons of Jupiter. Io, Europa, Ganymede, Callisto turned beneath his brown eyes. The moons of Saturn, under the diffuse illumination of the rings, rotated before his solitary inspection as he wandered out from the land compounds where he was stationed. He explored the gray craters, the gray mountains, valleys, and cañons through days and nights of blinding intensity. Moons are the same?

Had Katin been placed on any of them, and blindfold suddenly removed, petrological structure, crystalline formation, and general topography would have identified it for him immediately. Tall Katin was used to making subtle distinctions in both landscape and character. The passions that come through the diversity of a complete world, or a whole man, he knew—but did not like.

He dealt with this dislike two ways.

For the inner manifestations, he was writing a novel.

A jeweled recorder that his parents had given him when he won his scholarship hung from a chain at his waist. To date it contained some hundred thousand words of notes. He had not begun the first chapter.

For the outer manifestations, he had chosen this isolate life below his educational capacity, not even particularly in keeping with his temperament. He was slowly moving further and further away from the focus of human activity which for him was still a world called Earth. He had completed his course as a cyborg stud only a month ago. He had arrived on this last moon of Neptune—the last moon in the Solar System— that morning.

His brown hair was silky, unkempt, and long enough to grab in a fight (if you were that tall). His hands, under the belt, kneaded his flat belly. As he reached the walkway, he stopped. Someone was sitting on the railing playing a sensory-syrynx.

Several people had stopped to watch.

Colors sluiced the air with fugal patterns as a shape subsumed the breeze and fell, to form further on, a brighter emerald, a duller amethyst. Odors flushed the wind with vinegar, snow, ocean, ginger, poppies, rum. Autumn, ocean, ginger, ocean, autumn; ocean, ocean, the surge of ocean again, while light foamed in the dimming blue that underlit the Mouse's face. Electric arpeggios of a neo-raga rilled.

Perched on the railing, the Mouse looked between the images, implosions on bright implosion, and at his own brown fingers leaping on the frets, as light from the machine flowed on the backs of his hands. And his fingers fell. Images vaulted from under his palms.

Some two dozen people had gathered. They blinked, they turned their heads. Light from the illusion shook on the roofs of their eye sockets, flowed in the lines about their mouths, filled the ridges furrowing foreheads. One woman rubbed her ear and coughed. One man punched the bottom of his pockets.

Katin looked down over lots of heads.

Somebody was jostling forward. Still playing, the Mouse looked up.

Blind Dan lurched out, stopped, then staggered in the syrynx's fire.

"Hey, come on, get out of there—"

"Come on, old man, move—"

"We can't see what the kid's making—"

In the middle of the Mouse's creation, Dan swayed, head wagging.

The Mouse laughed; then his brown hand closed over the projection haft, and light and sounds and smells deflated around a single, gorgeous demon who stood before Dan, bleating, grimacing, flapping scaled wings that shifted color with each beat. It yowled like a trumpet, twisted its face to resemble Dan's own, but with a third eye spinning.

The people began to laugh.

The spectre leaped and squatted to the Mouse's fingers. Malevolently the gypsy grinned.

Dan staggered forward, one arm flailing through.

Shrieking, the demon turned its back, bent. There was a sound like a flutter valve and the spectators howled at the stink.

Katin, who was leaning on the rail next to the Mouse, felt embarrassment heat his neck.

The demon cavorted.

Then Katin reached down and put his palm over the visual inductance field and the image blurred.

The Mouse looked up sharply. "Hey—"

"You don't have to do that," Katin said, his big hand burying the Mouse's shoulder.

"He's blind," the Mouse said. "He can't hear, he can't smell—he doesn't know what's going on ..." Black brows lowered. But he had stopped playing.

Dan stood alone in the center of the crowd, oblivious. Suddenly he shrieked. And shrieked again. The sound clanged in his lungs. People fell back. The Mouse and Katin both looked in the direction Dan's arm flailed.

In dark blue vest with gold disk, his scar flaming beneath the blaze, Captain Lorq Von Ray left the line of people.

Dan, through his blindness, had recognized him. He turned, staggered from the circle. Pushing a man aside, striking a woman's shoulder with the side of his hand, he disappeared in the crowd.

Dan gone and the syrynx still, attention shifted to the captain. Von Ray slapped his thigh, making his palm on his black pants crack like a board. "Hold up! Stop yelling!"

The voice was big.

"I'm here to pick out a crew of cyborg studs for a long trip, probably along the inner arm." So alive, his yellow eyes. The features around the ropy scar, under rust-rough hair, grinned. But it took seconds to name the expression on the distorted mouth and brow. "All right, which one of you wants a hand-hold halfway to the night's rim? Are you sand-footed, or star steppers? You!" He pointed to the Mouse, still sitting on the rail. "You want to come along?"

The Mouse stepped down. "Me?"

"You and your infernal hurdy-gurdy! If you think you can watch where you're going, I'd like somebody to juggle the air in front of my eyes and tickle my earlobes. Take the job."

A grin struck the Mouse's lips back from his teeth. "Sure," and the grin went. "I'll go." The words came from the young gypsy in an old man's whisky whisper. "Sure I'll go, Captain." The Mouse nodded and his gold earring flashed above the volcanic crevice. Hot wind over the rail struck down hanks of his black hair.

"Do you have a mate you want to make the run with? I need a crew."

The Mouse, who didn't particularly like anyone in this port, looked up at the incredibly tall young man who had stopped his harassment of Dan. "What about shorty?" He thumbed at surprised Katin. "Don't know him, but he's mate enough."

"Right then. So I have . . ." Captain Von Ray narrowed his eyes a moment, appraising Katin's slump shoulders, narrow chest, high cheeks and weak blue eyes floating behind contact lenses ". . . two." Katin's ears warmed.

"Who else? What's the matter? Are you afraid to leave this little well of gravity funneling into that half-pint sun?" He jerked his chin toward the high-lighted mountains. "Who's coming with us where night means forever and morning's a recollection?"

A man stepped forward. Skin the color of an emperor grape, he was long-headed and full-featured. "I'm for out." When he spoke, the muscles under his jaw and high on his nappy scalp rolled.

"Have a mate?"

A second man stepped up. His flesh was translucent as soap. His hair was like white wool. It took a moment for the likeness of feature to strike. There were the same sharp cusp lines at the corner of the heavy lips, the same slant below the bell nostrils, the same break far front on the cheekbones:

twins. As the second man turned his head, the Mouse saw the blinking pink eyes, veiled with silver.

The albino dropped his broad hand—a sack of knuckles and work-ruined nails cabled to his forearm by thick livid veins—on his brother's shoulder. "We run together."

Their voices, slow with colonial drawl, were identical.

"Anyone else?" Captain Von Ray looked about the crowd.

"You me, Captain, want to take?"

A man pushed forward.

Something flapped on his shoulder.

His yellow hair shook with a wind not from the chasm. Moist wings crinkled, stretched again, like onyx, like isinglass. The man reached up to where black claws made an epaulet on his knotted shoulder and caressed the grappling pads with a spatulate thumb.

"Do you have any other mate than your pet?"

Her small hand in his, she stepped out, following him at the length of their two arms.

Willow bough? Bird's wing? Wind in spring rushes? The Mouse riffled his sensory store to equal her face in gentleness. And failed.

Her eyes were the color of steel. Small breasts rose beneath the laces of her vest, steady in breath. Then steel glittered as she looked about. (She's a strong woman, thought Katin, who could perceive such subtleties.)

Captain Von Ray folded his arms. "You two, and the beast on your shoulder?"

"We six pets, Captain, have," she said.

"As long as they're broken to ship, fine. But I'll jettison the first fluttering devil I trip on."

"Fair, Captain," the man said. The slanted eyes in his ruddy face crinkled with a smile. With his free hand now he grasped his opposite biceps and slid his fingers down the blond hair that matted each forearm, the back of each knuckle, till he held the woman's hand in both of his. They were the couple who had played cards in the bar, the Mouse realized. "When you us aboard want?"

"An hour before dawn. My ship goes up to meet the sun. It's the *Roc* on Stage Seventeen. How do your friends call you?"

"Sebastian." The beast beat on his golden shoulder.

"Tyÿ." Its shadow crossed her face.

Captain Von Ray bent his head and stared from beneath his rusty brows with tiger's eyes. "And your enemies?"

The man laughed. "Damned Sebastian and his flapping black gillies."

Von Ray looked at the woman. "And you?"

"Tyÿ." That, softly. "Still."

"You two." Von Ray turned to the twins. "Your names?"

"He's Idas—" the albino said, and once more put his hand on his brother's arm.

"—and he's Lynceos."

"And what would your enemies say if I asked them who you were?"

The dark twin shrugged. "Only Lynceos—"

"—and Idas."

"You?" Von Ray nodded toward the Mouse.

"You can call me the Mouse if you're my friend. You my enemy, and you never know my name."

Von Ray's lids fell halfway down the yellow balls as he looked at the tall one.

"Katin Crawford." Katin surprised himself by volunteering. "When my enemies tell me what they call me, I'll tell you, Captain Von Ray."

"We're on a long trip," Von Ray said. "And you'll face enemies you didn't know you had. We're running against Prince and Ruby Red. We fly a cargo ship out empty and come back—if the wheels of the machine run right—with a full hold. I want you to know this trip has been made twice before. Once it hardly got started. Once I got within sight of the goal. But the sight was too much for some of my crew. This time I intend to go out, fill my cargo hold, and come back."

"Where we for running are?" Sebastian asked. The creature on his shoulders stepped from one foot to the other, flapping to balance. Its wingspan was nearly seven feet. "What out there, Captain, is?"

Von Ray threw up his head as though he could see his destination. Then he looked down slowly. "Out there . . ."

The Mouse felt the skin on the back of his neck go funny, as though it were cloth and someone had just snagged a loose end and raveled the fabric.

"Somewhere out there," Von Ray said, "is a nova."

Fear?

The Mouse for one moment searched for stars and found Dan's ruined eye.

And Katin spun backward across the pits of many moons, his eyes bulged beneath the face-plate while somewhere, wombward, a sun collapsed.

"We're hunting a nova."

So that's *real* fear, the Mouse thought. More than just the beast flapping in the chest, lurching into the ribs.

It's the start of a million journeys, Katin reflected, with your feet stuck in the same place.

"We have to go to the flaming edge of that imploding sun. The whole continuum in the area of a nova is space that has been twisted away. We have to go to the rim of chaos and bring back a handful of fire, with as few stops as possible on the way. Where we're going all law has broken down."

"Which law do you mean?" Katin asked. "Man's, or the natural laws of physics, psychics, and chemistry?"

Von Ray paused. "All of them."

The Mouse pulled the leather strap across his shoulder and lowered the syrynx into its sack.

"This is a race," Von Ray said. "I tell you again. Prince and Ruby Red are our opponents. There is no human law I could hold them to. And as we near the nova, the rest break down."

The Mouse shook massed hair off his forehead. "It's going to be a changey trip, eh, Captain?" The muscles in his brown face jumped, quivered, fixed finally on a grin to hold his trembling. His hand, inside the sack, stroked the inlay on the syrynx. "A real changey trip." His woolly voice licked at the danger. "Sounds like a trip I'll be able to sing about." And licked again.

"About this . . . handful of fire we're bringing back," Lynceos began.

"A cargo hold full," Von Ray corrected. "That's seven tons. Seven slugs of a ton each."

Idas said: "You can't bring home seven tons of fire—"

"—so what are we hauling, Captain?" Lynceos finished.

The crew waited. Those standing near the crew waited.

Von Ray reached up and kneaded his right shoulder.

"Illyrion," he said. "And we're getting it from the source."
His hand fell. "Give me your classification numbers. After
that, the next time I want to see you is on the *Roc* an hour
before dawn."

"Take a drink—"

The Mouse pushed the hand away and kept dancing. Music
smashed over the metal chimes while red lights fled one
another around the bar.

"Take a—"

The Mouse's hips jerked against the music. Tyÿ jerked
against him, swinging dark hair back from a glistening shoulder. Her eyes were closed, her lips shook.

Someone was saying to someone else: "Here, I can't drink
this. Finish it for me."

She flapped her hands, coming toward him. Then the
Mouse blinked.

Tyÿ was beginning to flicker.

He blinked again.

Then his saw Lynceos holding the syrynx in his white
hands. His brother stood behind him; they were laughing.
Real Tyÿ sat at a corner table shuffling her cards.

"Hey," the Mouse said, and went over fast. "Look, don't
fool with my ax, please. If you can play it, fine. But ask me
first."

"Yeah," Lynceos said. "You were the only one who could
see it—"

"—it was on a directional beam," said Idas. "We're sorry."

"That's okay," the Mouse said, taking his syrynx back. He
was drunk and tired. He walked out of the bar, meandered
along the glowing lip of Hell³, finally to cross the bridge that
led toward Stage Seventeen. The sky was black. As he ran his
hand along the rail, his fingers and forearm were lit orange
from beneath.

Someone was leaning on the rail ahead of him.

He slowed.

Katin looked dreamily across the abyss, face devil-masked
by underlight.

At first the Mouse thought Katin was talking to himself.
Then he saw the jeweled contrivance in his hand.

"Cut into the human brain," Katin told his recorder. "Centered between cerebrum and medulla you will find a nerve cluster that resembles a human figure only centimeters high. It connects the sensory impressions originating outside the brain with the cerebral abstractions forming within. It balances the perception of the world outside with the knowledge of the world within.

"Cut through the loose tangle of intrigues that net world to world—"

"Hey, Katin."

Katin glanced at him as the hot air shook up from the lava.

"—ties star system to star system, that keeps the Sol-centered Draco sector, the Pleiades Federation, and the Outer Colonies each a single entity: you will find a whirl of diplomats, elected or self-appointed officials, honest or corrupt as their situations call for—in short, the governmental matrix that takes its shape from the worlds it represents. Its function is to respond to and balance the social, economic, and cultural pressures that shift and run through empire.

"And if one could cut directly through a star, centered in the flaming gas would be a bole of pure nuclear matter, condensed and volatile, crushed to this state by the weight of the matter around it, spherical or oblate as the shape of the sun itself. During a solar disturbance, this center carries vibrations from that disturbance directly through the mass of the star to cancel those vibrations racing the tidal shift on the sun's surface.

"Occasionally something goes wrong with the tiny bodies balancing the perceptual pressures on the human brain.

"Often the governmental and diplomatic matrix cannot handle the pressures of the worlds they govern.

"And when something goes wrong with the balancing mechanism inside a sun, the dispersal of incredible stellar power dephases into the titanic forces that make a sun go nova—"

"Katin?"

He switched off his recorder and looked at the Mouse.

"What you doing?"

"Making notes on my novel."

"Your what?"

"Archaic art form superseded by the psychorama. Alas, it

was capable of vanished subtleties, both spiritual and artistic, that the more immediate form has not yet equaled. I'm an anachronism, Mouse." Katin grinned. "Thanks for my job."

The Mouse shrugged. "What are you talking about?"

"Psychology." Katin put the recorder back in his pocket. "Politics, and Physics. The three *P's.*"

"Psychology?" the Mouse asked. "*Politics?*"

"Can you read and write?" Katin asked.

"Turkish, Greek, and Arabic. But not too good in English. The letters don't have nothing to do with the sounds you make."

Katin nodded. He was a little drunk too. "Profound. That's why English was such a fine language for novels. But I oversimplify."

"What about psychology and politics? I know the physics."

"Particularly," Katin said to the flowing, glowing strip of wet rock that wound two hundred meters below, "the psychology and politics of our captain. They intrigue me."

"What about them?"

"His psychology is, at this point, merely curious because it is unknown. I shall have a chance to observe that as we progress. But the politics are gravid with possibilities."

"Yeah? What's that mean?"

Katin locked his fingers and balanced his chin on a knuckle. "I attended an institution of higher learning in the ruins of a once great country. A bit across the quad was a building called the Von Ray Psycho-science Laboratory. It was a rather recent addition, from, I would guess, a hundred and forty years ago."

"Captain Von Ray?"

"Grandpa, I suspect. It was donated to the school in honor of the thirtieth anniversary of the grant of sovereignty to the Pleiades Federation by the Draco Courts."

"Von Ray is from out in the Pleiades? He don't talk like he is. Sebastian and Tyÿ, I could guess from them. Are you sure?"

"His family holdings are there, certainly. He's probably spent time all over the universe, traveling in the style we would like to be accustomed to. How much would you bet he owns his own cargo ship?"

"He's not working for some company combine?"

"Not unless his family owns it. The Von Rays are probably

the most powerful family in the Pleiades Federation. I don't
know if Captain there is a kissing cousin lucky enough to
have the same name, or whether he's the direct heir and
scion. But I do know that name is connected up with the
control and organization of the whole Pleiades Federation;
they're the sort of family with a summer home in the Outer
Colonies and a town house or two on Earth."

"Then he's a big man." The Mouse spoke hoarsely.

"He is."

"What about this Prince and Ruby Red he was talking
about?"

"Are you dense, or are you merely a product of thirty-
first-century over-specialization?" Katin asked. "Sometimes I
dream about a return of the great renaissance figures of the
twentieth century: Bertrand Russell, Susanne Langer, Pejt
Davlin." He looked at the Mouse. "Who makes every drive
system you can think of, interplanetary or interstellar?"

"Red-shift Limited—" The Mouse stopped. *"That* Red?"

"Were he not a Von Ray, I would assume he spoke of
some other family. Since he is, it is very probable that he
speaks of just those Reds."

"Damn," the Mouse said. Red-shift was a label that appeared so frequently you didn't even notice it. Red-shift
made the components for all conceivable space drives, the
tools for dismantling them, the machines for servicing them,
replacement parts.

"Red is an industrial family with its roots in the dawn of
space travel; it is very firmly fixed on Earth specifically, and
throughout the Draco system in general. The Von Rays are a
not so old, but powerful family of the Pleiades Federation.
And they are now in a race for seven tons of Illyrion.
Doesn't that make your political sensitivities quiver for the
outcome?"

"Why should it?"

"To be sure," Katin said, "the artist concerned with self-
expression and a projection of his inner world should, above
all things, be apolitical. But *really*, Mouse."

"What are you talking about, Katin?"

"Mouse, what does Illyrion mean to you?"

He considered. "An Illyrion battery makes my syrynx play.
I know they use it to keep this moon's core hot. Doesn't it
have something to do with the faster-than-light drive?"

Katin closed his eyes. "You are a registered, tested, competent cyborg stud, like me, right?" On "right," his eyes opened.

The Mouse nodded.

"Oh, for the rebirth of an educational system where understanding was an essential part of knowledge," Katin intoned to the flickering dark. "Where did you get your cyborg training, anyway, Australia?"

"Um-hm."

"Figures. Mouse, there is noticeably less Illyrion in your syrynx battery, by a factor of twenty or twenty-five, than there is, let's say, radium in the fluorescent paint on the numerals of a radium dial watch. How long does a battery last?"

"They're supposed to go to fifty years. Expensive as hell."

"The Illyrion needed to keep this moon's core molten is measured in grams. The amount needed to propel a starship is on the same order. To quantify the amount mined and free in the Universe, eight or nine thousand kilograms will suffice. And Captain Von Ray is going to bring back *seven tons!*"

"I guess Red-shift would be pretty interested in that."

Katin nodded deeply. "They might."

"Katin, what is Illyrion? I used to ask, at Cooper, but they told me it was too complicated for me to understand."

"Told me the same thing at Harvard," Katin said. "Psychophysics 74 and 75. *I* went to the library. The best definition is the one given by Professor Plovnievsky in his paper presented at Oxford in 2238 before the theoretical physics society. I quote: 'Basically, gentlemen, Illyrion is something else.' One wonders if it was a happy accident from lack of facility with the language, or a profound understanding of English subtlety. The dictionary definition, I believe, reads something like, '... general name for the group of trans three-hundred elements with psychomorphic properties, heterotropic with many of the common elements as well as the imaginary series that exist between 107 and 255 on the periodic chart.' How's your subatomic physics?"

"I am but a poor cyborg stud."

Katin raised a flickering brow. "You know that as you mount the chart of atomic numbers past 98, the elements become less and less stable, till we get to jokes like Einsteinium, Californium, Fermium with half lives of hundredths of a second—and mounting further, hundredths of thousandths of a second. The higher we go, the more unstable. For this reason, the whole series between 100 and 298 were labeled—mislabeled—the imaginary elements. They're quite real. They just don't stay around very long. At 296 or thereabouts, however, the stability begins to go up again. At three hundred we're back to a half life measurable in tenths of a second, and five or six above that and we've started a whole new series of elements with respectable half lives back in the millions of years. These elements have immense nuclei, and are *very* rare. But as far back as 1950, hyperons had been discovered, elementary particles bigger than protons and neutrons. These are the particles that carry the binding energies holding together these super nuclei, as ordinary mesons hold together the nucleus in more familiar elements. This group of super-heavy, super-stable elements go under the general heading of Illyrion. And to quote again the eminent Plovnievsky, 'Basically, gentlemen, Illyrion is something else.' As Webster informs us, it is both psychomorphic and heterotropic. I suppose that's a fancy way of saying Illyrion is many things to many men." Katin turned his back to the railing and folded his arms. "I wonder what it is to our captain?"

"What's *heterotropic?*"

"Mouse," said Katin, "by the end of the twentieth century mankind had witnessed the total fragmentation of what was then called 'modern science.' The continuum was filled with 'quasars' and unidentifiable radio sources. There were more elementary particles than there were elements to be created from them. And perfectly durable compounds that had been thought impossible for years were being formed left and right like KrI_4, H_4XeO_6, RrF_4; the noble gases were not so noble after all. The concept of energy embodied in the Einsteinian quantum theory was about as correct, and led to as many contradictions, as the theory three hundred years earlier that fire was a released liquid called phlogiston. The soft sciences—isn't that a delightful name?—had run amuck. The experiences opened by psychedelics were making everybody doubt everything anyway and it was a hundred and fifty years before the whole mess was put back into some sort of coherent order by those great names in the synthetic and

integrative sciences that are too familiar to both of us for me
to insult you by naming. And you—who have been taught
what button to push—want me—who am the product of a
centuries-old educational system founded not only on the
imparting of information, but a whole theory of social adjust-
ment as well—to give you a five-minute run-through of the
development of human knowledge over the last ten centuries?
You want to know what a heterotropic element is?"

"Captain says we got to be on board an hour before
dawn," the Mouse ventured.

"Never mind, never mind. I have a knack for this sort of
extemporaneous synthesis. Now let me see. First there was the
work of De Blau in France in two thousand, when he presented the first clumsy scale and his basically accurate method
for measuring the psychic displacement of electrical—"

"You're not helping." The Mouse grunted. "I want to find
out about Von Ray and Illyrion."

Wings gentled the air. Black shapes settled. Hand in hand,
Sebastian and Tyÿ came up the walkway. Their pets scuttled
about their feet, rose. Tyÿ pushed one away from her arm; it
soared. Two battled above Sebastian's shoulder for perch.
One gave, and the satisfied beast pulled his wings now,
brushing the Oriental's blond head.

"Hey!" the Mouse rasped. "You going back to the ship
now?"

"We go."

"Just a second. What does Von Ray mean to you? You
know his name?"

Sebastian smiled, and Tyÿ glanced at him with gray eyes.

"We from the Pleiades Federation are," Tyÿ said. "I and
these beasts under the Dim, Dead Sister, flock and master,
born."

"The Dim, Dead Sister?"

"The Pleiades used to be called the Seven Sisters in ancient
times because only seven of them could be seen from Earth,"
Katin explained to the Mouse's frown. "A few hundred B.C.
or so, one of the visible stars went nova and out. There are
cities now on the innermost of its charred planets. It's still
hot enough to keep things habitable, but that's about all."

"A nova?" the Mouse said. "What about Von Ray?"

Tyÿ made an inclusive gesture. "Everything. Great, good
family is."

"Do you know this particular Captain Von Ray?" Katin asked.

Tyÿ shrugged.

"What about Illyrion?" the Mouse asked. "What do you know about that?"

Sebastian squatted among his pets. Wings shed from him. His hairy hand went soothingly from head to head. "Pleiades Federation none have. Draco system none either have." He frowned.

"Von Ray a pirate some say," Tyÿ ventured.

Sebastian looked up sharply. "Von Ray great and good family is! Von Ray fine is! That why we with him go."

Tyÿ, more softly, her voice settling behind the gentle features: "Von Ray fine family is."

The Mouse saw Lynceos approaching over the bridge. And ten seconds later, Idas.

"You two are from the Outer Colonies?"

The twins stopped, shoulder brushing shoulder. Pink eyes blinked more than brown.

"From Argos," the pale twin said.

"Argos on Tubman B-12," specified the dark.

"The Far Out Colonies," Katin amended.

"What do you know about Illyrion?"

Idas leaned on the rail, frowned, then hoisted himself up so that he was sitting. "Illyrion?" He spread his knees and dropped his knotted hands between. "We have Illyrion in the Outer Colonies."

Lynceos sat beside him. "Tobias," he said. "We have a brother, Tobias." Lynceos moved on the bar closer to dark Idas. "We have a brother in the Outer Colonies named Tobias." He glanced at Idas, coral eyes netted with silver. "In the Outer Colonies, where there is Illyrion." He held his wrists together, but with fingers opened, like petals on a calloused lily.

"The worlds in the Outer Colonies?" Idas said. "Balthus—with ice and mud-pits and Illyrion. Cassandra—with glass deserts big as the oceans of Earth, and jungles of uncountable plants, all blue, with frothing rivers of galenium, and Illyrion. Salinus—combed through with mile-high caves and cañons, with a continent of deadly red moss, and seas with towered cities built of the tidal quartz on the ocean floor, and Illyrion—"

"—The Outer Colonies are the worlds of stars much young-

er than the stars here in Draco, many times younger than
the Pleiades," Lynceos put in.

"Tobias is in ... one of the Illyrion mines on Tubman,"
Idas said.

Their voices tensed; eyes stayed down, or leaped to one
another's faces. When black hands opened, white hands
closed.

"Idas, Lynceos, and Tobias, we grew up in the dry, equatorial stones of Tubman at Argos, under three suns and a
red moon—"

"—and on Argos too there is Illyrion. We were wild. They
called us wild. Two black pearls and a white, bouncing and
brawling through the streets of Argos—"

"—Tobias, he was black as Idas. I alone was white in the
town—"

"—but no less wild than Tobias for his whiteness. And
they say in wildness we, one night, out of heads on bliss—"

"—the gold powder that collects in the rock crevices and
when inhaled makes the eyes flicker with unnamed colors and
new harmonies reel in the ear's hollow, and the mind dilate—"

"—on bliss, we made an effigy of the mayor of Argos, and
fixed him with a clockwork flying mechanism, and set him
soaring about the city square, uttering satirical verses on the
leading personages of the city—"

"—for this we were banished from Argos into the wilds of
Tubman—"

"—and outside the town there is only one way to live, and
that is to descend beneath the sea and work off the days of
disgrace in the submarine Illyrion mines—"

"—and the three of us, who had never done anything in
bliss but laugh and leap, and had mocked no one—"

"—we were innocent—"

"—we went into the mines. There we worked in air masks
and wet suits in the underwater mines of Argos, for a year—"

"—a year on Argos is three months longer than a year on
Earth, with six seasons instead of four—"

"—and at the beginning of our second, algae-tinted autumn, we made ready to leave. But Tobias would not go. His
hands had taken up the rhythms of the tides, the weight of
ore became a comfort on his palms—"

"—so we left our brother in the Illyrion mines, and came
up among the stars, afraid—"

"—you see, we are afraid that as our brother, Tobias, found something that pulled him from us, so one of us may find something that will divide the remaining two—"

"—as we thought the three of us could never be divided." Idas looked at the Mouse. "And we are out of bliss."

Lynceos blinked. "That is what Illyrion means to us."

"Paraphrase," Katin said from the other side of the walk. "In the Outer Colonies, comprising to date forty-two worlds and circa seven billion people, practically the entire population at one time or another has something to do with the direct acquisition of Illyrion. And I believe approximately one out of three works in some facet of its development or production his entire life."

"Those are the statistics," Idas said, "for the Far Outer Colonies."

Black wings rose as Sebastian stood and took Tyÿ's hand.

The Mouse scratched his head. "Well. Let's spit in this river and get on to the ship."

The twins climbed down from the rail. The Mouse leaned out over the hot ravine and puckered.

"*What* are you doing?"

"Spitting into Hell[8]. A gypsy's got to spit three times in any river he crosses," the Mouse explained to Katin. "Otherwise, bad things."

"This *is* the thirty-first century we're living in. What bad things?"

The Mouse shrugged.

"*I* never spit in any river."

"Maybe it's just for gypsies."

"I it kind of a cute idea is think," Tyÿ said, and leaned across the railing beside Mouse. Sebastian loomed at her shoulder. Above them one of the beasts was caught in a hot updraft and flung into the dark.

"What that is?" Tyÿ frowned suddenly, pointing.

"Where?" The Mouse squinted.

She pointed past him to the cañon wall.

"Hey!" Katin said. "That's the blind man!"

"The one who busted up your playing!"

Lynceos pushed between them. "He's sick." He narrowed his blood-colored eyes. "That man there is sick."

Demoned by the flickering, Dan reeled down the ledges toward the lava.

"He'll burn up!" Katin joined them.

"But he can't feel the heat!" the Mouse exclaimed. "He can't see—he probably doesn't even know!"

Idas, then Lynceos, pushed away from the rail and ran up the bridge.

"Come on!" the Mouse cried, following.

Sebastian and Tyÿ came after, with Katin at the rear.

Ten meters below the rim, Dan paused on a rock, arms before him, preparing an infernal dive.

As they reached the head of the bridge—the twins were already climbing the rail—a figure appeared at the cañon's lips above the old man.

"Dan!" Von Ray's face flamed as the light fanned him. He vaulted. Shale struck from under his sandals and shattered before him as he crabbed down the slope. "Dan, don't—"

Dan did.

His body caught on an outcropping sixty feet below, then spun on, out, and down.

The Mouse clutched the rail, bruising his stomach on the bar as he leaned.

Katin was beside him a moment afterward, leaning even further.

"Ahhh!" the Mouse whispered and pulled back to avert his face.

Captain Von Ray reached the rock from which Dan had leaped. He dropped to one knee, both fists on the stone, staring over. Shapes fell at him (Sebastian's pets), rose again, casting no shadow. The twins had stopped, ledges above him.

Captain Von Ray stood. He looked up at his crew. He was breathing hard. He turned and made his way back up the slope.

"What happened?" Katin asked when they were all on the bridge again. "Why did he . . . ?"

"I was talking with him just a few minutes before," Von Ray explained. "He's crewed with me for years. But on the last trip, he was . . . was blinded."

The big captain; the scarred captain. And how old would he be, the Mouse wondered. Before, the Mouse had put him at forty-five, fifty. But this confusion lopped ten or fifteen years. The captain was aged, not old.

"I had just told him that I had made arrangements for him to return to his home in Australia. He'd turned around to go back across the bridge to the dormitory where I'd taken him a room. I glanced back . . . he wasn't on the bridge." The captain looked around at the rest of them. "Come on to the *Roc*."

"I guess you'll have to report this to the Patrol," Katin said.

Von Ray led them toward the gate to the take-off field, where *Draco* writhed up and down his hundred-meter column in the darkness.

"There's a phone right here at the head of the bridge—"

Von Ray's look cut Katin off. "I want to leave this rock. If we call from here, they'll have everybody wait around to tell his version in triplicate."

"I guess you can call from the ship," Katin suggested, "as we leave."

For a moment the Mouse doubted all over again his judgment of the captain's age.

"There's nothing we can do for the sad fool."

The Mouse cast an uncomfortable glance down the chasm, then followed along with Katin.

Beyond the hot drafts, night was chill, and fog hung coronas on the induced-fluorescent lamps that patterned the field.

Katin and the Mouse were at the group's tail.

"I wonder just what Illyrion means to handsome there," the Mouse commented softly.

Katin grunted and put his hands under his belt. After a moment he asked, "Say, Mouse what did you mean about that old man and all his senses having been killed?"

"When they tried to reach the nova the last time," the Mouse said, "he looked at the star too long through sensory input and all his nerve endings were seared. They weren't killed. They were jammed into constant stimulation." He shrugged. "Same difference. Almost."

"Oh," Katin said, and looked at the pavement.

Around them stood star-freighters. Between them, the much smaller, hundred-meter shuttles.

After he'd thought awhile, Katin said: "Mouse, has it occurred to you how much you have to lose on this trip?"

"Yeah."

"And you're not scared?"

The Mouse grasped Katin's forearm with his thin fingers. "I'm scared as hell," he rasped. He shook his hair back to look up at his tall shipmate. "You know that? I don't like things like Dan. I'm scared."

Chapter Three

Some stud had taken a black crayon and scrawled "Olga" across the vane-projector face.

"Okay," the Mouse said to the machine. "You're Olga."

Purr and blink, three green lights, four red ones. The Mouse began the tedious check of pressure distribution and phase readings.

To move a ship faster than light from star to star, you take advantage of the very twists in space, the actual distortions that matter creates in the continuum itself. To talk about the speed of light as the limiting velocity of an object is to talk about twelve or thirteen miles an hour as the limiting velocity of a swimmer in the sea. But as soon as one starts to employ the currents of the water itself, as well as the wind above, as with a sailboat, the limit vanishes. The starship had seven vanes of energy acting somewhat like sails. Six projectors controlled by computers sweep the vanes across the night. And each cyborg stud controls a computer. The captain controls the seventh. The vanes of energy had to be tuned to the shifting frequencies of the stasis pressures; and the ship itself was quietly hurled from this plane of space by the energy of the Illyrion in its core. That was what Olga and her cousins did. But the control of the shape and the angling of the vane was best left to a human brain. That was the Mouse's job—under the captain's orders. The captain also had blanket control of many of the sub-vane properties.

The cubicle's walls were covered with graffiti from former crews. There was a contour couch. The Mouse adjusted the inductance slack in a row of seventy-microfarad coil-condensers, slid the tray into the wall, and sat.

He reached around to the small of his back beneath his

vest, and felt for the socket. It had been grafted onto the
base of his spinal cord back at Cooper. He picked up the first
reflex cable that looped across the floor to disappear into the
computer's face, and fiddled with it till the twelve prongs
slipped into his socket and caught. He took the smaller,
six-prong plug and slipped it into the plug on the underside of
his left wrist; then the other into his right. Both radial nerves
were connected with Olga. At the back of his neck was
another socket. He slipped the last plug in—the cable was
heavy and tugged a little on his neck—and saw sparks. This
cable could send impulses directly to his brain that could
bypass hearing and sight. There was a faint hum coming
through already. He reached over, adjusted a knob on Olga's
face, and the hum cleared. Ceiling, walls, and floor were
covered with controls. The room was small enough so that he
could reach most of them from the couch. But once the ship
took off, he would touch none of them, but control the vane
directly with the nervous impulses from his body.

"I always feel like I'm getting ready for the Big Return,"
Katin's voice sounded in his ear. In their cubicles throughout
the ship, as they plugged themselves in, the other studs joined
contact. "The base of the spine always struck me as an
unnatural place from which to drag your umbilical cord. It
better be an interesting marionette show. Do you really know
how to work this thing?"

"If you don't know by now," the Mouse said, "too bad."

Idas: "This show's about Illyrion—"

"—Illyrion and a nova": Lynceos.

"Say, what are you doing with your pets, Sebastian?"

"A saucer of milk them feed."

"With tranquilizers," Tyÿ's soft voice came. "They now
sleep."

And lights dimmed.

The captain hooked in. The graffiti, the scars on the walls,
vanished. There were only the red lights chasing one another
on the ceiling.

"A shook up go game," Katin said, "with iridescent
stones." The Mouse pushed his syrynx case beneath the couch
with his heel and lay down. He straightened the cable under
his back, beneath his neck.

"All secure?" Von Ray's voice rang through the ship.
"Open the fore vanes."

The Mouse's eyes began to flicker with new sight—

—the space port: lights over the field, the lavid fissures of the crust fell to dim, violet quiverings at the spectrum's tip. But above the horizon, the 'winds' were brilliant.

"Pull open the side vane seven degrees."

The Mouse flexed what would have been his left arm. And the side vane lowered like a wing of mica. "Hey, Katin," the Mouse whispered. "Ain't that something! Look at it—"

The Mouse shivered, crouched in a shield of light. Olga had taken over his breathing and heartbeat while the synapses of the medulla were directed to the workings of the ship.

"For Illyrion, and Prince and Ruby Red!" from one of the twins.

"Hold your vane!" the captain ordered.

"Katin, look—"

"Lie back and relax, Mouse," Katin whispered. "I shall do just that and think about my past life."

The void roared.

"You really feel like that, Katin?"

"You can be bored with anything if you try hard enough."

"You two, look up," from Von Ray.

They looked.

"Cut in stasis shifters."

A moment Olga's lights pricked his vision. And were gone; winds swept against him. And they were cartwheeling from the sun.

"Good-bye, moon," Katin whispered.

And the moon fell into Neptune; Neptune fell into the sun. And the sun began to fall.

Night exploded before them.

What were the first things?

His name was Lorq Von Ray and he lived at 12 Extol Park in the big house up the hill: New Ark (N.W. 73), Ark. That was what you told somebody on the street if you should get lost, and that person would help you find home. The streets of Ark were set with transparent wind shields, and the evenings from the months of April to Iumbra were blasted with colored fumes that snagged, ripped free, and writhed above the city on the crags of Tong. His name was Lorq Von Ray and he lived . . . Those were the childish things, the things that persisted, the first learned. Ark was the greatest city in the Pleiades Federation. Mother and Father were important people and were often away. When they were home they talked of Draco, its capital world Earth; they talked of the realignment, the prospect of sovereignty for the Outer Colonies. They had guests who were senator this, and representative that. After Secretary Morgan married Aunt Cyana, they came to dinner and Secretary Morgan gave him a hologram map of the Pleiades Federation that was just like a regular piece of paper, but when you looked at it under the tensor beam, it was like looking through a night window with dots of light flickering at different distances, and nebulous gases winding. "You live on Ark, the second planet of that sun there," his father said, pointing down where Lorq had spread the map over the rock table beside the glass wall. Outside, spidery tilda trees writhed in the evening gale.

"Where's Earth?"

His father laughed, loud and alone, in the dining room. "You can't see it on that map. It's just the Pleiades Federation."

Morgan put his hand on the boy's shoulder. "I you a map of Draco next time bring." The secretary, whose eyes were almond-shaped, smiled.

Lorq turned to his father. "I want to go to Draco!" And then back to Secretary Morgan: "I some day to Draco want to go!" Secretary Morgan spoke like many of the people in his school at Causby; like the people on the street who had helped him find his way home when he had gotten lost when he was four (but not like his father or Aunt Cyana) and Mommy and Daddy had been so terribly upset ("We were so worried! We thought you'd been kidnapped. But you mustn't go to those cardplayers on the street, even if they did bring you home!"). His parents smiled when he spoke like that to them, but they wouldn't smile now, because Secretary Morgan was a guest.

His father humphed. "A map of Draco! That's all he needs. Oh yes, Draco!"

Aunt Cyana laughed; then Mother and Secretary Morgan laughed too.

They lived on Ark but often they went on big ships to other worlds. You had a cabin where you could pass your hand in front of colored panels and have anything to eat you wanted any time, or you could go down to the observation deck and watch the winds of the void translated to visible patterns of light over the bubble ceiling, flailing colors among stars that drifted by—and you knew you were going faster and faster than anything.

Sometimes his parents went to Draco, to Earth, to cities called New York and Peking. He wondered when they would take him.

But every year, the last week in Saluary, they would go on one of the great ships to another world that was also not on the map. It was called New Brazillia and was in the Outer Colonies. He lived in New Brazillia too, on the island of São Orini, because his parents had a house there near the mine.

The first time he heard the names Prince and Ruby Red it was at the São Orini house. He was lying in the dark, screaming for light.

His mother came at last, pushed away the insect netting (it wasn't needed because the house had sonics to keep away the tiny red bugs that occasionally bit you outside and made you feel funny for a few hours, but Mother liked to be safe). She lifted him. "Shhh! Shhh! It's all right. Don't you want to go to sleep? Tomorrow is the party. Prince and Ruby will be here. Don't you want to play with Prince and Ruby at the party?" She carried him around the nursery, stopping to push the wall switch by the door. The ceiling began to rotate till the polarized pane was transparent. Through the palm fronds lapping the roof, twin moons splattered orange light. She laid him back in the bed, caressed his rough, red hair. After a while she started to leave.

"Don't turn it off, Mommy!"

Her hand fell from the switch. She smiled at him. He felt warm, and rolled over to stare through the meshed fronds at the moons.

Prince and Ruby Red were coming from Earth. He knew that his mother's parents were on Earth, in a country called Senegal. His father's great-grandparents were also from Earth, from Norway. Von Rays, blond and blustering, had been speculating in the Pleiades now for generations. He wasn't sure what they speculated, but it must have been successful. His family owned the Illyrion mine that operated just beyond the northern tip of São Orini. His father occasionally joked with him about making him the little foreman of the mines. That's what "speculation" probably was. And the moons were drifting away; he was sleepy.

He did not remember being introduced to the blue-eyed, black-haired boy with the prosthetic right arm, nor his spindly sister. But he recalled the three of them—himself, Prince, and Ruby—playing together the next afternoon in the garden.

He showed them the place behind the bamboo where you could climb up into the carved stone mouths.

"What are *those?*" Prince asked.

"Those are the dragons," Lorq explained.

"There aren't any dragons," Ruby said.

"Those are dragons. That's what Father says."

"Oh." Prince caught his false hand over the lower lip and hoisted himself up. "What are they for?"

"You climb up in them. Then you can climb down again. Father says the people who lived here before us carved them."

"Who lived here before?" Ruby asked. "And what did they want with dragons? Help me up, Prince."

"I think they're silly." Prince and Ruby were now both standing between the stone fangs above him. (Later he would learn that "the people who had lived here before" were a race extinct in the Outer Colonies for twenty thousand years; their carvings had survived, and on these ruined foundations, Von Ray had erected this mansion.)

Lorq sprang for the jaw, got his fingers around the lower lip, and started scrambling. "Give me a hand?"

"Just a second," Prince said. Then, slowly, he put his shoe on Lorq's fingers and mashed.

Lorq gasped and fell back on the ground, clutching his hand.

Ruby giggled.

"Hey!" Indignation throbbed, confusion welled. Pain beat in his knuckles.

"You shouldn't make fun of his hand," Ruby said. "He doesn't like it."

"Huh?" Lorq looked at the metal and plastic claw directly for the first time. "I didn't make fun of it!"

"Yes you did," Prince said evenly. "I don't like people who make fun of me."

"But I—" Lorq's seven-year-old mind tried to comprehend

this irrationality. He stood up again. "What's wrong with your hand?"

Prince lowered himself to his knees, reached out, and swung at Lorq's head.

"Watch—!" He leaped backward. The mechanical limb had moved so fast the air hissed.

"Don't talk about my hand any more! There's nothing wrong! Nothing at all!"

"If you stop making fun of him," Ruby commented, looking at the rugae on the roof of the stone mouth, "he'll be friends with you."

"Well, all right," Lorq said warily.

Prince smiled. "Then we'll be friends now." He had very pale skin and his teeth were small.

"All right," Lorq said. He decided he didn't like Prince.

"If you say something like, 'let's shake on it,'" Ruby said, "he'll beat you up. And he can, even though you're bigger than he is."

Or Ruby either.

"Come on up," Prince said.

Lorq climbed into the mouth beside the other two children.

"Now what do we do?" Ruby asked. "Climb down?"

"You can look into the garden from here," Lorq said. "And watch the party."

"Who wants to watch an old party," Ruby said.

"I do," said Prince.

"Oh," Ruby said. "You do. Well, all right then."

Beyond the bamboo, the guests walked in the garden. They laughed gently, talked of the latest psychorama, politics, drank from long glasses. His father stood by the fountain, discussing with several people his feelings about the proposed sovereignty of the Outer Colonies—after all, he had a home out here and had to have his finger on the pulse of the situation. It was the year that Secretary Morgan had been assassinated. Though Underwood had been caught, there were still theories going around as to which faction was responsible.

A woman with silver hair flirted with a young couple who had come with Ambassador Selvin, who was also a cousin. Aaron Red, a portly, proper gentleman, had cornered three young ladies and was pontificating on the moral degeneration of the young. Mother moved through the guests, the hem of her red dress brushing the grass, followed by the humming buffet. She paused here and there to offer canapés, drinks, and her opinion of the new realignment proposal. Now, after a year of phenomenal popular success, the intelligentsia had accepted the *Tohu-bohus* as legitimate music; the jarring rhythms tumbled across the lawn. A light sculpture in the corner twisted, flickered, grew with the tones.

Then his father let out a booming laugh that made everyone look. "Listen to this! Just hear what Lusuna has said to me!" He was holding the shoulder of a university student who had come with the young couple. Von Ray's bluster had apparently prompted the young man to argument. Father gestured for him to repeat.

"I only said that we live in an age where economic, political, and technological change have shattered all cultural tradition."

"My Lord," laughed the woman with silver hair, "is that all?"

"No, no!" Father waved his hand. "We have to listen to what the younger generation thinks. Go on, sir."

"There's no reservoir of national, or world solidarity, even on Earth, the center of Draco. The past half dozen generations have seen such movement of peoples from world to world, there can't be any. This pseudo-interplanetary society that has replaced any real tradition, while very attractive, is totally hollow and masks an incredible tangle of decadence, scheming, corruption—"

"Really, Lusuna," the young wife said, "your Scholarship is showing." She had just taken another drink at the prompting of the woman with the silver hair.

"—and piracy."

(With the last word, even the three children crouching in the mouth of the carved lizard could tell from the looks passing on the guests' faces that Lusuna had gone too far.)

Mother came across the lawn, the bottom of her red sheath brushing back from gilded nails. She held her hands out to Lusuna, smiling. "Come, let's continue this social dissection over dinner. We're having a totally corrupt mango-bongoou with untraditional loso ye mbiji a meza, and scathingly decadent mpati a nsengo." His mother always made the old Senegal dishes for parties. "And if the oven cooperates, we'll end up with dreadfully pseudo-interplantary tiba yoka flambé."

The student looked around, realized he was supposed to smile, and did one better by laughing. With the student on her arm, Mother led everyone into dinner— "Didn't someone tell me you had won a scholarship to Draco University at Centauri? You must be quite bright. You're from Earth, I gather from your accent. Senegal? Well! So am I. What city . . . ?" And Father, relieved, brushed back oak-colored hair and followed everyone into the jalousied dining pavilion.

On the stone tongue, Ruby was saying to her brother, "I don't think you should do that."

"Why not?" said Prince.

Lorq looked back at the brother and sister. Prince had picked up a stone from the floor of the dragon's mouth in his mechanical hand. Across the lawn stood the aviary of white cockatoos Mother had brought from Earth on her last trip.

Prince aimed. Metal and plastic blurred.

Forty feet away, birds screamed and exploded in the cage. As one fell to the floor, Lorq could see, even at this distance, blood in the feathers.

"That's the one I was aiming for." Prince smiled.

"Hey," Lorq said. "Mother's not going to . . ." He looked again at the mechanical appendage strapped to Prince's shoulder over the stump. "Say, you throw better with—"

"Watch it." Prince's black brows lowered on chipped blue glass. "I told you not to make fun of my hand, didn't I?" The hand drew back, and Lorq heard the motors—whirr, click, whirr—in wrist and elbow.

"It's not his fault he was born that way," Ruby said. "And it's impolite to make remarks about your guests. Aaron says you're all barbarians out here anyway, doesn't he, Prince?"

"That's right." He lowered his hand.

A voice came over the loudspeaker into the garden. "Children, where are you? Come in and get your supper. Hurry."

They climbed down and went out through the bamboo.

Lorq went to bed still excited by the party. He lay under the doubled shadows of the palms above the nursery ceiling, transparent from the night before.

A whisper: "Lorq!"

And: "Shhh! Don't be so loud, Prince."

More softly: "Lorq?"

He pushed back the netting and sat up in bed. Imbedded in the plastic floor, tigers, elephants, and monkeys glowed. "What do you want?"

"We heard them leaving through the gate." Prince stood in the nursery doorway in his shorts. "Where did they go?"

"We want to go too," Ruby said from her brother's elbow.

"Where did they go?" Prince asked again.

"Into town." Lorq stood up and padded across the glowing menagerie. "Mommy and Daddy always take their friends down into the village when they come for the holidays."

"What do they do?" Prince leaned against the jamb.

"They go . . . well, they go into town." Where ignorance had been, curiosity came to fill it.

"We jimmied the baby sitter," said Ruby.

"You don't have a very good one; it was easy. Everything is so old-fashioned out here. Aaron says only Pleiades barbarians could think it quaint to live out here. Are you going to take us to go see where they went?"

"Well, I . . ."

"We want to go," said Ruby.

"Don't you want to go see too?"

"All right." He had planned to refuse. "I have to put my sandals on." But childish curiosity to see what adults did when children were not about was marking foundations on which adolescent, and later, adult consciousness would stand.

The garden lisped about the gate. The lock always opened to Lorq's handprint during the day, but he was still surprised when it swung back now.

The road threaded into the moist night.

Past the rocks and across the water one low moon turned the mainland into a tongue of ivory lapping at the sea. And through the trees, the lights of the village went off and on like a computer checkboard. Rocks, chalky under the high, smaller moon, edged the roadway. A cactus raised spiky paddles to the sky.

As they reached the first of the town's cafés, Lorq said "hello" to one of the miners who sat at a table outside the door.

"Little Senhor." The miner nodded back.

"Do you know where my parents are?" Lorq asked.

"They came by here," he shrugged, "the ladies with the fine clothes, the men in their vests and their dark shirts. They came by, half an hour ago, an hour."

"What language is he talking?" Prince demanded.

Ruby giggled. "You understand *that?*"

Another realization hit Lorq; he and his parents spoke to the people of São Orini with a completely different set of words than they spoke to each other and their guests. He had learned the slurred dialect of Portuguese under the blinking lights of a hypno-teacher sometime in the fog of early childhood.

"Where did they go?" he asked again.

The miner's name was Tavo; for a month last year when the mine shut down, he had been plugged into one of the clanking gardeners that had landscaped the park behind the house. Dull grown-ups and bright children form a particularly tolerant friendship. Tavo was dirty and stupid; Lorq accepted this. But his mother had put an end to the relation when, last year, he came back from the village and told how he had watched Tavo kill a man who had insulted the miner's ability to drink.

"Come on, Tavo. Tell me where they went?"

Tavo shrugged.

Insects beat about the illuminated letters over the café door.

Crepe paper left from the Sovereignty Festival, blew from the awning posts. It was the anniversary of Pleiades Sovereignty, but the miners celebrated it out here both in hope for their own and for Mother and Father.

"Does he know where they went?" Prince asked.

Tavo was drinking sour milk from a cracked cup along with his rum. He patted his knee and Lorq, glancing at Prince and Ruby, sat down.

Brother and sister looked at each other uncertainly.

"You sit down too," Lorq said. "On the chairs."

They did.

Tavo offered Lorq his sour milk. Lorq drank half of it, then passed it to Prince. "You want some?"

Prince raised the cup to his mouth, then caught the smell. "You drink this?" He wrinkled his face and set the cup down sharply.

Lorq picked up the glass of rum. "Would you prefer . . . ?"

But Tavo took the glass out of his hand. "That's not for you, Little Senhor."

"Tavo, where are my parents?"

"Back up in the woods, at Alonza's."

"Take us, Tavo?"

"Who?"

"We want to go see them."

Tavo deliberated. "We can't go unless you have money." He roughed Lorq's hair. "Hey, Little Senhor, you have any money?"

Lorq took out the few coins from his pocket.

"Not enough."

"Prince, do you or Ruby have any money?"

Prince had two pounds @sg in his shorts.

"Give it to Tavo."

"Why?"

"So he'll take us to see our parents."

Tavo reached across and took the money from Prince, then raised his eyebrows at the amount.

"Will he give this to me?"

"If you take us," Lorq told him.

Tavo tickled Lorq's stomach. They laughed. Tavo folded one bill and put it in his pocket. Then he ordered another rum and sour milk. "The milk is for you. Some for your friends?"

"Come on, Tavo. You said you'd take us."

"Be quiet," the miner said. "I'm thinking whether we should go up there. You know I must go plug in at work tomorrow morning." He tapped the socket on one wrist.

Lorq put salt and pepper in the milk and sipped it.

"I want to try some," Ruby said.

"It smells awful," said Prince. "You shouldn't drink it. Is he going to take us?"

Tavo gestured to the owner of the café. "Lots of people up at Alonza's tonight?"

"It's Friday night, isn't it?" said the owner.

"The boy wants me to take him up there," said Tavo, "for the evening."

"You're taking Von Ray's boy up to Alonza's?" The owner's purple birthmark crinkled.

"His parents are up there." Tavo shrugged. "The boy

wants me to take them. He told me to take them, you know? And it will be more fun than sitting here and swatting redbugs." He bent down, tied the thongs of his discarded sandals together, and hung them around his neck. "Come on, Little Senhor. Tell the one-armed boy and the girl to behave."

At the reference to Prince's arm, Lorq jumped.

"We are going now."

But Prince and Ruby didn't understand.

"We're going," Lorq explained. "Up to Alonza's."

"What's Alonza's?"

"Is that like the places Aaron is always taking those pretty women in Peking?"

"They don't have anything out here like in Peking," Prince said. "Silly. They don't even have anything like Paris."

Tavo reached down and took Lorq's hand. "Stay close. Tell your friends to stay close too." Tavo's hand was all sweat and callus. The jungle chuckled and hissed over them.

"Where are we going?" Prince asked.

"To see Mother and Father." Lorq's voice sounded uncertain. "To Alonza's."

Tavo looked over at the word and nodded. He pointed through the trees, dappled with double moons.

"Is it far, Tavo?"

Tavo just cuffed Lorq's neck, took his hand again, and went on.

At the top of the hill, a clearing: light seeped beneath the edge of a tent. A group of men joked and drank with a fat woman who had come out for air. Her face and shoulders were wet. Her breasts gleamed before falling under the orange print. She kept twiddling her braid.

"Stay," whispered Tavo. He pushed his children back.

"Hey, why—"

"We have to stay here," Lorq translated for Prince who had stepped forward after the miner.

Prince looked around, then came back and stood by Lorq and Ruby.

Joining the men, Tavo intercepted the raffia-covered bottle as it swung from arm to arm. "Hey, Alonza, are the Senhores Von Ray . . . ?" He thumbed toward the tent.

"Sometimes they come up. Sometimes they bring their

guests with them," Alonza said. "Sometimes they like to see—"

"Now," Tavo said. "Are they here now?"

She took the bottle and nodded.

Tavo turned and beckoned the children.

Lorq, followed by the wary siblings, went to stand beside him. The men went on talking in blurry voices that undercut the shrieks and laughter from the tarpaulin. The night was hot. The bottle went around three more times. Lorq and Ruby got some. And the last time Prince made a face, but drank too.

Finally Tavo pushed Lorq's shoulder. "Inside."

Tavo had to duck under the low door. Lorq was the tallest of the children and the top of his head just brushed the canvas.

A lantern hung from the center pole: harsh glare on the roof, harsh light in the shell of an ear, on the rims of nostrils, on the lines of old faces. A head fell back in the crowd, expelling laughter and expletives. A wet mouth glistened as a bottle neck dropped. Loose, sweaty hair. Over the noise, somebody was ringing a bell. Lorq felt excitement tingling in his palms.

People began to crouch. Tavo squatted. Prince and Ruby did too. So did Lorq, but he held on to Tavo's wet collar.

In the pit, a man in high boots tramped back and forth, motioning the crowd to sit.

On the other side, behind the rail, Lorq suddenly recognized the silver-haired woman. She was leaning on the shoulder of the Senegalese student, Lusuna. Her hair stuck to her forehead like confused and twisted knives. The student had opened his shirt. His vest was gone.

The pitman shook the bell rope again. A piece of down had fallen on his gleaming arm and adhered, even as he waved and shouted at the crowd; now he rapped his brown fist on the tin wall for silence.

Money was wedged between the boards of the rail. The wagers were jammed between the planks. As Lorq looked along the rail, he saw the young couple further down. He was leaning over, trying to point out something to her.

The pitman stamped across the mash of scales and feather. His boots were black to the knees.

When the people were nearly quiet, he went to the near side of the pit where Lorq couldn't see, bent down—

A cage door slammed back. With a yell, the pitman vaulted onto the fence and grabbed the center post. The spectators shouted and surged up. Those squatting began to stand. Lorq tried to push forward.

Across the pit, he saw his father rise, streaming face twisted below blond hair; Von Ray shook his fist toward the arena. Mother, hand at her neck, pressed against him. Ambassador Selvin was trying to push between two miners shouting at the rail.

"There's Aaron!" Ruby exclaimed.

"No!" from Prince.

But now there were so many people standing, Lorq could no longer see anything. Tavo stood up and began to shout for people to sit, till someone passed him a bottle.

Lorq moved left to see; then right when the left was blocked. Unfocused excitement pounded in his chest.

The pitman stood on the railing above the crowd. Jumping, he had struck the lantern with his shoulder so that shadows staggered on the canvas. Leaning against the pole, he frowned at the swaying light, rubbed his bulging arms. Then he noticed the fluff. Carefully he pulled it off, then began to search his matted chest, his shoulders.

The noise exploded at the pit's edge, halted, then roared. Somebody was waving a vest in the air.

The pitman, finding nothing, leaned against the pole again.

Excited, fascinated, at the same time Lorq was slightly ill with rum and stench. "Come on," he shouted to Prince, "let's go up where we can see!"

"I don't think we ought to," Ruby said.

"Why not!" Prince took a step forward. But he looked scared.

Lorq barged ahead of him.

Then someone caught him by the arm and he whirled around. "*What* are you doing out here?" Von Ray, angry and confused, was breathing hard. "Who told you you could bring those children up here!"

Lorq looked around for Tavo. Tavo was not there.

Aaron Red came up behind his father. "I *told* you we should have left somebody with them. Your baby sitters are so old-fashioned out here. Any clever child could fix it!"

Von Ray turned briskly. "Oh, the children are perfectly all right. But Lorq knows he's not supposed to go out in the evening by himself!"

"I'll take them home," Mother said, coming up. "Don't be upset, Aaron. They're all right. I'm terribly sorry, really I am." She turned to the children. "Whatever possessed you to come out here?"

The miners had gathered to watch.

Ruby began to cry.

"Dear me, now what's the matter?" Mother looked concerned.

"There's nothing wrong with her," Aaron Red said. "She knows what's going to happen when I get her home. They know when they do wrong."

Ruby, who hadn't thought about what was going to happen at all, began to cry in earnest.

"Why don't we talk about this tomorrow morning." Mother cast Von Ray a despairing glance. But Father was too upset by Ruby's tears and chagrined by Lorq's presence to respond.

"Yes, you take them home, Dana." He looked up to see the miners watching. "Take them home now. Come, Aaron, you needn't worry yourself."

"Here," Mother said. "Ruby, Prince, give me your hands. Come, Lorq, we're going right—"

Mother had extended her hands to the children.

Then Prince reached with his prosthetic arm, and yanked—

Mother screamed, staggered forward, beating at his wrist with her free hand. Metal and plastic fingers locked her own.

"Prince!" Aaron reached for him, but the boy ducked away, twisted, then dodged across the floor.

Mother went to her knees on the dirt floor, gasping, letting out tiny sobs. Father caught her by the shoulders. "Dana! What did he do? What happened?" Mother shook her head.

Prince ran straight against Tavo.

"Catch him!" Father shouted in Portuguese.

And Aaron bellowed, "Prince!"

At the word, resistance left the boy; he sagged in Tavo's arms, face white.

Mother was on her feet now, grimacing on Father's shoulder. ". . . and one of my white birds . . ." Lorq heard her say.

"Prince, come here!" Aaron commanded.

Prince walked back, his movements jerky and electric.

"Now," Aaron said. "You go back to the house with Dana. She's sorry she mentioned your hand. She didn't mean to hurt your feelings."

Mother and Father looked at Aaron, astounded. Aaron Red turned to them. He was a small man. The only thing red about him Lorq could see were the corners of his eyes. "You see"—Aaron looked tired—"I never mention his deformity. Never." He looked upset. "I don't want him to feel inferior. I don't let anyone point him out as different at all. You must never talk about it in front of him, you see. Not at all."

Father started to say something. But the initial embarrassment of the evening had been his.

Mother looked back and forth between the two men, then at her hand. It was cradled in her other palm, and she made stroking motions. "Children," she said. "Come with me."

"Dana, are you sure that you're—"

Mother cut him off with a look. "Come with me, children," she repeated. They left the tent.

Tavo was outside. "I go with you, Senhora. I will go back to the house with you, if you wish."

"Yes, Tavo," Mother said. "Thank you." She held her hand against the stomach of her dress.

"That boy with the iron hand." Tavo shook his head. "And the girl, and your son. I brought them here, Senhora. But they asked me to, you see. They told me to bring them here."

"I understand," Mother said.

They didn't go down through the jungle this time, but took the wider road that led past the launch from where the aquaturbs took the miners to the undersea mines. The high forms swayed in the water, casting double shadows on the waves.

As they reached the gate of the park, Lorq was suddenly sick to his stomach. "Hold his head, Tavo," Mother instructed. "See, this excitement isn't good for you, Lorq. And you were drinking that milk again. Do you feel any better?"

He hadn't mentioned the rum. The smell in the tent, as well as the odor that lingered around Tavo kept his secret. Prince and Ruby watched him quietly, glancing at one another.

Upstairs Mother got the sitter back in order, and secured Prince and Ruby in their room. Finally she came into the nursery.

"Does your hand still hurt, Mommy?" he asked from the pillow.

"It does. Nothing's broken, though I don't know why not. I'm going to get the medico-unit soon as I leave you."

"They wanted to go!" Lorq blurted. "They said they wanted to see where you all had gone."

Mother sat down on the bed and began to rub his back with her good hand. "And didn't you want to see too, just a little bit?"

"Yes," he said, after a moment.

"That's what I thought. How does your stomach feel? I don't care what they say, I still don't see how that sour milk could be any good for you."

He still hadn't mentioned the rum.

"You go to sleep now." She went to the nursery door.

He remembered her touching the switch.

He remembered a moon darkening through the rotating roof.

Lorq always associated Prince Red with the coming and going of light.

He was sitting naked by the swimming pool on the roof, reading for his petrology exam, when the purple leaves at the rock entrance shook. The skylight hummed with the gale outside; the towers of Ark, vaned to glide in the wind, were distorted behind the glittering frost.

"Dad!" Lorq snapped off the reader and stood up. "Hey, I came in third in senior mathematics. Third!"

Von Ray, in fur-rimmed parka stepped through the leaves. "And I suppose you call yourself studying now. Wouldn't it be easier in the library? How can you concentrate up here with all this distraction?"

"Petrology," Lorq said, holding up his note-recorder. "I don't really have to study for that. I've got honors already."

Only in the last few years had Lorq learned to relax under his parents' demand for perfection. Having learned, he had discovered that the demands were now ritual and phatic, and gave way to communication if they were allowed to ride out.

"Oh," his father said. "You did." Then he smiled. The frost on his hair turned to water as he unlaced his parka. "At least you've been studying instead of crawling through the bowels of *Caliban*."

"Which reminds me, Dad. I've registered her in the New Ark Regatta. Will you and Mother go up to see the finish?"

"If we can. You know Mother hasn't been feeling too well recently. This past trip was a little rough. And you worry her with your racing."

"Why? I haven't let it interfere with my schoolwork."

Von Ray shrugged. "She thinks it's dangerous." He laid the parka over the rock. "We read about your prize at Trantor last month. Congratulations. She may worry about you, but she was as proud as a partridge when she could tell all those stuffy club women you were her son."

"I wish you'd been there."

"We wanted to be. But there was no way to cut a month off the tour. Come, I've got something to show you."

Lorq followed his father along the stream that curled from the pool. Von Ray put his arm around his son's shoulder as they started the steps that dropped beside the waterfall into the house. At their weight, the steps began to escalate.

"We stopped on Earth, this trip. Spent a day with Aaron Red. I believe you met him a long time ago. Red-shift Limited?"

"Out on New Brazillia," Lorq said. "At the mine."

"Do you remember that far back?" The stairs flattened and carried them across the conservatory. Cockatoos sprung from the brush, beat against the transparent wall where snow lay outside the bottom panes, then settled in the bloodflowers, knocking petals to the sand. "Prince was with him. A boy your age, perhaps a little older." Lorq had been vaguely aware of Prince's doings over the years as a child is aware of the activity of the children of parents' friends. Some time back, Prince had changed schools four times very rapidly, and the rumor that had filtered to the Pleiades was that only the fortunes of Red-shift, Ltd., kept the transfers from being openly labeled expulsion.

"I remember him," Lorq said. "He only had one arm."

"He wears a black glove to the shoulder with a jeweled armband at the top, now. He's a very impressive young man. He said he remembered you. You two got into some mischief or other back then. He, at least, seems to have quieted down some."

Lorq shrugged from under his father's arm and stepped onto the white rugs that scattered the winter garden. "What do you want to show me?"

Father went to one of the viewing columns. It was a transparent column four feet thick supporting the clear roofing with a capital of floral glass. "Dana, do you want to show Lorq what you brought for him?"

"Just a moment." His mother's figure formed in the column. She was sitting in the swan chair. She took a green cloth from the table beside her and opened it on the quilted brocade of her lap.

"They're beautiful!" Lorq claimed. "Where did you find heptodyne quartz?"

The stones, basically silicon, had been formed at geological pressures so that in each crystal, about the size of a child's fist, light flowed along the shattered blue lines within the jagged forms.

"I picked them up when we stopped at Cygnus. We were staying near the Exploding Desert of Krall. We could see it flashing from our hotel window beyond the walls of the city. It was quite as spectacular as it's always described. One afternoon when your father was off in conference, I took the tour. When I saw them, I thought of your collection and bought these for you."

"Thanks." He smiled at the figure in the column.

Neither he nor his father had seen his mother in person for four years. Victim of a degenerative mental and physical disease that often left her totally incommunicative, she had retired to her suite in the house with her medicines, her diagnostic computers, her cosmetics, her gravothermy and reading machines. She—or more often one of her androids programmed to her general response pattern—would appear in the viewing columns and present a semblance of her normal appearance and personality. In the same way, through android and telerama report, she "accompanied" Von Ray on his business travels, while her physical presence was confined in the masked, isolate chambers that no one was allowed to enter except the psychotechnician who came quietly once a month.

"They're beautiful," he repeated, stepping closer.

"I'll leave them in your room this evening." She picked one up with dark fingers and turned it over. "I find them fascinating myself. Almost hypnotic."

"Here." Von Ray turned to one of the other columns. "I have something else to show you. Aaron had apparently heard of your interest in racing, and knew how well you were doing." Something was forming in the second column. "Two of his engineers had just developed a new ion-coupler. They told us it was too sensitive for commercial use and wouldn't be profitable for them to manufacture on any large scale. But Aaron said the response level would be excellent for small-scale racing craft. I offered to buy it for you. He wouldn't hear of it; he's sent it to you as a gift."

"He did?" Lorq felt excitement lap above surprise. "Where is it?"

In the column a crate stood on the corner of a loading platform. The fence of Nea Limani Yacht Basin diminished in the distance between the guide towers. "Over at the field?" Lorq sat down in the green hammock hanging from the ceiling. "Good! I'll look at it when I go down this evening. I still have to get a crew for the race."

"You just pick your crew from people hanging around the spacefield?" Mother shook her head. "That always worries me."

"Mom, people who like racing, kids who are interested in racing ships, people who know how to sail, they hang around the shipyards. I know half the people at Nea Limani anyway."

"I still wish you'd get your crew from among your school friends, or people like that."

"What wrong is with people who like this talk?" He smiled slightly.

"I didn't say anything of that nature at all. I just meant you should use people you know."

"After the race," his father cut in, "what do you intend to do with the rest of your vacation?"

Lorq shrugged. "Do you want me to foreman out at the São Orini mine like last year?"

His father's eyebrows separated, then snarled over the vertical crevices above his nose. "After what happened with that miner's daughter . . . ?" The brows unsnarled again. "Do you *want* to go out there again?"

Lorq shrugged once more.

"Have you thought of anything that you'd like to do?" This from his mother.

"Ashton Clark will send me something. Right now I've got to pick up my crew." He stood up from the hammock. "Mom, thanks for the stones. We'll talk about vacation when school is really over."

He started for the bridge that arched the water.

"You won't be too—"

"Before midnight."

"Lorq. One more thing."

He stopped at the crest of the bridge, leaning on the aluminum banister.

"Prince is having a party. He sent you an invitation. It's at Earth, Paris, on the Ile St.-Louis. But it's just three days after the Regatta. You wouldn't be able to get there—"

"*Caliban* can make Earth in three days."

"No, Lorq! You're not going to go all the way to Earth in that tiny—"

"I've never been to Paris. The last time I was on Earth was the time you took me when I was fifteen and we went to Peking. It'll be easy sailing down into Draco." Leaving, he called back to them, "If I don't get my crew, I won't even get back to school next week." He disappeared down the other side of the bridge.

His crew was two fellows who volunteered to help him unpack the ion-coupler. Neither one was from the Pleiades Federation.

Brian, a boy Lorq's age who had taken a year off from Draco University and flown out to the Outer Colonies, was now working his way back; he had done both captaining and studding on racing yachts, but only in the co-operative yachting club sponsored by his school. Based on common interest in racing-ships, their relation was one of mutual awe. Lorq was silently agape at the way Brian had taken off to the other end of the galaxy and was beating his way without funds or forethought; while Brian had at last met, in Lorq, one of the mythically wealthy who could own his own boat and whose name had, till then, been only an abstraction on the sports tapes—Lorq Von Ray, one of the youngest and most spectacular of the new crop of racing captains.

Dan, who completed the crew of the little three-vaned racer, was a man in his forties, from Australia on Earth. They had met him in the bar where he had started a whole series of tales about his times as a commercial stud on the big transport freighters, as well as racing captains he had occasionally crewed for—though he had never captained himself. Barefoot, a rope around pants torn off at the knees, Dan was a lot more typical of the studs that hung around the heated walkways of Nea Limani. The high wind-domes broke the hurricane gusts that rolled from Tong across glittering Ark—it was the month of Iumbra when there were only three hours of daylight in the twenty-nine-hour day. The mechanics, officers, and studs drank late, talked currents and racing at the bars and the sauna baths, the registration offices and the service pits.

Brian's reaction to continuing on after the race down to Earth: "Fine. Why not? I have to get back into Draco in time for vacation classes anyway."

Dan's: "Paris? That's awful close to Australia, ain't it? I got a kid and two wives in Melbourne, and I ain't so anxious for them to catch hold of me. I suppose if we don't stay too long—"

When the Regatta swept past the observation satellite circling Ark, looped the inner edge of the cluster to the Dim, Dead Sister, and returned to Ark again, it was announced that *Caliban* had placed second.

"All right. Let's get out of here. To Prince's party!"

"Be careful now . . ." His mother's voice came over the speaker.

"Give our regards to Aaron. And congratulations again, son," Father said. "If you wreck that brass butterfly on this silly trip, don't expect me to buy a new one."

"So long, Dad."

The *Caliban* rose from among the ships clustered at the viewing station where the spectators had come to observe the Regatta's conclusion. Fifty-foot windows flashed in starlight below them (behind one, his father and an android of his mother stood at the railing, watching the ship pull away), and in a moment they were wheeling through the Pleiades Federation, then toward Sol.

A day out, they lost six hours in a whirlpool nebula ("Now

if you had a real ship instead of this here toy," Dan complained over the intercom, "it'd be a sneeze to get out of this thing." Lorq turned the frequency of the scanner higher on the ion-coupler. "Point two-five down, Brian. Then catch it up fast—there!"), but made up the time and then some on the Outward Tidal Drift.

A day later, and Sol was a glowing, growing light in the cosmos raging.

Shaped like the figure eight of a Mycenaean shield, De Blau Field tilted miles below the sweeping vans. Cargo shuttles left from here for the big star-port on Neptune's second moon. The five-hundred-meter passenger liners glittered across the platforms. *Caliban* fell toward the inset of the yacht basin, coming down like a triple kite. Lorq sat up from the couch as the guide beams caught them. "Okay, puppets. Cut the strings." He switched off *Caliban*'s humming entrails a moment after touchdown. Banked lights died around him.

Brian hopped into the control cabin, tying his left sandal. Dan, unshaven, his vest unlaced, ambled from his projection chamber. "Guess we got here, Captain." He stooped to finger dirt between his toes. "What kind of party is this you kids are going to?"

As Lorq touched the unload button, the floor began to slant and the ribbed covering rolled back till the lower edge of the floor hit the ground. "I'm not sure," Lorq told him. "I suppose we'll all find out when we get there."

"*Ohhh* no," Dan drawled as they reached the bottom. "I don't go for this society stuff." They started from beneath the shadow of the hull. "Find me a bar, and just pick me up when you come back."

"If you two don't want to come," Lorq said, looking around the field, "we'll stop off for something to eat, and then you can stay here."

"I . . . well, sort of wanted to go." Brian looked disappointed. "This is as close as I'll ever get to going to a party given by Prince Red."

Lorq looked at Brian. The stocky, brown-haired boy with coffee-colored eyes had changed his scuffed leather work-vest for a clean one with iridescent flowers. Lorq was only beginning to realize how dazzled this young man, who had hitched across the universe, was before the wealth, visible and implied, that went with a nineteen-year-old who could race his own yacht and just took off to parties in Paris.

It had not occurred to Lorq to change his vest at all.

"You come on then," Lorq said. "We'll get Dan on the way back."

"Just *you* two don't get so drunk you can't carry *me* back on board."

Lorq and Dan laughed.

Brian was staring around at the other yachts in the basin. "Hey! Have you ever worked a tri-vaned Zephyr?" He touched Lorq's arm, then pointed across to a graceful, golden hull. "I bet one of those would really twirl."

"Pickup is slow on the lower frequencies." Lorq turned back to Dan. "You make sure you get back on board by take-off time tomorrow. I'm not going to go running around looking for you."

"With me this close to Australia? Don't worry, Captain. By the by, you wouldn't get upset if I should happen to bring a lady onto the ship?" He grinned at Lorq, then winked.

"Say," Brian said. "How do those Boris-27s handle? Our club at school was trying to arrange a swap with another club that had a ten-year-old Boris. Only they wanted money too."

"As long as she doesn't leave the ship with anything she didn't bring," Lorq told Dan. He turned to Brian again. "I've never been on a Boris more than three years old. A friend of mine had one a couple of years back. It worked pretty well, but it wasn't up to *Caliban*."

They walked through the gate of the landing field, started down the steps to the street, and passed through the shadow from the column of the coiled snake.

Paris had remained a more or less horizontal city. The only structures interrupting the horizon to any great extent were the Eiffel Tower to their left and the spiring structure of Les Halles: seventy tiers of markets were enclosed in transparent panes, tessellated with metal scrollwork—it was the focus of food and produce for the twenty-three million inhabitants of the city.

They turned up Rue des Astronauts past the restaurants and hotel marquees. Dan dug under the rope around his middle to scratch his stomach, then pushed his long hair from his forehead. "Where do you get drunk around here if you're a working cyborg stud?" Suddenly he pointed down a smaller street. "There!"

At the bend of the L-shaped street was a small café-bar with a crack across the window, Le Sidéral. The door was closing behind two women.

"Fine," Dan drawled, and loped ahead of Lorq and Brian.

"I envy someone like that, sometimes," Brian said to Lorq, softly.

Lorq looked surprised.

"You really don't care," Brian went on, "I mean if he brings a woman on the ship?"

Lorq shrugged. "I'd bring one on."

"Oh. You must have it pretty easy with girls, especially with a racing ship."

"I guess it helps."

Brian bit at his thumbnail and nodded. "That would be nice. Sometimes I think girls have forgotten I'm alive. Probably be the same, yacht or no." He laughed. "You ever . . . brought a girl onto your ship?"

Lorq was silent a moment. Then he said, "I have three children."

Now Brian looked surprised.

"A boy and two girls. Their mothers are miners on a little Outer Colony world, New Brazillia."

"Oh, you mean you . . ."

Lorq cupped his left hand on his right shoulder, right hand on his left.

"We lead very different sorts of lives, I think," Brian said slowly, "you and I."

"That's what I was thinking." Then Lorq grinned.

Brian's smile returned uneasily.

"Hold on, you there!" from behind them. "Wait!"

They turned.

"Lorq? Lorq Von Ray?"

The black glove Lorq's father had described was now a silver one. The armband, high on his biceps, was set with diamonds.

"Prince?"

Vest, pants, boots were silver. "I almost missed you!" The bony face beneath black hair animated. "I had the field call me as soon as you got clearance at Neptune. Racing yacht, huh? Sure took your time. Oh, before I forget; Aaron told me if you did come, I should ask you to give his regards to your Aunt Cyana. She stayed with us for a weekend at the beach on Chobe's World last month."

"Thanks. I will if I see her," Lorq said. "If she was with you last month, you've seen her more recently than I have. She doesn't spend much time on Ark any more."

"Cyana . . ." Brian began. ". . . Morgan?" he finished in astonishment. But Prince was already going on: "Look." He dropped his hands on the shoulders of Lorq's leather vest (Lorq tried to detect a difference in pressure between gloved and ungloved fingers), "I've got to get to Mt. Kenyuna and back before the party. I have every available bit of transportation bringing people down from all over everywhere. Aaron's not co-operating. He's refused to have anything more to do with the party; he thinks it's gotten out of hand. I'm afraid I've been throwing his name around to get things I needed in a few places he didn't approve. But he's somewhere off on Vega. Do you want to run me over to the Himalayas?"

"All right." Lorq started to suggest that Prince stud with Brian. But perhaps with his arm Prince might not be able to plug in properly. "Hey, Dan!" he shouted down the street. "You're still working."

The Australian had just opened the door. Now he turned around, shook his head, and started back.

"What are we going for?" Lorq asked as they started back toward the field.

"Tell you on the way."

As they passed the gate (and the Draco column ringed with the Serpent gleaming in the sunset), Brian hazarded conversation. "That's quite an outfit," he said to Prince.

"There'll be a lot of people on the Ile. I want everybody to be able to see where I am."

"Is that glove something new they're wearing here on Earth?"

Lorq's stomach caught itself. He glanced quickly between the two boys.

"Things like that," Brian went on, "they never get out to Centauri till a month after everybody's stopped wearing them on Earth. And I haven't even been in Draco for ten months anyway."

Prince looked at his arm, turned his hand over.

Twilight washed the sky.

Then lights along the top of the fence flicked on: light lined the folds on Prince's glove.

"My personal style." He looked up at Brian. "I have no right arm. This"—he made a fist of silver fingers—"is all metal and plastic and whirring doo-hickeys." He laughed sharply. "But it serves me . . . about as well as a real one."

"Oh." Embarrassment wavered through Brian's voice. "I didn't know."

Prince laughed. "Sometimes I almost forget too. Sometimes. Which way is your ship?"

"There." As Lorq pointed, he was acutely aware of the dozen years between his and Prince's first and present meetings.

"All plugged?"

"You're paying me, Captain," Dan's voice grated through. "Strung up and out."

"Ready, Captain," from Brian.

"Open your low vanes—"

Prince sat behind Lorq, one hand on Lorq's shoulder (his real hand). "Everybody and his brother is coming to this thing. You just got here tonight, but people have been arriving all week. I invited a hundred people. There're at least three hundred coming. It grows, it grows!" As the inertia field caught them up, De Blau dropped, and the sun, which had set, rose in the west and crescented the world with fire. The blue rim burned. "Anyway, Che-ong brought a perfectly wild bunch with her from somewhere on the edge of Draco—"

Brian's voice came over the speaker. "Che-ong, you mean the psychorama star?"

"The studio gave her a week's vacation, so she decided to come to my party. Day before yesterday, she took it into her head to go mountain climbing, and flew off to Nepal."

The sun passed overhead. To travel between two points on one planet, you just had to go up and come down in the right place. In a vane-projector craft, you had to ascend, circle the Earth three or four times, and glide in. It took the same seven/eight minutes to get from one side of the city to the other as it did to get to the other side of the world.

"Che radioed me this afternoon they were stuck three

quarters of the way up Mt. Kenyuna. There's a storm below
them, so they can't get through to the rescue station in
Katmandu for a helicopter to come and pick them up. Of
course, the storm doesn't stop her from getting a third of the
way around the world to tell me her troubles. Anyway, I
promised her I'd think of something."

"How the hell are we supposed to get them off the mountain?"

"*You* fly within twenty feet of the rock face and hover.
Then *I'll* climb down and bring them up."

"Twenty feet!" The blurred world slowed beneath them.
"You want to get to your party alive?"

"Did you get that ion-coupler Aaron sent?"

"I'm using it now."

"It's supposed to be sensitive enough for that sort of
maneuvering. And you're a crack racing captain. Yes or no?"

"I'll try it," Lorq said warily. "I'm a bigger fool than you
are." Then he laughed. "We'll try it, Prince!"

Reticulations of snow and rock glided under them. Lorq
set the loran co-ordinates of the mountain as Prince had
given them. Prince reached over Lorq's arm and tuned the
radio . . .

A girl's voice tumbled into the cabin:

". . . Oh, there! Look, do you think that's them? Prince!
Prince, darling, have you come to rescue us? We're hanging
here by our little frozen nubs and just miserable. Prince
. . . ?" There was music behind her voice; there was a babble
of other voices.

"Hold on, Che," Prince said into the mike. "Told you we'd
do something." He turned to Lorq. "There! They should be
right down there."

Lorq cut the frequency filter till *Caliban* was sliding down
the gravitational distortion of the mountain itself. The peaks
rose, chiseled and flashing.

"Oh, look, everybody! Didn't I tell you Prince wouldn't let
us languish away up here and miss the party?"

And in the background:

"Oh, Cecil, I can't do that step—"

"Turn the music up louder—"

"But I don't *like* anchovies—"

"Prince," cried Che, "do hurry! It's started to snow again.

You know this would never have happened, Cecil, if you hadn't decided to do parlor tricks with the hobenstocks."

"Come on, sweetheart, let's dance!"

"I told you, no! We're too close to the edge!"

Below Lorq's feet, on the floor screen, transmitting natural light, ice and gravel and boulders shone in the moonlight as the *Caliban* lowered.

"How many of them are there?" Lorq asked. "The ship isn't that big."

"They'll squeeze."

On the icy ledge that slipped across the screen, som: were seated on a green poncho with wine bottles, cheeses, and baskets of food. Some were dancing. A few sat around on canvas chairs. One had scrambled to a higher ledge and was shading his eyes, staring up at the ship.

"Che," Prince said, "we're here. Get everything packed. We can't wait around all day."

"Good heavens! That *is* you up there. Come on, everybody, we're on our way! Yes, that's Prince!"

There was an explosion of activity on the ledge. The youngsters began to run about, picking things up, putting them in knapsacks; two people were folding the poncho.

"Edgar! *Don't* throw that away! It's 'forty-eight, and you can't just pick up a bottle any old where. Yes, Hillary, you *may* change the music. *No!* Don't turn the heater off *yet!* Oh, Cecil, you *are* a fool. Brrrr!—well, I suppose we'll be off in a moment or two. Of course I'll dance with you, honey. Just not so close to the edge. Wait a second. Prince? Prince . . . !"

"Che!" Prince called as Lorq settled still closer. "Do you have any rope down there?" He put his hand over the mike. "Did you see her in *Mayham's Daughters* where she acted the wacky, sixteen-year-old daughter of that botanist?"

Lorq nodded.

"That wasn't acting." He took his hand from the mike again. "Che! Rope! Do you have any rope?"

"Oodles! Edgar, where's all that rope? But we climbed up here on *something!* There it is! Now, what do I do?"

"Tie big knots in it every couple of feet. How far are we above you?"

"Forty feet? Thirty feet? Edgar! Cecil! José! You heard him. Tie knots!"

On the floor screen Lorq watched the shadow of the yacht slip over the bergs; he let the boat fall even lower.

"Lorq, open the hatch in the drive-room when we're—"

"We're seventeen feet above them," Lorq called over his shoulder. "That's it, Prince!" He reached forward. "And it is open."

"Fine!"

Prince ducked through the doorway into the drive-room. Cold air slapped Lorq's back. Dan and Brian held the ship steady in the wind.

On the floor screen Lorq saw one of the boys fling the rope up at the ship—Prince would be standing in the open hatchway to catch it in his silver glove. It took three tries. Then Prince's voice came back over the wind: "Right! I've got it tied. Come on up!" And one after another they mounted the knotted rope.

"There you go. Watch it—"

"Man, it's cold out there! Soon as you get past the heating field—"

"I've got you. Right in—"

"Didn't think we'd make it. Hey, you want some Châteauneuf du Pape 'forty-eight? Che says you can't get—"

The voices filled the drive-room. Then:

"Prince! Luscious of you to rescue me! Are you going to have any nineteenth-century Turkish music at your party? We couldn't get any local stations, but there was this educational program beaming up from New Zealand. Airy! Edgar invented a new step. You get down on your hands and knees and just swing your up and down. José, don't fall back onto that silly mountain! Come in here this instant and meet Prince Red. He's the one who's giving the party, and his father has ever so many more millions than yours. Close the door now and let's get out of the engine room. All these machines and things. It isn't me."

"Come inside, Che, and annoy the captain awhile. Do you know Lorq Von Ray?"

"My goodness, the boy who's winning all those races? Why, he's got even more money than you—"

"*Shhhhh!*" Prince said in a stage whisper as they came into the cabin. "I don't want *him* to know."

Lorq pulled the ship away from the mountain, then turned.

"You *must* be the one who won those prizes: You're so handsome!"

Che-ong wore a completely transparent cold suit.

"Did you win them with this ship?"

She looked around the cabin, still panting from the climb up the rope. Rouged nipples flattened on vinyl with each breath.

"This is lovely. I haven't been on a yacht in days."

And the crowd surged in behind her:

"Doesn't anybody want any of this 'forty-eight—"

"I can't get any music in here. Why isn't there any music—"

"Cecil, do you have any more of that gold powder?"

"We're above the ionosphere, stupid, and electromagnetic waves aren't reflected any more. Besides, we're moving too—"

Che-ong turned to them all. "Oh, Cecil, where has that marvelous golden dust got to? Prince, Lorq, you must try this. Cecil is the son of a mayor—"

"Governor—"

"—on one of those tiny worlds we're always hearing about, very far away. He had this gold powder that they collect from crevices in the rocks. Oh, look, he's still got lots and lots!"

The world began to spin beneath them.

"See, Prince, you breathe it in, like this. Ahhhh! It makes you see the most marvelous colors in everything you look at and hear the most incredible sounds in everything you hear, and your mind starts running about and filling in absolutely paragraphs between each word. Here, Lorq—"

"Watch it!" Prince laughed. "He's got to get us back to Paris!"

"Oh!" exclaimed Che, "it won't bother him. We'll just get there a little faster, that's all."

Behind them the others were saying:

"Where did she say this goddamn party was?"

"Ile St.-Louis. That's in Paris."

"Where—?"

"Paris, baby, Paris. We're going to a party in—"

In the middle of the fourth century the Byzantine Emperor Julian, tiring of the social whirl of the Cité de Paris (whose population, then under a thousand, dwelt mostly in skin huts clustered about a stone and wooden temple sacred to the

Great Mother), moved across the water to the smaller island.

In the first half of the twentieth century, the queen of a worldwide cosmetic industry, to escape the pretensions of the Right Bank and the bohemian excesses of the Left, established here her Paris *pied à terre*, the walls of which were lined with a fortune in art treasures (while across the water, a twin-towered cathedral had replaced the wooden temple).

At the close of the thirty-first century, its central avenue hung with lights, the side alleys filled with music, menageries, drink, and gaming booths, while fireworks boomed in the night, the Ile St.-Louis held Prince Red's party.

"This way! Across here!"

They trooped over the trestled bridge. The black Seine glittered. Across the water, foliage dripped the stone balustrades. The sculptured buttresses of Notre Dame, floodlit now, rose behind the trees in the park on the Cité.

"No one can come onto my island without a mask!" Prince shouted.

As they reached the bridge's center, he vaulted to the rail, grabbed one of the beams, and waved over the crowd with his silver hand. "You're at a party! You're at Prince's party! And everybody wears a mask!" Spheres of fireworks, blue and red, bloomed on the dark behind his bony face.

"Airy!" squealed Che-ong, running to the rail. "But if I wear a mask, nobody will recognize me, Prince! The studio only said I could come if there was publicity!"

He jumped, grabbed her vinyl glove, and led her down the steps. There, on racks, hundreds of full-headed masks glared.

"But I have a special one for you, Che!" He pulled down a two-foot, transparent rat's head, ears rimmed with white fur, eyebrows sequined, jewels shaking at the end of each wire whisker.

"Airy!" squealed Che as Prince clapped the shape over her shoulders.

Through the transparent leer, her own delicate, green-eyed face twisted into laughter.

"Here, one for you!" Down came a saber-toothed panther's head for Cecil; an eagle for Edgar, with iridescent feathers; José's dark hair disappeared under a lizard's head.

A lion for Dan (who had come protesting at everyone's insistence, though they had forgotten him the moment he had given his belligerent consent) and a griffon for Brian (whom everyone had ignored till now, though he'd followed eagerly).

"And you!" Prince turned to Lorq. "I have a special one for you too!" Laughing, he lifted down a pirate's head, with eyepatch, bandana, scarred cheek, and a dagger in bared teeth. It went lightly over Lorq's head: he was looking through mesh eyeholes in the neck. Prince slapped him on the back. "A pirate, that's for Von Ray!" he called as Lorq started across the cobble street.

More laughter as others arrived at the bridge.

Above the crowd, girls in powdered, towering, twenty-third-century, pre-Ashton Clark coiffures, tossed confetti from a balcony. A man was pushing up the street with a bear. Lorq thought it was someone in costume till the fur brushed his shoulder and he smelled the musk. The claws clicked away. The crowd caught him up.

Lorq was ears.

Lorq was eyes.

Bliss filed the receptive surface of each sense glass-smooth. Perception turned suddenly in (as the vanes of a ship might turn) as he walked the brick street, mortared with confetti. He felt the presence of his centered self. His world focused on the now of his hands and tongue. Voices around him caressed his awareness.

"Champagne! Isn't that just airy!" The transparent plastic rat had cornered the griffon in the flowered vest at the wine table. "Aren't you having fun? I just love it!"

"Sure," Brian answered. "But I've never been to a party like this. People like Lorq, Prince, you—you're the sort of people I only used to hear about. It's hard to believe you're real."

"Just between us. I've occasionally had the same problem. It's good to have you here to remind us. Now you just keep telling us—"

Lorq passed on to another group.

". . . on the cruise boat up from Port Said to Istanbul, there was this fisherman from the Pleiades who played the most marvelous things on the sensory-syrynx . . ."

". . . and then we had to hitchhike all the way across Iran because the mono wasn't working. I really think Earth is coming apart at the seams . . ."

". . . beautiful party. Perfectly airy . . ."

The very young, Lorq thought; the very rich; and wondered what limits of difference those conditions defined.

Barefoot, with a rope belt, the lion leaned against the side of a doorway, watching. "How you doing, Captain?"

Lorq raised his hand to Dan, walked on.

Now, specious and crystal, was within him. Music invaded his hollow mask where his head was cushioned on the sound of his own breath. On a platform at a harpsichord a man was playing a Byrd pavane. Voices in another key grew over the sound as he moved further on; on a platform on the other side of the street, two boys and two girls in twentieth-century mod re-created a flowing antiphonal work of the Mommas and the Poppas. Turning down a side street, Lorq moved into a crowd that pushed him forward, till at last he confronted the towering bank of electronic instruments that were reproducing the jarring, textured silences of the *Tohu-bohus*. Responding with the nostalgia produced by ten-year-old popular music, the guests, in their bloated mâché and plastic heads, broke off in twos, threes, fives, and sevens to dance. A swan's head swayed to the right. Left, a frog's face wobbled on sequined shoulders. As he moved even further, into his ear threaded the thirdless modulations that he had heard over the speaker of the *Caliban*, hovering above the Himalayas.

They came running through the dancers. "He did it! Isn't Prince a darling!" They shouted and cavorted. "He's got that old Turkish music!"

Hips and breasts and shoulders gleaming beneath the vinyl (the material had pores that opened in warm weather to make the transparent costume cool as silk), Che-ong swung around, holding her furry ears.

"Down, everybody! Down on all fours! We're going to show you our new step! Like this: just swing your—"

Lorq turned under the exploding night, a little tired, a little excited. He crossed the street edging the island and leaned on the stone near one of the floodlights that shone back on the buildings of the Ile. Across the water on the opposite quay people strolled, in couples or singly, gazing at the fireworks or simply watching the gaiety here.

Behind him a girl laughed sharply. He turned to her—

—head of a bird of paradise, blue feathers about red foil eyes, red beak, red rippling comb—

—as she pulled away from the group to sway against the low wall. The breeze shook the panels of her dress so that they tugged at the scrolled brass fastenings at shoulder, wrist, and thigh. She rested her hip on the stone, one sandaled toe touching the ground, one an inch above it. With long arms (her nails were crimson) she removed her mask. As she set it on the wall, the breeze shook out her black hair, dropped it to her shoulders, raised it. The water reticulated below them as under flung sand.

He looked away. He looked back. He frowned.

There are two beauties (her face struck the thought in him, articulate and complete): with the first, the features and the body's lines conform to an averaged standard that will offend no one: this was the beauty of model and popular actresses; this was the beauty of Che-ong. Second, there was this: her eyes were smashed disks of blue jade, her cheekbones angled high over the white hollows of her wide face. Her chin was wide; her mouth, thin, red, and wider. Her nose fell straight from her forehead to flare at the nostrils (she breathed in the wind—and watching her, he became aware of the river's odor, the Paris night, the city wind); these features were too austere and violent on the face of such a young woman. But the authority with which they set together would make him look again, he knew, once he looked away; make him remember, once he had gone away. Her face compelled in the way that makes the merely beautiful gnaw the insides of their cheeks.

She looked at him: "Lorq Von Ray?"

His frown deepened inside his mask.

She leaned forward, above the paving that lipped the river. "They're all so far away." She nodded toward the people on the quay. "They're so much farther away than we think, or they think. What would they do at our party?"

Lorq took off his mask and placed the pirate beside her crested bird.

She glanced back at him. "So that's what you look like. You're handsome."

"How did you know who I was?" Thinking he might somehow have missed her in the crowd that had first come across the bridge, he expected her to say something about the pictures of him that occasionally appeared across the galaxy when he won a race.

"Your mask. That's how I knew."

"Really?" He smiled. "I don't understand."

Her eyebrows' arch sharpened. There were a few seconds of laughter, too soft and gone too fast.

"You. Who are you?" Lorq asked.

"I'm Ruby Red."

She was still thin. Somewhere a little girl had stood above him in the mouth of a beast—

Lorq laughed now. "What was there about my mask that gave me away?"

"Prince has been gloating over the prospect of making you wear it ever since he extended the invitation through your father and there was the faintest possibility that you would actually come. Tell me, is it politeness that makes you indulge him in his nasty prank by wearing it?"

"Everyone else has one. I thought it was a clever idea."

"I see." Her voice hung above the tone of general statement. "My brother tells me we have all met a long time ago." It returned. "I . . . wouldn't have recognized you. But I remember you."

"I remember you."

"Prince does too. He was seven. That means I was five."

"What have you been doing for the last dozen years?"

"Growing older gracefully, while you've been the *enfant terrible* in the raceways of the Pleiades, flaunting your parents' ill-gotten gains."

"Look!" He gestured toward the people watching from the opposite bank. Some apparently thought he waved; they waved back.

Ruby laughed and waved too. "Do they realize how special we are? I feel very special tonight." She raised her face with eyes closed. Blue fireworks tinted her lids.

"Those people, they're too far away to see how beautiful you are."

She looked at him again.

"It's true. You are—"

"We are . . ."

"—very beautiful."

"Don't you think that's a dangerous thing to say to your hostess, Captain Von Ray?"

"Don't you think that was a dangerous thing to say to your guest?"

"But we're unique, young Captain. If we want, we're allowed to flirt with dan—"

The streetlights about them extinguished.

There was a cry from the side street; the strings of colored bulbs as well were dead. As Lorq turned from the embankment, Ruby took his shoulder.

Along the island, lights and windows flickered twice. Someone screamed. Then the illumination returned, and with it laughter.

"*My* brother!" Ruby shook her head. "Everyone told him he was going to have power trouble, but he insisted on having the whole island wired for electricity. He thought electric light would be more romantic than the perfectly good induced-fluorescence tubes that were here yesterday—and have to go back up tomorrow by city ordinance. You should have seen him trying to hunt up a generator. It's a lovely six-hundred-year-old museum piece that fills up a whole room. I'm afraid Prince is an incurable romantic—"

Lorq placed his hand over hers.

She looked. She took her hand away. "I have to go now. I promised I'd help him." Her smile was not a happy thing. The piercing expression etched itself on his heightened senses. "Don't wear Prince's mask any more." She lifted the bird of paradise from the rail. "Just because he choses to insult you, you needn't display that insult to everyone here."

Lorq looked down at the pirate's head, confused.

Foil eyes glittered at him from blue feathers. "Besides"—her voice was muffled now—"you're too handsome to cover yourself up with something so mean and ugly." And she was crossing the street, was disappearing in the crowded alley.

He looked up and down the sidewalk, and did not want to be there.

He crossed after her, plunged into the same crowd, only realizing halfway down the block that he was following her.

She *was* beautiful.

That was not bliss.

That was not the party's excitement.

That was her face and the way it turned and formed to her words.

That was the hollow in him so evident now because moments before, during a few banal exchanges, it had been so full of her face, her voice.

". . . trouble with all of this is that there's no cultural solidity underneath." (Lorq glanced to the side where the griffon was speaking to earnest armadillos, apes, and others.) "There's been so much movement from world to world that we have no real art any more, just a pseudo-interplanetary . . ."

In the doorway, on the ground, lay a lion's head and a frog's. Back in the darkness, Dan, his back sweating from the dance, nuzzled the girl with sequined shoulders.

And halfway down the block, Ruby passed up a set of steps behind scrolled iron.

"Ruby!"

He ran forward—

"Hey, watch—"

"Look out. Where do you—"

"Slow down—"

—swung round the banister, and ran up the steps after her, "Ruby Red!" and through a door. "Ruby . . . ?"

Wide tapestries between thin mirrors cut all echo from his voice. The door by the marble table was ajar. So he crossed the foyer, opened it.

She turned on swirling light.

Beneath the floor, tides of color flowed the room, flickering on the heavy, black-in-crystal legs of Vega Republic furniture. Without shadow, she stepped back. "Lorq! *Now* what are you doing here?" She had just placed her bird mask on one of the circular shelves that drifted at various levels around the room.

"I wanted to talk to you some more."

Her brows were dark arches over her eyes. "I'm sorry. Prince has planned a pantomime for the float that goes down the middle of the island at midnight. I have to change."

One of the shelves had drifted toward him. Before it could respond to his body temperature and float away, Lorq removed a liquor bottle from the veined glass panel. "Do you have to rush?" He raised the bottle. "I want to find out who you are, what you do, what you think. I want to tell you all about me."

"Sorry." She turned toward the spiral lift that would take her up to the balcony.

His laughter stopped her. She turned back to see what had caused it.

"Ruby?"

And continued turning till she faced him again.

He crossed the surging floor and put his hands on the smooth cloth falling at her shoulders. His fingers closed on her arms. "Ruby Red." His inflection brought puzzlement to her face. "Leave here with me. We can go to another city, on another world, under another sun. Don't the configurations of the stars bore you from here? I know a world where the constellations are called the Mad Sow's Litter, the Greater and Lesser Lynx, the Eye of Vahdamin."

She took two glasses from a passing shelf. "What are you high on anyway?" Then she smiled. "Whatever it is, it becomes you."

"Will you go?"

"No."

"Why not?" He poured frothing amber into tiny glasses.

"First." She handed him the glass as he placed the bottle on another passing shelf. "Because it's terribly rude—I don't know how you do it back on Ark—for a hostess to run out on her party before midnight."

"After midnight then?"

"Second." She sipped the drink and wrinkled her nose (he was surprised, shocked that her clear, clear skin could support anything so human as a wrinkle). "Prince has been planning this party for months, and I don't want to upset him by not showing up when I promised." Lorq touched his fingers to her cheek. "Third." Her eyes snapped from the brim of her glass to lock his. "I'm Aaron Red's daughter and you are the dark, redhaired, high, handsome son"—she turned her head away—"of a blond thief!" Cold air on his fingertips where her warm arm had been.

He put his palm against her face, slid his fingers into her hair. She turned away from his hand and stepped onto the spiral lift. She rose up and away, adding, "And you haven't got much pride if you let Prince mock you the way he does."

Lorq jumped onto the edge as the lift came around. She stepped back, surprised.

"What's all this talk of thieves, piracy, and mocking mean?" Anger, not at her but at the confusion she caused. "I don't understand and I don't know if it sounds like anything I want to. I don't know how it is on Earth, but on Ark you don't make fun of your guests."

Ruby looked at her glass, his eyes, her glass again. "I'm sorry." And then his eyes. "Go outside, Lorq. Prince will be here in a few minutes. I shouldn't have spoken to you at all—"

"Why?" The room revolved, falling. "Whom you should speak to, whom you shouldn't; I don't know what brings this all up, but you're talking as if we were little people." He laughed again, a slow low sound in his chest, rising to shake his shoulders. "You're Ruby Red?" He took her shoulders and pulled her forward. For a moment her blue eyes beat. "And you take all this nonsense that little people say seriously?"

"Lorq, you'd better—"

"I'm Lorq Von Ray! And you're Ruby, Ruby, Ruby Red!" The lift had already taken them past the first balcony.

"Lorq, please. I've got to—"

"You've got to come with me! Will you go over the rim of Draco, with me, Ruby? Will you come to Ark, where you and your brother have never been? Or come with me to São Orini. There's a house there that you'd remember if you saw it, there at the galaxy's edge." They rose by the second balcony, rotated toward the third. "We'll play behind the bamboo on the stone lizards' tongues—"

She cried out. Because veined glass struck the lift ceiling and rained fragments over them.

"Prince!" She pulled away from Lorq, and stared down over the lift's edge.

"*Get* AWAY FROM HER!" His silver glove snatched another of the shelves from the inductance field that caused it to float around the room, and sailed it at them. "Damn you, you . . ." His voice rasped to silence on his anger, then broke: "Get *away!*"

The second disk hissed by their shoulders and smashed on the balcony bottom. Lorq flung up his arm to knock aside the shards.

Prince ran across the floor to the stairway that mounted at the left side of the tiered chamber. Lorq ran from the lift across the carpeted balcony till he reached the head of the same stairway—Ruby behind him—and started down.

They met on the first balcony. Prince grasped both rails, panting with fury.

"Prince, what the hell is the matter with—"

Prince lunged for him. His silver glove clanged the railing where Lorq had been standing. The brass bar caved, the metal tore. "Thief! Marauder!" Prince hissed, "Murderer! Scum—"

"What are you talking—"

"—spawn of scum. If you touch my—" His arm lashed again.

"No, Prince!" (That was Ruby.)

Lorq vaulted the balcony and dropped twelve feet to the floor. He landed, falling to his hands and knees in a pool of red that faded to yellow, was cut by drifting green.

"Lorq—!" (Ruby again.)

He flipped, rolling on multichrome (and saw Ruby at the rail, hands at her mouth; then Prince cleared the rail, was in the air, was falling at him). Prince struck the place Lorq's head had been with his silver fist.

Crack!

Lorq staggered back to his feet and tried to regain his breath. Prince was still down.

The multichrome had smashed under his glove. Cracks zagged a yard out from the impact. The pattern had frozen in a sunburst around the glaring point.

"You . . ." Lorq began. Words floundered under panting. "You and Ruby, are you crazy—?"

Prince rocked back to his knees. Fury and pain hooked his face up in outrage. The lips quivered about small teeth, the lids about turquoise eyes. "You clown, you pig, you come to Earth and dare to put your hands, your *hands* on my—"

"Prince, *please*—*!*" Her voice tautened above them. Anguish. Her violent beauty shattered with a cry.

Prince reeled to his feet, grasped another floating shelf. He flung it, roaring.

Lorq cried as it cut his arm and crashed into the French doors behind him.

Cooler air swept the room as the panels swung. Laughter poured from the street.

"I'll get you; I'll catch you, and"—he rushed Lorq—"I'll hurt you!"

Lorq turned, jumped the wrought iron and crashed against the crowd.

They screamed as he barreled through. Hands struck his face, pushed his chest, grabbed his shoulders. The screaming—

and the laughter—increased. Prince was behind him because:

"What are they . . . ? Hey, watch out—"

"They're fighting! Look, that's Prince—"

"Hold them! Hold them! What are they—"

Lorq broke from the crowd and stumbled against the balustrade. For a moment the rushing Seine and wet rock were below. He pulled back and turned to see.

"Let *go* of me!" Prince's voice howled from the crowd. "Let go of my hand! My *hand*, let go of my hand!"

Memories struck up, shaking. What was confusion before, was fear now.

Beside him stone steps led to the river's walkway. He fled down, and heard others behind him as he reached the bottom.

Then lights ground on his eyes. Lorq shook his head. Light across the wet pavement, the mossy stone wall beside him—someone had swung a floodlight over to watch.

"Let go of my—" He heard Prince's voice, cutting through the others. "I'm going to *get* him!"

Prince raced down the steps, reflections glancing from the rocks. He balanced at the bottom, squinting by the floodlit river.

His vest had been pulled from one shoulder. In the scuffle he had lost the long glove.

Lorq backed away.

Prince raised his arm:

Copper mesh and jeweled capacitors webbed black metal bone; pulleys whirred in the clear casing.

Lorq took another step.

Prince lunged.

Lorq dodged for the wall; the two boys spun around each other.

The guests crowded the rail, pushed at the banister. Foxes and lizards, eagles and insects joggled one another to see. Someone stumbled against the floodlight, and the inverted gallery in the water shook.

"Thief!" Prince's narrow chest was in spasm. "Pirate!" A rocket flared overhead. The explosion thudded after. "You're dirt, Lorq Von Ray! You're less than—"

Now Lorq lunged.

Anger snapped in his chest, his eyes, his hands. One fist

caught the side of Prince's head, the other jabbed his stomach. He came with blasted pride, fury compelled by bewilderment, with dense humiliation breaking his breath against his ribs as he fought below the fantastic spectators. He struck again, not knowing where.

Prince's prosthetic arm swung up.

It caught him under the chin, bright fingers flat. It crushed skin, scraped bone, went on up, opening lip and cheek and forehead. Fat and muscle tore.

Lorq screamed, bloody mouthed, and fell.

"Prince!" Ruby (struggling to see, it was she who had jarred the light) stood on the wall. Red dress and dark hair whipped behind her in the river wind. "Prince, *no!*"

Panting, Prince stepped back, back again. Lorq lay face-down, one arm in the water. Beneath his head blood slurred the stone.

Prince turned sharply, and walked to the steps. Someone swung the floodlight back up. The people watching from the quay across the Seine were momentarily illuminated. Then the light went up and over, fixing on the building.

People turned from the rail.

Someone started to come down the steps, confronted Prince. After a second he turned back. A plastic rat's face left the rail. Someone took the transparent vinyl shoulder, led her away. Music from a dozen epochs clashed across the island.

Lorq's head rocked by the dark water. The river sucked his arm.

Then a lion climbed the wall, dropped barefoot to the stone. A griffon ran down the steps and fell to one knee beside him.

Dan pulled off his false head and tossed it against the steps. It thumped, rolled a foot. The griffon head followed.

Brian turned Lorq over.

Breath caught in Dan's throat, then came out whistling. "He sure messed up Captain, huh?"

"Dan, we've got to get the patrol or something. They can't do something like this!"

Dan's shaggy brows rose. "What the hell makes you think they can't? I've worked for bastards with a lot less money than Red-shift who could do a lot more."

Lorq groaned.

"A medico-unit!" Brian said. "Where do you get a medico-unit here?"

"He ain't dead. We get him back to the ship. When he comes to, I get my pay and off this damn planet!" He looked over the river from the twin spires of Notre Dame to the opposite bank. "Earth just ain't big enough for me and Australia both. I'm willing to leave." He got one arm under Lorq's knees, the other under his shoulders, and stood up.

"You're going to carry him?"

"Can you think of another way to get him back?" Dan turned toward the steps.

"But there must be—" Brian followed him. "We have to do—"

Something hissed on the water. Brian looked back.

The wing of a skimmer-boat scraped the shore. "Where are you taking Captain Von Ray?" Ruby, in the front seat, wore a dark cloak now.

"Back to his yacht, ma'am," Dan said. "It doesn't look like he's welcome here."

"Bring him on the boat."

"I don't think we should leave him in anybody's hands on this world."

"You're his crew?"

"That's right," Brian said. "Were you going to take him to a doctor?"

"I was going to take him to De Blau Field. You should get off Earth as soon as possible."

"Fine by me," Dan said.

"Put him back there. There's a pre-med kit under the seat. See if you can stop him from bleeding."

Brian stepped on the swaying skimmer and dug under the seat among the rags and chains to bring out the plastic box. The skimmer doffed again as Dan stepped aboard. In the front seat Ruby took the control line and plugged it into her wrist. They moved forward, hissing. The small boat mounted above the spray on its hydrofoils and sped. Pont St.-Michel, Pont Neuf, and Pont des Arts dropped their shadows over the boat. Paris glittered on the shores.

Minutes later the struts of the Eiffel Tower cleared the buildings left, spotlighted on the night. Right, above slanted stone and behind sycamores, the last late strollers moved under the lamps along the Allée des Cygnes.

"All right," his father said. "I'll tell you."

"I think he should get that scar . . ." his mother's image spoke from the viewing column. "It's been three days, and the longer he lets the scar go . . ."

"If he wants to go around looking as though there was an earthquake in his head, that's his business," Father said. "But right now I want to answer his question." He turned back to Lorq. "But to tell you"—he walked to the wall and gazed out across the city—"I have to tell you some history. And not what you learned at Causby."

It was high summer on Ark.

Wind tossed salmon clouds about the sky beyond the glass walls. When a gust was too strong, the blue veins of the irises in the windward wall contracted to bright mandalas, then dilated when the eighty-mile winds had passed.

His mother's fingers, dark and jeweled, moved on the rim of her cup.

His father folded his hands behind his back as he watched the clouds torn up like rags and flung from Tong.

Lorq leaned against the back of the mahogany chair, waiting.

"What strikes you as the most important factor in today's society?"

Lorq ventured after a moment: "The lack of a solid cultural—?"

"Forget Causby. Forget the things that people babble to one another when they feel they have to say something profound. You're a young man who may someday control one of the largest fortunes in the galaxy. If I ask you a question, I want you to remember who you are when you answer me. This is a society where, given any product, half of it may be grown on one world, the other half mined a thousand light-years away. On Earth, seventeen out of the hundreds of possible elements make up ninety per cent of the planet. Take any other world, and you'll find a different dozen making up ninety to ninety-nine per cent. There are two hundred and sixty-five inhabited worlds and satellites in the hundred and seventeen sun systems that make up Draco.

Here in the Federation we have three quarters the population of Draco spread over three hundred and twelve worlds. The forty-two populated worlds of the Outer Colonies—"

"Transportation," Lorq said. "Transportation from one world to the other. That's what you mean?"

His father leaned against the stone table. "The cost of transportation is what I mean. And for a long time the biggest factor in the cost of transportation was Illyrion, the only way to get enough power to hurl the ships between worlds, between stars. When my grandfather was your age, Illyrion was manufactured artificially, a few billion atoms at a time, at great cost. Just about then it was discovered there was a string of stars, younger stars, much further out from the galactic center whose planets still possessed minute quantities of natural Illyrion. And it has only been since you were born that large-scale mining operations have been feasible on those planets that now make up the Outer Colonies."

"Lorq knows this," his mother said. "I think he should have—"

"Do you know why the Pleiades Federation is a political entity separate from Draco? Do you know why the Outer Colonies will soon be a separate political entity from either Draco or the Pleiades?"

Lorq looked at his knee, his thumb, his other knee. "You're asking me questions and you're not answering mine, Dad."

His father took a breath. "I'm trying to. Before there was any settling in the Pleiades at all, expansion throughout Draco was carried on by national governments on Earth, or by corporations, ones comparable to Red-shift—corporations and governments that could afford the initial cost of transportation. The new colonies were subsidized, operated, and owned by Earth. They became part of Earth, and Earth became the center of Draco. At that time another technical problem that was being solved by the early engineers of Red-shift Limited was the construction of spaceships with more sensitive frequency ranges that could negotiate the comparatively 'dusty' areas of space, as in the free-floating interstellar nebulas, and in regions of dense stellar population like the Pleiades, where there was a much higher concentration of sloughed-off interstellar matter. Something like a whirlpool nebula still gives your little yacht trouble. It would have completely immobilized a ship made two hundred and fifty years ago. Your great-great-grandfather, when exploration was just beginning in the Pleiades, was very much aware of what I've just told you: the cost of transportation is the most important factor in our society. And within the Pleiades itself, the cost of transportation is substantially less than in Draco."

Lorq frowned. "You mean the distances . . . ?"

"The central section of the Pleiades is only thirty light-years across and eighty-five long. Some three hundred suns are packed into this space, many of them less than a light-year apart. The suns of Draco are scattered over one whole arm of the galaxy, almost sixteen thousand light-years from end to end. There's a big difference in cost when you only have to jump the tiny distances within the Pleiades cluster as compared with the huge expanses of Draco. So you had a different kind of people coming into the Pleiades: small businesses that wanted to pick up and move themselves lock, stock, and barrel; co-operative groups of colonists; even private citizens—rich private citizens, but private nevertheless. Your great-great-grandfather came here with three commercial liners filled with junk, prefab hot and cold shelters, discarded mining and farming equipment for a whole range of climates. Most of it he'd been paid to haul away from Draco. Two of the liners had been stolen, incidentally. He also had gotten hold of a couple of atomic cannons. He went around to every new settlement and offered his goods. And everyone bought from him."

"He forced them to buy at cannon point?"

"No. He also offered them a bonus service that made it worthwhile to take the junk. You see, the fact that transportation costs were lower hadn't stopped the governments and big corporations from trying to move in. Any ship that came bearing a multimillon-dollar name out of Draco, any emissary from some Draco monopoly trying to extend itself into new territory—Grandfather blew them up."

"Did he loot them too?" Lorq asked. "Did he pick over the remains?"

"He never told me. I only know he had a vision—a selfish, mercenary, ego-centered vision that he implemented in any way he could, at anyone's expense. During the formative years of its existence, he did not let the Pleiades become an extension of Draco. He saw in Pleiades independence a chance to become the most powerful man in a political entity that might someday rival Draco. Before my father was your age, Great-grandfather had accomplished that."

"I still don't understand what that has to do with Red-shift."

"Red-shift was one of the mega-companies that made the most concerted efforts to move into the Pleiades. They tried to claim the thorium mines that are now run by your school friend's father, Dr. Setsumi. They attempted to begin harvesting the plastic lichens on Circe IV. Each time, Granddad blew them up. Red-shift *is* transportation, and when the cost of transportation goes down compared to the number of ships made, Red-shift feels its throat throttled."

"And this is why Prince Red can call us pirates?"

"A couple of times Aaron Red the first—Prince's father is the third—sent one of his more uppity nephews to head his expeditions into the Pleiades. Three of them, I believe. They never got back. Even in my father's time the feud was pretty much a personal matter. There'd been retaliation, and it had gone on well beyond the declaration of sovereignty that the Pleiades Federation made in 'twenty-six. One of my personal projects as a young man your age was to end it. My father gave a lot of money to Harvard on Earth, built them a laboratory, and then sent me to the school. I married your mother, from Earth, and I spent a lot of time talking with Aaron—Prince's father. It wasn't too difficult to effect, since the sovereignty of the Pleiades had been an accepted fact for a generation, and Red-shift had long since stopped teetering under any direct threat from us. My father purchased the Illyrion mine out at New Brazillia—this was back when the mining operations were just beginning in the Outer Colonies— mainly as an excuse to have some reason to deal formally with Red-shift. I never mentioned the feud to you, because I thought there was no need to."

"Prince is just crazy then, breaking out an old grudge that you and Aaron settled before we were born."

"I can't comment on Prince's sanity. But you have to bear in mind: what's the biggest factor affecting the cost of transportation today?"

"The Illyrion mines in the Outer Colonies."

"There's a hand around Red-shift's throat again," his father said. "Can you see it?"

"Mining Illyrion naturally is much cheaper than manufacturing it."

"Even if it takes plugging in a population of millions upon millions. Even if three dozen competing companies from both Draco and the Pleiades have opened mines all over the Outer Colonies and subsidized vast migrations of labor from all over the galaxy. What strikes you as different about the set-up of the Outer Colonies as opposed to Draco and the Pleiades?"

"It has, comparatively, all the Illyrion it wants right there."

"Yes. But also this: Draco was extended by the vastly monied classes of Earth. The Pleiades was populated by a comparatively middle-class movement. Though the Outer Colonies have been prompted by those with money both in the Pleiades and Draco, the population of the colonies comes from the lowest economic strata of the galaxy. The combination of cultural difference—and I don't care what your social studies teachers at Causby say—and the difference in the cost of transportation is what assures the eventual sovereignty of the Outer Colonies. And suddenly Red-shift is striking out at anyone who has their hands on Illyrion again." He gestured toward his son. "You've been hit."

"But we've only got one Illyrion mine. Our money comes from the control of how many dozen different types of businesses all over the Pleiades, a few of them in Draco now—the mine on São Orini is a trifle—"

"True. But have you ever noticed the businesses we *don't* handle?"

"What do you mean, Dad?"

"We have very little money in shelter or food production. We are in computers, small technical components; we make the housing for Illyrion batteries; we make plugs and sockets; we mine heavily in other areas. The last time I saw Aaron, on this past trip, I said to him, jokingly of course: 'You know, if the price of Illyrion were only at half the price it is now, in a year I could be making spaceships at *less* than half the price you manufacture them.' And do you know what he said to me, jokingly?"

Lorq shook his head.

" 'I've known that for ten years.' "

His mother's image put her cup down. "I think he must have his face fixed. You're such a fine-looking boy, Lorq, it's been three days since that Australian brought you back home. That scar is just going to—"

"Dana," his father said. "Lorq, can you think of any way to lower the price of Illyrion by half?"

Lorq frowned. "Why?"

"I've figured that at the present rate of expansion, in fifteen years the Outer Colonies will be able to lower the cost of Illyrion by almost a quarter. During that time, Red-shift is going to try to kill us." He paused. "Knock everything out from under the Von Rays, and ultimately, the whole Pleiades Federation. We have a long way to fall. The only way we can survive is to kill them first; and the only way we can do that is to figure out a way to get Illyrion down to half price before it goes down to three quarters, and make those ships." His father folded his arms. "I didn't want to get you involved in this, Lorq. I saw the termination of the whole affair coming in my lifetime. But Prince has taken it on himself to strike the first blow at you. It's only fair you be told what's happening."

Lorq was looking down at his hands. After a while he said, "I'll strike a blow back."

"No," his mother said. "That's not the way to handle this, Lorq. You can't get back at Prince; you can't think of getting back at—"

"I'm not." He stood up and walked to the curtains. "Mom, Dad, I'm going out."

"Lorq," his father said, unfolding his arms, "I didn't mean to upset you. But I just wanted you to know . . ."

Lorq pushed back the brocade curtains. "I'm going down to the *Caliban*. Good-bye." The drape swung.

"Lorq—"

His name was Lorq Von Ray and he lived at 12 Extol Park in Ark, the capital city of the Pleiades Federation. He walked beside the moving road. Through the wind shields, the winter gardens of the city bloomed. People looked at him. That was because of the scar. He was thinking about Illyrion. People looked, then looked away when they saw him look back. Here, in the center of the Pleiades, he himself was a center, a focus. He had once tried to calculate the amount of money that devolved from his immediate family. He was the focus of billions, walking along by the clear walls of the covered streets of Ark, listening to the glistening lichens ululate in the winter gardens. One out of five people on the street—so one of his father's accountants had informed them—was being paid a salary either directly or indirectly by Von Ray. And Red-shift was making ready to declare war on the whole structure that was Von Ray, that focused on himself as the Von Ray heir. At São Orini, a lizard-like animal with a mane of white feathers roamed and hissed in the jungles. The miners caught them, starved them, then turned them on one another in the pit to wager on the outcome. How many millions of years back, those three-foot lizards' ancestors had been huge, hundred-meter beasts, and the intelligent race which had inhabited New Brazillia had worshiped them, carving life-sized stone heads about the foundations of their temples. But the race—that race was gone. And the offspring of that race's gods, dwarfed by evolution, were mocked in the pits by drunken miners as they clawed and screeched and bit. And he was Lorq Von Ray. And somehow Illyrion had to have its price lowered by half. You could flood the market with the stuff. But where could you go to get what was probably the rarest substance in the universe? You couldn't fly into the center of a sun and scoop it out of the furnace where all the substances of the galaxy were smelted from raw nuclear matter by units of four. He caught his reflection in one of the mirrored columns, and he stopped just before the turnoff to Nea Limani. The fissure dislocated his features, full-lipped, yellow-eyed. But where the scar entered the kinky red, he noticed something. The new hair growing was the same color and texture as his father's, soft and yellow as flame.

Where do you get that much Illyrion (he turned from the mirrored column)? Where?

"You're asking me, Captain?" From the revolving stage in the floor Dan lifted his mug to his knee. "If I knew, I wouldn't be bumming around this field now." He reached down, took the handle of the mug from his toes, and drank half. "Thanks for the drink." With his wrist he scrubbed his mouth, ringed with stubble and mustached with foam. "When are you going to get your face put back together . . . ?"

But Lorq was leaning back on the seat, looking through the ceiling. The lights about the field left only the hundred brightest stars visible. On the ceiling, the kaleidoscopic wind-iris was shutting. Centered among the blue, purple, and vermilion vanes was a star.

"Say, Captain, if you want to go up in the balcony . . ."

On the second level of the bar, visible through falling water, the freighter officers and some of the liner crew mixed with the sportsmen discussing currents and cosmic conditions. The lower level was crowded with mechanics and commercial studs. Card games progressed in the corner.

"I got to get me a job, Captain. Letting me sleep in the back chamber of *Caliban*, then getting me drunk every night doesn't help much. I've got to turn you loose."

Wind passed again; the iris shuddered about the star. "Dan, have you," Lorq mused, "ever realized that every sun, as we travel between them, is a furnace where the very worlds of empire are smelted? Every element among the hundreds is fused from their central nuclear matter. Take that one there—" He pointed at the transparent roof. "—or any one: gold is fusing there right now, and radium, nitrogen, antimony, in amounts that are huge—bigger than Ark, bigger than Earth. And there's Illyrion there too, Dan." He laughed. "Suppose there were some way to dip into one of those stars and ladle out what I wanted." He laughed again; the sound caught in his chest, where anguish, despair, and fury fused. "Suppose we could stand at the edge of some star gone nova and wait for what we wanted to be flung out, and catch it as it flamed by—but novas are implosions, not explosions, hey, Dan?" He pushed the stud's shoulder playfully. Drink sloshed from the mug's rim.

"Me, Captain, I was in a nova, once." Dan licked the back of his hand.

"Were you now?" Lorq pressed his head against the cushion. The haloed star flickered.

"Ship I was on got caught in a nova—must be about ten years ago."

"Aren't *you* glad you weren't on it."

"I was. We got out again too."

Lorq looked down from the ceiling.

Dan sat forward on the green bench, knobby elbows on his knees; his hands wrapped the mug.

"You did?"

"Yeah." Dan glanced at his shoulder where the broken lace on his vest was clumsily knotted. "We fell in, and we got out."

Puzzlement surfaced on Lorq's face.

"Hey, Captain! You look fierce, don't you!"

Five times now Lorq had passed his face in a mirror, thinking it bore one expression, to discover the scar had translated it into something that totally amazed. "What happened, Dan?"

The Australian looked at his mug. There was only foam at the bottom of the glass.

Lorq pressed the order plate on the bench arm. Two more mugs circled toward them, foam dissolving.

"Just what I needed, Captain." Dan reached out his foot "One for you. There you go. And one for me."

Lorq sipped his drink and stuck his feet out to rest on the sandal heels. Nothing moved on his face. Nothing moved behind it.

"You know the Alkane Institute?" Dan raised his voice above the cheers and laughter from the corner where two mechanics had begun wrestling on the trampoline. Spectators waved their drinks. "On Vorpis in Draco they got this big museum with laboratories and stuff, and they study things like novas."

"My aunt's a curator there." Lorq's voice was low, words clearing beneath the shouts.

"Yeah? Anyway, they send out people whenever they get reports of some star acting up—"

"Look! She winning is!"

"No! He her arm watch pull!"

"Hey, Von Ray, you the man or woman will win think?" A group of officers had come down the ramp to watch the match. One slapped Lorq's shoulder, then turned his hand up. There was a ten-pound @sg piece in his palm.

"I not tonight wager make." Lorq pushed the hand away.

"Lorq, I double this on the woman lay—"

"Tomorrow your money I take," Lorq said. "Now you go."

The young officer made a disgusted sound and drew his finger down his face, shaking his head to his companions.

But Lorq was waiting for Dan to go on.

Dan turned from the wrestling. "It seems a freighter got lost in a tidal drift and noticed something funny about the spectral lines of some star a couple of solars away. Stars are mostly hydrogen, yeah, but there was a big build-up of heavy materials on the gases of the surface; that means something odd. When they finally got themselves found, they reported the condition of the star to the cartographic society of the Alkane, who took a guess at what it was—the build-up of a nova. Because the make-up of a star doesn't change in a nova, you can't detect the build-up over any distance with spectranalysis or anything like that; Alkane sent out a team to watch the star. They've studied some twenty or thirty of them in the last fifty years. They put up rings of remote-control stations as close to the star as Mercury is to Sol; they send televised pictures of the star's surface; these stations burn the second the sun goes. They put rings of stations further and further out that send second-by-second reports of the whole thing. At about one light-week they have the first manned stations; even these are abandoned for stations further out soon as the nova begins. Anyway, I was on a ship that was supposed to bring supplies to one of these manned stations that was sitting around waiting for the sun to blow. You know the actual time it takes for the sun to go from its regular brightness to maximum magnitude twenty or thirty thousand times as bright is only about two or three hours."

Lorq nodded.

"They still can't judge exactly when a nova that they've been watching is going to go. Now I don't understand it exactly, but somehow the sun we were coming to went up just before we reached our stop-off station. Maybe it was a twist in space itself, or a failure of instruments, but we overshot the station and went right on into the sun, during the first hour of implosion." Dan lowered his mouth to sip off foam.

"All right," Lorq said. "From the heat, you should have been atomized before you were as close to the sun as Pluto is from Sol. You should have been crushed by the actual physical battering. The gravitational tides should have torn you to pieces. The amount of radiation the ship was exposed to should have, first, knocked apart every organic compound in the ship, and second, fissioned every atom down into ionized hydrogen—"

"Captain, I can think of seven more things without trying. The ionization frequencies should have—" Dan stopped. "But none of them did. Our ship was funneled directly through the center of the sun—and *out* the other side. We were deposited safely about two light-weeks away. The captain, as soon as he realized what was happening, pulled his head in and turned off all our sensory-input scanners so that we were falling blind. An hour later he peeked out and was very surprised to find we still were—period. But the instruments recorded our path. We had gone straight through the nova." Dan finished his drink. He looked sideways at Lorq. "Captain, you're looking all fierce again."

"What's the explanation?"

Dan shrugged. "They came up with a lot of suggestions when Alkane got hold of us. They got these bubbles, see, exploding on the surface of any sun, two or three times the size of medium-sized planets, where the temperature is as low as eight hundred or a thousand degrees. That sort of temperature might not destroy a ship. Perhaps we were caught in one of those and carried on through the sun. Somebody else suggested perhaps the energy frequencies of a nova are all polarized in one direction while something caused the ship's energies to polarize in another so that they sort of passed through one another just like they didn't touch. But other people came up with just as many theories to knock those down. What seems most likely is that when time and space are subject to such violent strains like you get in a nova, the laws that govern the natural machinery of physics and physical happenings as we know them just don't work right." Dan shrugged again. "They never did get it settled."

"Look! Look, he her down has!"

"One, two—no, she away pulls—"

"No! He her has! He her has!"

On the trampoline the grinning mechanic staggered over his opponent. Half a dozen drinks had already been brought for him; by custom he had to finish as many as he could, and the loser drink the rest. More officials had come down to congratulate him and stake wagers on the next match.

"I wonder . . ." Lorq frowned.

"Captain, I know you can't help it, but you *shouldn't* look like that."

"I wonder if the Alkane has any record of that trip, Dan."

"I guess they do. Like I say, it was about ten years . . ."

But Lorq was looking at the ceiling. The iris had shut under the wind that wracked Ark's night. The clashing mandala completely covered the star.

Lorq raised his hands to his face. His lips fell back as he hunted at the roots of the idea pushing through his mind. Fissured flesh translated his expression to beatific torture.

Dan started to speak again. Then he moved away, his gristly face filled with puzzlement.

His name was Lorq Von Ray. He had to repeat it silently, secure it with repetition; because an idea had just split his being. As he sat, looking up, he felt totally shaken. Something central had been parted as violently as Prince's hand had parted his face. He blinked to clear the stars. And his name . . .

"Yes, Captain Von Ray?"

"Pull in the side vanes."

The Mouse pulled in.

"We're hitting the steady stream. Side vanes in completely. Lynceos and Idas, stay on your vanes and take the first watch. The rest of you can break out for a while." Lorq's voice boomed over the sounds of space.

Turning from the vermilion rush, in which hung the charred stars, the Mouse blinked and realized the chamber once more.

Olga blinked.

The Mouse sat up on the couch to unplug.

"I'll see you in the commons," the captain continued. "And Mouse, bring your . . ."

Chapter Four

The Mouse pulled the leather sack from under the couch and slung it over his shoulder.

". . . sensory-syrynx with you."

The door slid back and the Mouse stood at the top of three steps above the blue carpet of the *Roc's* commons:

A stairway spiraled in a fall of shadows: tongues of metal twisting under the lights on the ceiling sent flashings over the wall and the leaves of the philodendrons before the mirrored mosaic.

Katin had already seated himself before the layered gaming board for three-D chess and was setting up pieces. A final rook clicked to its corner, and the bubble chair, a globe of jellied glycerin contoured to the body, bobbed. "All right, who's going to play me first?"

Captain Von Ray stood at the head of the spiral steps. As he started down, his smashed reflection graveled down the mosaic.

"Captain?" Katin raised his chin. "Mouse? Which one of you wants the first game?"

Tyÿ and Sebastian came through the arched door and across the ramp that spanned the lime-banked pool filling a third of the room.

A breeze.

The water rippled.

Darknesses sailed in over their heads.

"Down!" from Sebastian.

His arm jerked in its socket, and the beasts wheeled on steel leashes. The huge pets collapsed about him like rags.

"Sebastian? Tyÿ? Do you play?" Katin turned to the ramp.

"It used to be a passion with me, but my game has gone off a bit." He gazed up the steps, picked up the rook again, and examined the black-cored crystal. "Tell me, Captain, are these pieces original?"

At the bottom of the steps Von Ray raised red eyebrows. "No."

Katin grinned. "Oh."

"What are they?" The Mouse came across the carpet and looked over Katin's shoulder. "I've never seen pieces like that before."

"Funny style for chess pieces," Katin observed. "Vega Republic. But you see it a lot in furniture and architecture."

"Where's the Vega Republic?" The Mouse took up a pawn: inside crystal, a sun system, a jewel in the center, circled a tilted plane.

"It isn't anywhere any more. It refers to an uprising in twenty-eight hundred when Vega tried to secede from Draco. And failed. The art and architecture from that period have been taken up by our artier intellectuals. I suppose there was something heroic about the whole business. They certainly tried as hard as they could to be original—last stand for cultural autonomy and all that. But it's become sort of a polite parlor game to trace influences." He picked up another piece. "I still like the stuff. They did produce three gold musicians and one incredible poet. Though only one of the musicians had anything to do with the uprising. But most people don't know that."

"No kidding?" the Mouse said. "All right. I'll play you a game." He walked around the chessboard and sat on the green glycerin. "What do you want, black or yellow?"

Von Ray reached over the Mouse's shoulder for the control panel that had surfaced on the chair arm and pressed a micro-switch.

The lights in the gaming board went out.

"Hey, why . . . ?" The Mouse's rough whisper halted on chagrin.

"Take your syrynx, Mouse." Lorq walked to the sculptured rock on the yellow tiles. "If I told you to make a nova, Mouse, what would you do?" He sat on a stone outcrop.

"I don't know. What do you mean?" The Mouse lifted his instrument from its sack. His thumb ran the finger board. His fingers walked the inductance plate; the pinky staggered on its stilted nail.

"I'm telling you now. Make a nova."

The Mouse paused. Then, "All right," and his hand jumped.

Sound rumbled after the flash. Colors behind the after-image blotted vision, swirled in a diminishing sphere, were gone.

"Down!" Sebastian was saying. "Down now . . ."

Lorq laughed. "Not bad. Come here. No, bring your hell-harp." He shifted on the rock to make room. "Show me how it works."

"Show you how to play the syrynx?"

"That's right."

There are expressions that happen on the outside of the face; there are expressions that happen on the inside, with only quivers on the lips and eyelids. "I don't usually let people fool with my ax." Lips and eyelids quivered.

"Show me."

The Mouse's mouth thinned. He said: "Give me your hand." As he positioned the captain's fingers across the saddle of the image-resonance board, blue light glowed before them. "Now look down here." The Mouse pointed to the front of the syrynx. "These three pin-lenses have hologramic grids behind them. They focus where the blue light is and give you a three-dimensional image. Brightness and intensity you control here. Move your hand forward."

The light increased—

"Now back."

—and dimmed.

"How do you make an image?"

"Took me a year to learn, Captain. Now, these strings control the sound. Each one isn't a different note; they're different sound textures. The pitch is changed by moving your fingers closer or further away. Like this." He drew a chord of brass and human voices that glissandoed into uncomfortable subsonics. "You want to smell up the place? Back here. This knob controls the intensity of the image. You can make the whole thing highly directional by—"

"Suppose, Mouse, there was a girl's face that I wanted to re-create; the sound of her voice saying my name; the smell of her too. Now, I have your syrynx in my hands." He lifted the instrument from the Mouse's lap. "What should I do?"

"Practice. Captain, look, I really don't like other people fooling with my ax—"

He reached for it.

Lorq lifted it out of the Mouse's reach. Then he laughed. "Here."

The Mouse took the syrynx and went quickly to the chessboard. He shook the sack and slipped the instrument inside.

"Practice," repeated Lorq. "I don't have time. Not if I'm to beat Prince Red to that Illyrion, hey?"

"Captain Von Ray?"

Lorq looked up.

"Are you going to tell us what's going on?"

"What do you want to know?"

Katin's hand hung on the switch that would reactivate the chessboard. "Where are we going? How are we going to get there? And why?"

After moments, Lorq stood. "What are you asking me, Katin?"

The chessboard flicked on, lighting Katin's chin. "You're in a game, playing against Red-shift Limited. What are the rules? What's the prize?"

Lorq shook his head. "Try again."

"All right. How do we get the Illyrion?"

"Yes, how we it get?" Tyÿ's soft voice made them look around. At the foot of the bridge, beside Sebastian, she had been shuffling her deck of cards. She stopped when they looked. "Into the blasting sun, plunge?" She shook her head. "How, Captain?"

Lorq's hands capped the bone knots of his knees. "Lynceos? Idas?"

On opposite walls hung two six-foot gilt frames. In the one just over the Mouse's head, Idas lay on his side under his computer's lights. Across the room in the other frame, hair and eyelashes glittering, pale Lynceos was curled on his cables.

"While you sail us, keep an ear on."

"Right, Captain," Idas mumbled, as a man talks in sleep.

Lorq stood up and clasped his hands. "It's been a good

number of years since I first had to ask that question. The person who answered it for me was Dan."

"Blind Dan?"—the Mouse.

"Dan who jumped?"—Katin.

Lorq nodded. "Instead of this hunk of freighter"— He glanced up where simulated stars hurled on the high, dark ceiling to remind them that, among pools and ferns and shapes of rock, they sped between worlds— "I had a racing boat that Dan was studding for. I stayed out too late at a party one night in Paris, and Dan got me home to Ark. He flew me there all the way by himself. My other stud, some college kid, got scared and ran off." He shook his head. "Just as well. But there I was. How could I get hold of enough Illyrion to topple Red-shift before they toppled us? How many people would like to know that? I mentioned it to Dan one evening when we were drinking around the yacht basin. Get it out of a sun? He stuck his thumb in his belt and looked at one of the wind irises dilating over the bar and said, 'I was caught in a nova once.' " Lorq looked around the room. "It made me sit up and listen."

"What happened to him?" the Mouse asked.

"How come he was around long enough to get into another one? That's what I want to know." Katin returned the rook to the board and lounged back on the jelly. "Come on: where was Dan through all the fireworks?"

"He was in the crew of a ship that was bringing supplies to one of the Alkane Institute's study stations when the star blew."

The Mouse glanced back at Tyÿ and Sebastian, who listened from the steps at the end of the ramp. Tyÿ was shuffling her cards again.

"After a thousand years of study, from close up and far away, it's a bit unnerving how much we don't know about what happens in the center of the most calamitous of stellar catastrophes. The make-up of the star stays the same, only the organization of the matter within the star is disrupted by a process that is still not quite understood. It could be an effect of tidal harmonics. It could even be a prank of Maxwell's demon. The longest build-ups observed have been a year and a half, but these were always caught after they were under way. The actual time a nova takes to reach its peak intensity from the time it blows is a few hours. In the case of a super-nova—and there have only been two on record in our galaxy, one in the thirteenth century in Cassiopeia, and an unnamed star in twenty-four hundred, and neither of those could be studied up close—the blow takes perhaps two days; in a super-nova the brightness increases by a factor of several hundred thousand. The resultant light and radio disturbance of a super-nova is more than the combined light of all the stars in the galaxy. Alkane has discovered other galaxies simply because a super-nova occurred inside them and the near-total annihilation of a single star made the whole galaxy of several billion stars visible."

Tyÿ flicked cards from hand to hand.

Sebastian asked, "What to Dan happened?" He reined his pets closer to his knees.

"His ship overshot and was funneled through the center of the sun in the middle of its first hour of implosion—and then funneled out the other side." Yellow eyes fixed Katin. On the ruptured features it was hard to read subtleties in Lorq's emotions.

Katin, used to hard readings, dropped his shoulders and tried to sink into the chair.

"They only had seconds' warning. All the captain could do was switch off all incoming sensory inputs in the studs."

"They blind flew?" asked Sebastian.

Lorq nodded.

"This was a nova Dan was in, before he even met you; the first," confirmed Katin.

"That's right."

"What happened in the second?"

"One more thing that happened in the first. I went to the Alkane and looked up the whole business. The hull of the ship was scarred from bombardment with loose drifting matter at about the time it was in the nova's center. The only matter that could break off and drift into the area of protection around the ship must have been formed from the almost solid nuclear matter in the sun's center. It would have to be formed of elements with immense nuclei, at least three or four times the size of uranium."

"You mean the ship was bombarded with meteors of Illyrion?" the Mouse demanded.

"One of the things that happened in the *second* nova"—

Lorq looked at Katin again—"was that after our expedition was organized in complete secrecy, after a new nova had been located with my aunt's help from the Alkane Institute without letting anyone know why we wanted to go there, after the expedition was launched and under way, I was trying to re-create the original conditions of the first accident when Dan's ship had fallen into the sun, as closely as possible, by flying the whole maneuver blind; I gave an order to the crew to keep the sensory input off in their perception chambers. Dan, going against orders, decided he wanted to take a look at what he hadn't seen last time." Lorq stood up and turned his back to the crew. "We weren't even in an area where there might have been any physical danger to the ship. Suddenly I felt one vane of the ship flailing wild. Then I heard Dan screaming." He turned to face them. "We pulled out and limped back to Draco and took the tidal drift down to Sol and landed on Triton Station. The secrecy ended two months back."

"Secrecy?" Katin asked.

The twisted thing that was Lorq's smile rose in the muscles of his face. "Not any more. I came to Triton Station in Draco rather than shelter in the Pleiades. I dismissed my whole crew with instructions to tell as many people as they could all they knew. I let that madman stagger around the port babbling till Hell[3] swallowed him. I waited. And I waited till what I was waiting for came. Then I picked you up right off the port's concourse. I told you what I was going to do. Who did you tell? How many people heard me tell you? How many people did you mutter to, scratching your heads, 'That's a funny thing to do, huh?' " Lorq's hand knotted on a spike of stone.

"What were you waiting for?"

"A message from Prince."

"Did you get it?"

"Yes."

"What did it say?"

"Does it matter?" Lorq made a sound nearly laughter. Only it came from his belly. "I haven't played it yet."

"Why not?" the Mouse asked. "Don't you want to know what he says?"

"I know what I'm doing. That's enough. We'll return to the Alkane and locate another ... nova. My mathematicians came up with two dozen theories that might explain the phenomenon that lets us enter the sun. In all of them, the effect would reverse at the end of those first few hours during which the brightness of the star rose to peak intensity."

"How long a nova to die takes?" Sebastian asked.

"A few weeks, perhaps two months. A super-nova can take up to two years to dwindle."

"The message," the Mouse said. "You don't want to see what Prince says?"

"*You* do?"

Katin suddenly leaned over the chessboard. "Yes."

Lorq laughed. "All right." He strode across the room. Once more he touched the control panel on the Mouse's chair.

In the largest frame on the high wall the light fantasy faded in the two-meter oval of gilded leaves.

"So. That's what you've been doing all these years!" Prince said.

The Mouse watched the gaunt jaws and his own jaws clamped; his eyes raised to Prince's thin, high hair, and the Mouse's own forehead tightened. He pushed forward in the chair, his fingers twitching to shape, as on a syrynx, the bladed nose, the wells of blue.

Katin's eyes widened. His sandal heels grabbed the carpet as involuntarily he pushed away.

"I don't know what you think you're going to accomplish. Nor do I care. But . . ."

"That Prince is?" Tyÿ whispered.

". . . you'll fail. Believe me." Prince smiled.

And Tyÿ's whisper became a gasp.

"No. I don't even know where you're going. But watch. I'll get there first. Then"—he raised his black-gloved hand —"we'll see." He reached forward so that his palm filled the screen. Then the fingers flicked; there was a tinkle of glass—

Tyÿ gave a little scream.

Prince had snapped his finger against the lens of the message camera, shattering it.

The Mouse glanced at Tyÿ; she had dropped her cards.

The beasts flapped at the leash; the wind scattered Tyÿ's cards on the carpet.

"Here," Katin was saying, "I'll get them!" He leaned from

his seat and reached about the floor with gawky arms. Lorq had begun to laugh again.

A card overturned on the rug by the Mouse's foot. Three-dimensional within laminated metal, a sun flared above a black sea. Over the sea wall the sky was alive with flame. On shore two naked boys held hands. The dark one squinted at the sun, his face amazed and luminous. The tow-headed one looked at their shadows on the sand.

Lorq's laughter, like multiple explosions, rolled in the commons. "Prince has accepted the challenge." He slapped the stone. "Good! Very good! Hey, and you think we'll meet under the sun afire?" His hand went up, a fist. "I can feel his claw. Good! Yes, good!"

The Mouse picked up the card quickly. He looked from the captain to the viewing screen where the multichrome's shifting hues had replaced the face, the hand. (And there, on opposite walls, were dim Idas and pale Lynceos in their smaller frames.) His eyes fell back to the two boys beneath the erupting sun.

As he looked, his left toes clawed the carpet, his right clutched his boot sole; fear pawed behind his thighs, tangled in the nerves along his backbone. Suddenly he slipped the card into his syrynx sack. His fingers lingered inside the leather, becoming sweaty on the laminate. Unseen, the picture was even more frightening. He took his hand out and wiped it on his hip, then looked to see if anyone watched.

Katin was looking through the cards he had picked up. "This is what you've been playing with, Tyÿ? The Tarot?" He looked up. "You're a gypsy, Mouse. I bet you've seen these before." He held the cards up so the Mouse might see.

Not looking, the Mouse nodded. He tried to keep his hand from his hip. (There had been a big woman sitting behind the fire—in the dirty print skirt—and the mustachioed men sat around under the flickering overhang of rock, watching while the cards flashed and flashed in her fat hands. But that had been ...)

"Here," Tyÿ said. "You to me them give." She reached.

"May I look through the whole set?" asked Katin.

Her gray eyes widened. "No." Surprise was in her voice.

"I'm ... sorry," Katin began, confused. "I didn't mean to ... "

Tyÿ took the cards.

"You ... do you read the cards?" Katin tried to keep his face from freezing.

She nodded.

"Tarot reading is common over the Federation," Lorq said. He was sitting on the sculpture. "Of Prince's message, your cards anything have to say?" As he turned, his eyes flashed like jasper, like gold. "Perhaps your cards of Prince and me will speak?"

The Mouse was surprised how easily the captain slipped on the Pleiades dialect. The expression inside was a quick smile.

Lorq left the stone. "What the cards about this swing into the night say?"

Sebastian, gazing from under thick blond brows, pulled his dark shapes closer.

"I their patterns want to see. Yes. Where Prince and myself among the cards fall?"

If she read, he would have an opportunity to see more of the cards: Katin grinned. "Yes, Tyÿ. Give us a reading on Captain's expedition. How well does she read them, Sebastian?"

"Tyÿ never wrong is."

"You for a few seconds only Prince's face have seen. In the face the lines of a man's fate mapped are." Lorq put his fists on his hips. "From the crack across mine, you where those lines my fate can tell will touch?"

"No, Captain—" Her eyes dropped to her hands. The cards looked much too big for her still fingers. "I the cards only array and read."

"I haven't seen anybody read the Tarot since I was in school." Katin looked back at the Mouse. "There was one character from the Pleiades in my philosophy seminar who knew his cards. I suppose at one time you could have called me quite an amateur aficionado of the *Book of Toth*, as they were incorrectly labeled in the seventeenth century. I would say rather"—he paused for Tyÿ's corroboration—"the *Book of the Grail?*"

None came.

"Come. Give me a reading, Tyÿ." Lorq dropped his fists to his sides.

Tyÿ's fingertips rested on the golden backs. From her seat

at the bottom of the ramp, gray eyes halved by epicanthi, she looked between Katin and Lorq.

She said: "I will."

"Mouse," Katin called, "come on and take a look at this. Give us your opinion on the performance—"

The Mouse stood up in the light of the gaming table. "Hey . . . !"

They turned at the wrecked voice.

"*You* believe in that?"

Katin raised an eyebrow.

"You call *me* superstitious because I spit in the river? Now you tell the future with cards! *Ahnnn!*" which is not really the sound he made. Still it meant disgust. His gold earring shook and flashed.

Katin frowned.

Tyÿ's hand hung over the deck.

The Mouse dared half the distance of the rug. "You're really going to try and tell the future with cards? That's silly. *That's* superstitious!"

"No it's not, Mouse," Katin countered. "One would think that you of all people—"

The Mouse waved his hand and barked hoarse laughter. "You, Katin, and them cards. That's something!"

"Mouse, the cards don't actually predict anything. They simply propagate an educated commentary on present situations—"

"Cards aren't educated! They're metal and plastic. They don't know—"

"Mouse, the seventy-eight cards of the Tarot present symbols and mythological images that have recurred and reverberated through forty-five centuries of human history. Someone who understands these symbols can construct a dialogue about a given situation. There's nothing superstitious about it. *The Book of Changes,* even *Chaldean Astrology* only become superstitious when they are abused, employed to direct rather than guide and suggest."

The Mouse made that sound again.

"Really, Mouse! It's perfectly logical; you talk like somebody living a thousand years ago."

"Hey, Captain?" The Mouse closed the rest of the distance and, peering around Lorq's elbow, squinted at the deck in

Tyӱ's lap. "You believe in those things?" His hand fell on Katin's forearm, as though holding it, he might keep it still.

Tiger eyes beneath rusted brows showed agony; Lorq was grinning. "Tyӱ, me the cards read."

She turned the deck over and passed the pictures— "Captain, you one choose"—from hand to hand.

Lorq squatted to see. Suddenly he stopped the passing cards with his forefinger. "The *Kosmos*, it looks like." He named the card his finger had fallen on. "In this race, the universe the prize is." He looked up at the Mouse and Katin. "Do you think I should pick the *Kosmos* to start the reading?" Framed by the bulk of his shoulders, the "agony" grew subtle.

The Mouse answered with a twist of dark lips.

"Go ahead," Katin said.

Lorq drew the card:

Morning fog wove birch and yew and holly trees; in the clearing a naked figure leaped and cavorted in the blue dawn.

"Ah," said Katin, "the Dancing Hermaphrodite, the union of all male and female principles." He rubbed his ear between two fingers. "You know, for about three hundred years or so, from about eighteen-ninety to after space travel began, there was a highly Christianized set of Tarot cards designed by a friend of William Butler Yeats that became so popular, they almost obliterated the true images."

As Lorq tilted the card, diffraction images of animals flashed and disappeared in the mystic grove. The Mouse's hand tightened on Katin's arm. He raised his chin to question.

"The beasts of the apocalypse," Katin answered. He pointed over the captain's shoulder to the four corners of the grove: "Bull, Lion, Eagle, and that funny little ape-like creature back there is the dwarf god Bes, originally of Egypt and Anatolia, protector of women in labor, the scourge of the miserly, a generous and terrible god. There's a statue of him that's fairly famous: squat, grinning, fanged, copulating with a lioness."

"Yeah," the Mouse whispered. "I seen that statue."

"You have? Where?"

"Some museum." He shrugged. "In Istanbul, I think. A tourist took me there when I was a kid."

"Alas," mused Katin, "I have been content with three-dimensional holograms."

"Only it's no dwarf. It's"—the Mouse's rasp halted as he

looked up at Katin—"maybe twice as tall as you." His pupils, rolling in sudden recollection, showed veined whites.

"Captain Von Ray, you well the Tarot know?" Sebastian asked.

"I've had my cards read perhaps a half dozen times," Lorq explained. "My mother didn't like my stopping to listen to the readers who would have their little tables set up under the wind-shield junctions on the streets. Once, when I was five or six, I managed to get lost. While I was wandering around a part of Ark I'd never seen before, I stopped and got my fortune read." He laughed; the Mouse, who had not judged the gathering expression right, had expected anger. "When I did get home and told my mother, she grew very upset and told me I mustn't do it again."

"She knew it was all stupid!" the Mouse whispered.

"What had the cards said?" Katin asked.

"Something about a death in my family."

"Did anyone die?"

Lorq's eyes narrowed. "About a month later my uncle was killed."

Katin reflected on the sound of m's. Captain Lorq Von Ray's uncle?

"But well the cards you do not know?" Sebastian asked once more.

"Only the names of a few—the *Sun*, the *Moon*, the *Hanged-man*. But I on their meanings never studied."

"Ah." Sebastian nodded. "The first card picked always yourself is. But the *Kosmos* a card of the Major Arcana is. A human being it can't represent. Can't pick."

Lorq frowned. Puzzlement looked like rage. Misinterpreting, Sebastian stopped.

"What it is," Katin went on, "in the Tarot pack there are fifty-six cards of the Minor Arcana—just like the fifty-two playing cards, only with pages, knights, queens, and kings for court cards. These deal with ordinary human affairs: love, death, taxes—things like that. There are twenty-two other cards: the Major Arcana, with cards like the *Fool* and the *Hanged-man*. They represent primal cosmic entities. You can't very well pick one of them to represent yourself."

Lorq looked at the card a few seconds. "Why not?" He looked up at Katin. All expression was gone now. "I like this card. Tyÿ said choose, and I chose."

Sebastian's hand rose. "But—"

Tyÿ's slender fingers caught her companion's hairy knuckles. "He chose," she said. The metal of her eyes flashed from Sebastian to the captain, to the card. "There it place." She gestured for him to lay the card down. "The captain which card he wants can choose."

Lorq laid the card on the carpet, the dancer's head toward himself, the feet toward Tyÿ.

"The *Kosmos* reversed," muttered Katin.

Tyÿ glanced up. "Reversed for you, upright for me is." Her voice was sharp.

"Captain, the first card you pick doesn't predict anything," Katin said. "Actually, the first card you take removes all the possibilities it represents from your reading."

"What does it represent?" Lorq asked.

"Here male and female unite," Tyÿ said. "The sword and the chalice, the staff and the dish join. Completion and certain success it means; the cosmic state of divine awareness it signifies. Victory."

"And that's all been cut from my future?" Lorq's face assumed agony again. "Fine! What sort of a race would it be if I knew I was going to win?"

"Reserved it means obsession with one thing, stubbornness," Katin added. "Refusal to learn—"

Tyÿ suddenly closed the cards. She held out the deck. "You, Katin, the reading will complete?"

"Huh? . . . I . . . Look, I'm sorry. I didn't . . . Anyway, I only know the meaning of about a dozen cards." His ears blushed along the rims. "I'll be quiet."

A wing brushed the floor.

Sebastian stood and pulled his pets away. One flapped to his shoulder. A breeze, and the Mouse's hair tickled his forehead.

All were standing now except Lorq and Tyÿ, who squatted with the Dancing Hermaphrodite between.

Once more Tyÿ shuffled and fanned the cards, this time face down. "Choose."

Broad fingers with thickened nails clamped the card, drew:

A workman stood before a double vault of stone, a stone-cutter plugged into his wrists. The machine was carving its third five-pointed star into the transom. Sunlight lit the mason and the building face. Through the doorway, darkness sank away.

"The Three of Pentacles. This card you covers."

The Mouse looked at the captain's forearm. The oval socket was almost lost between the double tendon along his wrist.

The Mouse fingered the socket on his own arm. The plastic inset was a quarter the width of his wrist: both sockets were the same size.

The captain lay the Three of Pentacles on the *Kosmos*.

"Again choose."

The card came out upside down:

A black-haired youngster in brocade vest, with boots of tooled leather, leaned on the hilt of a sword on which was a jeweled silver lizard. The figure stood in shadow under crags; the Mouse couldn't tell if it were boy or girl.

"The Page of Swords reversed. This card you crosses."

Lorq placed the card crosswise on the Three of Pentacles.

"Again choose."

Above a seaside, in a clear sky with birds, a single hand, extending from coils of mist, held a five-pointed star-form in a circle.

"The Ace of Pentacles." Tyÿ pointed below the crossed cards. Lorq placed the card there. "This card beneath you lies. Choose."

A big blond fellow stood on the flag path within a garden. He looked up, his hand back. A red bird was about to light on his wrist. On the stones of the court, nine star-shapes were cut.

"The Nine of Pentacles." She pointed beside the pattern on the rug. "This card behind you lies."

Lorq placed the card.

"Choose."

Upside down again:

Between storm clouds burned a violet sky. Lightning had ignited the top of a stone tower. Two men had leaped from the upper balcony. One wore rich clothing. You could even see his jeweled rings and the gold tassels on his sandals. The other wore a common work vest, was barefoot, bearded.

"The *Tower*, reversed!" Katin whispered. "Uh-oh. I know what—" and stopped because Tyÿ and Sebastian looked.

"The *Tower* reversed." Tyÿ pointed above the pattern. "This above you lies."

Lorq placed the card, then drew a seventh.

"The Two of Swords, reversed."

Upside down:

A blindfolded woman sat on a chair before the ocean, holding two swords crossed on her breasts.

"This before you lies."

With three cards in the center and four around, the first seven cards formed a cross.

"Again choose."

Lorq chose.

"The King of Swords. Here it place."

The King went to the left of the cross.

"And once more."

Lorq drew his ninth card.

"The Three of Wands reversed."

Which went below the King.

"The *Devil*—"

Katin looked at the Mouse's hand. The fingers arched and the little nail bit Katin's arm.

"—reversed."

The fingers relaxed; Katin looked back at Tyÿ.

"Here place." The upside-down *Devil* went below the Wands. "And choose."

"The Queen of Swords. This final card here place."

Beside the cross there was now a vertical row of four cards.

Tyÿ squared the pack.

She brushed her fingers under her chin. As she bent over the vivid dioramas, her iron-colored hair broke on her shoulder.

"Do you see Prince in there?" Lorq asked. "Do you see me, and the sun I'm after?"

"You I see; and Prince. A woman also, somehow related to Prince, a dark woman—"

"Black hair, but blue eyes?" Lorq said. "Prince's eyes are blue."

Tyÿ nodded. "Her too I see."

"That's Ruby."

"The cards mostly swords and pentacles are. Much money I see. Also much struggle about and around it there is."

"With seven tons of Illyrion?" the Mouse mumbled. "You don't have to read cards to see—"

"Shhh ..." from Katin.

"The only positive influence from the Major Arcana the *Devil* is. A card of violence, of revolution, of struggle it is. But also the birth of spiritual understanding it signifies. Pentacles at the beginning of your reading lay. They cards of money and wealth are. Swords them overtake; cards of power and conflict. The wand the symbol of intellect and creativity is. Though the number of the wands three and low is, high the reading it comes. That good is. But no cups—the symbol of the emotions and particularly love—there are. Bad is. To be good, wands must cups have." She lifted the cards in the center of the cross: the *Kosmos*, the Three of Pentacles, the Page of Swords.

"Now ..." Tyÿ paused. The four men breathed together. "You yourself as the world see. The card covering you of nobility, of aristocracy speaks. As well, some skill which you possess—"

"You said you used to be a racing captain, didn't you?" asked Katin.

"That with material increase you are concerned, this card reveals. But the Page of Swords you crosses."

"That's Prince?"

Tyÿ shook her head. "A younger person it is. Someone already close to you now it is. Someone you know. A dark, very young man perhaps—"

Katin was first to look at the Mouse.

"—who somehow between you and your flaming sun will come."

Now Lorq looked up over his shoulder.

"Hey, now. Look ..." The Mouse frowned at the others. "What are you going to do? Fire me the first stopover because of some stupid cards? You think I want to cross you up?"

"Even if he you fired," Tyÿ said, glancing up, "it would nothing change."

The captain slapped the Mouse's hip. "Don't mind it, Mouse."

"If you don't believe in them, Captain, why waste your time listening to ... ?" and stopped because Tyÿ had replaced the cards.

"In your immediate past," Tyÿ went on, "the Ace of Pentacles lies. Again, much money, but toward a purpose pointed."

"Setting up this expedition must have cost an arm and a leg," Katin commented.

"And an eye and an ear?" Sebastian's knuckles rippled on the head of one of his pets.

"In the far past, the Nine of Pentacles lies. Again a card of wealth it is. You success are used to. The best things you have enjoyed. But in your immediate future the *Tower* reversed is. In general this signifies—"

"—go directly to jail. Do not pass go. Do not"—Katin's ears glowed again as Tyÿ narrowed her eyes at him—"collect two hundred pounds @sg." He coughed.

"Imprisonment this card signifies; a great house topples."

"The Von Rays have had it?"

"Whose house I did not say."

At that Lorq laughed.

"Beyond it, the Two of Swords reversed lies. Of unnatural passion, Captain, beware."

"What's *that* supposed to mean?" the Mouse whispered.

But Tyÿ had moved from the cross of seven cards to the row of four.

"At the head of your endeavors the King of Swords sits."

"That's my friend Prince?"

"It is. Your life he can affect. He a strong man is, and easily to wisdom he you may lead; also your death." Then she looked up, her face sharply distraught. "As well, all our lives . . . He—"

When she did not go on, Lorq asked, "What, Tyÿ?" Her voice calmed already, became a deeper, solider thing.

"Below him—"

"What was it, Tyÿ?"

"—the Three of Wands reversed lies. Of offered his beware. The best defense against disappointment expectation is. The foundation of this the Devil is. But reversed. You the spiritual understanding of which I spoke will receive in the—"

"Hey." The Mouse looked up at Katin. "What'd she see?"

"Shhh."

"—coming struggle, the surface of things away will fall. The workings beneath strange and stranger will seem. And though the King of Swords the walls of reality back will pull, behind them the Queen of Swords you will discover."

"That's . . . Ruby? Tell me, Tyÿ: do you see the sun?"

"No sun. Only the woman, dark and powerful as her brother, her shadow casts—"

"From the light of what star?"

"Her shadow across both you and Prince falls—"

Lorq waved his hands over the cards. "And the sun?"

"Your shadow in the night is cast. Stars in the sky I see. But still no single sun—"

"No!" Only it was the Mouse. "It's all stupid! Nonsense! Nothing, Captain!" His nail dug, and Katin jerked his arm away. "She can't tell you anything with them!" Suddenly he lurched to the side. His booted foot kicked among Sebastian's creatures. They rose and beat at the end of their chains.

"Hey, Mouse! What are you—"

He swept his bare foot across the patterned cards.

"Hey!"

Sebastian pulled flapping shadows back. "Come, still now be!" His hand moved from head to head, knuckle and thumb working quiet behind dark ears and jaws.

But the Mouse had already stalked up the ramp across the pool. His sack banged his hip at each step till he disappeared.

"I'll go after him, Captain." Katin ran up the ramp.

As wings settled by Sebastian's sandals, Lorq stood.

On her knees Tyÿ picked up her scattered cards.

"You two back on vanes I put. Lynceos and Idas I'll relieve." As humor translated to agony, so concern appeared a grin. "You to your chambers, go."

Lorq took Tyÿ's arm as she stood. Three expressions struck her face, one after the other: surprise, fear, and the third was when she recognized his.

"For what you in the cards have read, Tyÿ, I you thank."

Sebastian moved to take her hand from the captain's.

"Again, I you thank."

In the corridor to the *Roc's* bridge, projected stars drifted on the black wall. Against the blue one, the Mouse sat cross-legged on the floor, sack in lap. His hand molded shapes in the leather. He stared at the circling lights.

Katin strolled up the hall, hands behind his back. "What the hell's wrong with you?" he inquired amicably.

The Mouse looked up, and let his eyes catch a star emerging from Katin's ear.

"You certainly like to make things complicated for yourself."

The star drifted down, disappeared at the floor.

"And by the way, what was the card you stuck in your sack?"

The Mouse's eyes came back to Katin's fast. He blinked.

"I'm very good at picking up on that sort of thing." Katin leaned back on the star-flecked wall. The ceiling projector that duplicated the outside night flashed dots of light across his short face, his long, flat belly. "This isn't the best way to get on the captain's good side. You've got some odd ideas, Mouse—admitted, they're fascinating. If somebody had told me I'd be working in the same crew, today in the thirty-first century, with somebody who could honestly be skeptical about the Tarot, I don't think I would have believed it. You're really from Earth?"

"Yeah, I'm from Earth."

Katin bit at a knuckle. "Come to think of it, I doubt if such fossilized ideas could have come from anywhere else but Earth. As soon as you have people from the times of the great stellar migrations, you're dealing with cultures sophisticated enough to comprehend things like the Tarot. I wouldn't be surprised if in some upper Mongolian desert town there isn't someone who still thinks Earth floats in a dish on the back of an elephant who stands on a serpent coiled on a turtle swimming in the sea of forever. In a way I'm glad I wasn't born there, fascinating place that it is. It produces some spectacular neurotics. There was one character at Harvard—" He paused and looked back at the Mouse. "You're a funny kid. Here you are, flying this star-freighter, a product of thirty-first-century technology, and at the same time your head full of a whole handful of petrified ideas a thousand years out of date. Let me see what you swiped?"

The Mouse jammed his forearm into the sack, pulled out the card. He looked at it, back and front, till Katin reached down and took it.

"Do you remember who told you not to believe in the Tarot?" Katin examined the card.

"It was my . . ." The Mouse took the sack rim in his hands

and squeezed. "This woman. Back when I was a real little kid, five or six."

"Was she a gypsy too?"

"Yeah. She took care of me. She had cards, like Tyÿ's. Only they weren't three-D. And they were old. When we were going around in France and Italy, she gave readings for people. She knew all about them, what the pictures meant and all. And she told me. She said no matter what anybody said, it was all phony. It was all just fake and didn't mean anything. She said gypsies had given the Tarot cards to everybody else."

"That's right. Gypsies probably brought them from the East to the West in the eleventh and twelfth centuries. And they certainly helped distribute them about Europe for the next five hundred years."

"That's what she told me, that the cards belonged to the gypsies first, and the gypsies knew: they're just fake. And never to believe them."

Katin smiled. "A very romantic notion. I cotton to it myself: the idea that all those symbols, filtered down through five thousand years of mythology, are basically meaningless and have no bearing on man's mind and actions, strikes a little bell of nihilism ringing. Unfortunately I know too much about these symbols to go along with it. Still, I'm interested in what you have to say. So this woman you lived with when you were a child, she read Tarot cards, but she still insisted they were false?"

"Yeah." He let go of the sack. "Only . . ."

"Only what?" Katin asked when the Mouse did not go on.

"Only, there was one night—just before the end. There was no one there but gypsies. We were waiting in a cave, at night. We were all afraid, because something was going to happen. They whispered about it, and if any of the kids came around, they shut up. And that night, she read the cards— only not like it was phony. And they all sat around the fire in the dark, listening to her tell the cards. And the next morning somebody woke me up early, while the sun was still coming up over the city between the mountains. Everybody was leaving. I didn't go with Moma—the woman who read the cards. I never saw any of them again. The ones I went with, they disappeared soon. I ended up getting to Turkey all by myself." The Mouse thumbed a form beneath the leather. "But that night, when she was reading the cards in the firelight, I remember I was awful scared. They were scared too, see. And they wouldn't tell us about what. But it made them scared enough to ask the cards—even though they knew it was all phony."

"I guess when the situation gets serious, people will use their common sense and give up their superstitions long enough to save their necks." Katin was frowning. "What do you think it was?"

The Mouse shrugged. "Perhaps people were after us. You know with gypsies. Everybody thinks that gypsies steal things. We did, too. Maybe they were going to come after us from the town. Nobody likes gypsies, on Earth. That's cause we don't work."

"You work hard enough, Mouse. That's why I wonder that you get involved in all this other mess back with Tyÿ. You'll spoil your good name."

"I haven't been with gypsies steady since I was seven or eight. Besides, I got my sockets. Though I didn't get them till I was at Cooper Astronautics in Melbourne."

"Really? Then you must have been at least fifteen or sixteen. That certainly is late. On Luna we got ours when we were three or four so we could operate teaching computers at school." Katin's expression suddenly concentrated. "You mean there was a whole group of grown men and women, with children, wandering around from town to town, country to country, on Earth *without* sockets?"

"Yeah. I guess there was."

"Without sockets there's not much in the line of work you can do."

"Sure isn't."

"No wonder your gypsies were being hounded. A group of adults traveling around without plug facilities!" He shook his head. "But why didn't you get them?"

"That's just gypsies. We never had them. We never wanted them. I took them because I was by myself, and—well, I guess it was easier." The Mouse hung his forearms over his knees. "But that was still no reason for them to come and run us out of town whenever we got settled. Once, I remember, they got two gypsies, and killed them. They beat them up till they were half dead, and then cut their arms off and hung them head down from trees to bleed to death—"

"Mouse!" Katin's face twisted.

"I was only a kid, but I remember. Maybe that's what made Moma finally decide to ask the cards what to do even though she didn't believe. Maybe that's what made us break up."

"Only in Draco," Katin said. "Only on Earth."

The dark face turned up at him. "Why, Katin? Go on, you tell me, why did they do that to us." No question mark at the end of his sentence. Hoarse outrage instead.

"Because people are stupid, and narrow, and afraid of anything different." Katin closed his eyes. "That's why I prefer moons. Even on a big one, it's hard to get so many people together that that sort of thing happens." His eyes opened. "Mouse, consider this. Captain Von Ray has sockets. He's one of the richest men in the universe. And so does any miner, or street cleaner, or bartender, or file clerk, or you. In the Pleiades Federation or in the Outer Colonies, it's a totally cross-cultural phenomenon—part of a way of considering all machines as a direct extension of man that has been accepted by all social levels since Ashton Clark. Up until this conversation, I would have said it was a totally cross-cultural phenomenon on Earth as well. Until you reminded me that on our strange ancestral home world, some incredible cultural anachronisms have managed to dodder on until today. But the fact that a group of non-socketed gypsies, impoverished, trying to work where there's no work to do, telling fortunes by a method that they have totally ceased to understand while the rest of the universe has managed to achieve the understanding these same gypsies' ancestors had fifteen hundred years back—lawless eunuchs moving into a town couldn't have been more upsetting to the ordinary socketed workingman or woman. Eunuchs? When you plug into a big machine, you call that studding; you wouldn't believe where that expression came from. No, I don't understand why it happened. But I do understand a little of the how." He shook his head. "Earth is a funny place. I was there in school four years, and I had just begun to learn how much of it I didn't understand. Those of us who weren't born there probably will never be able to figure it completely. Even in the rest of

Draco, we lead much simpler lives, I think." Katin looked at the card in his hand. "You know the name of this card you swiped?"

The Mouse nodded. "The *Sun*."

"You know if you go around pinching cards, they can't very well show up in the reading. Captain was rather anxious to see this one."

"I know." He ran his fingers along the strap of his sack. "The cards were already talking about me coming between Captain and his sun; and I'd just pinched the card from the deck." The Mouse shook his head.

Katin held the card out. "Why don't you give it back? While you're at it, you might apologize for kicking up that fuss."

The Mouse looked down for half a minute. Then he stood, took the card, and started up the hall.

Katin watched him turn the corner. Then he crossed his arms and dropped his head to think. And his mind drifted to the pale dusts of remembered moons.

Katin mulled in the quiet hall; finally he closed his eyes. Something tugged at his hip.

He opened them. "Hey—"

Lynceos (with Idas a shadow at his shoulder) had come up to him and pulled the recorder out of his pocket by the chain. He had held up the jeweled box. "What's this—"

"—thing do?" Idas finished.

"You mind giving that back?" The foundations for Katin's annoyance were laid at their interruption of his thoughts. It was built on their presumption.

"We saw you fooling with it back at the port." Idas took it from his brother's white fingers—

"Look—" Katin began.

—and handed it back to Katin.

"Thanks!" He started to put it back into his pocket.

"Show us how it works—"

"—and what you use it for?"

Katin paused, then turned the recorder in his hand. "It's just a matrix recorder where I can dictate notes and file them. I'm using it to write a novel."

Idas said, "Hey, I know what that—"

"—me too. Why do you want to—"

"—have to make one of—"

"—why don't you just make a psychorama—"

"—is so much easier. Are we—"

"—in it?"

Katin found himself starting to say four things. Then he laughed. "Look, you glorified salt and pepper shakers, I can't think like that!" He pondered a moment. "I don't know why I want to write one. I'm sure it would be easier to make a psychorama if I had the equipment, the money, and the connections in a psychorama studio. But that's not what I want. And I have no idea whether you'll be 'in it' or not. I haven't begun to think about the subject. I'm still making notes on the form." They frowned. "On structure, the aesthetics of the whole business. You can't just sit down and write, you know. You have to think. The novel was an art form. I have to invent it all over again before I can write one. The one I want to write, anyway."

"Oh," Lynceos said.

"You sure you know what a novel—"

"—of course I do. Did you experience *War*—"

"—*and Peace*. Yeah. But that was a psychorama—"

"—with Che-ong as Natasha. But it was—"

"—taken from a novel? That's right, I—"

"—you remember now?"

"Um-hm," Idas nodded darkly behind his brother. "Only"— He was talking to Katin now—"how come you don't know what you want to write about?"

Katin shrugged.

"Then maybe you'll write something about us if you don't know yet what—"

"—can we sue him if he says something that isn't—"

"Hey," Katin interrupted. "I have to find a subject that can support a novel. I told you, I can't tell you if you're going to be in it or—"

"—what sort of things you got in there anyway?" Idas was saying around Lynceos' shoulder.

"Huh? Like I said, notes. For the book."

"Let's hear."

"Look, you guys don't . . ." Then he shrugged. He dialed the ruby pivots on the recorder's top, then flicked it to play-back:

"Note to myself number five thousand three hundred and

seven. Bear in mind that the novel—no matter how intimate, psychological, or subjective—is always a historical projection of its own time." The voice played too high, and too fast. But it facilitated review. "To make my book, I must have an awareness of my time's conception of history."

Idas' hand was a black epaulet on his brother's shoulder. With eyes of bark and coral, they frowned, flexed their attention.

"History? Thirty-five hundred years ago Herodotus and Thucydides invented it. They defined it as the study of whatever had happened during their own lives. And for the next thousand years it was nothing else. Fifteen hundred years after the Greeks, in Constantinople, Anna Comnena, in her legalistic brilliance (and in essentially the same language as Herodotus) wrote history as the study of those events of man's actions that had been documented. I doubt if this charming Byzantine believed things only happened when they were written about. But incidents unchronicled were simply not considered the province of history in Byzantium. The whole concept had transformed. In another thousand years we had reached that century which began with the first global conflict and ended with the first conflict between globes brewing. Somehow the theory had arisen that history was a series of cyclic rises and falls as one civilization overtook another. Events that did not fit on the cycle were defined as historically unimportant. It's difficult for us today to appreciate the differences between Spengler and Toynbee, though from all accounts their approaches were considered polar in their day. To us they seem merely to be quibbling over when or where a given cycle began. Now that another thousand years has passed, we must wrestle with De Eiling and Broblin, 34-Alvin and the Crespburg Survey. Simply because they are contemporary, I know they must inhabit the same historic view. But how many dawns did I see flickering beyond the docks of the Charles while I stalked and pondered whether I held with Saunder's theory of Integral Historical Convection or was I still with Broblin after all. Yet I have enough prospective to know that in another thousand years these differences will seem as minute as the controversy of two medieval theologians disputing whether twelve or twenty-four angels can dance on the head of a pin.

"Note to myself number five thousand three hundred and

eight. Never loose the pattern of stripped sycamores against vermilion—"

Katin flicked off the recorder.

"Oh," Lynceos said. "That was sort of odd—"

"—interesting," Idas said. "Did you ever figure it out—"

"—he means about the history—"

"—about our time's historical concept?"

"Well, actually, I did. It's quite an interesting theory, really. If you just—"

"I imagine it must be very complicated," Idas said. "I mean—"

"—for people living now to grasp—"

"Surprisingly enough, it isn't." (Katin) "All you have to do is realize how we regard—"

"—Maybe for people who live later—"

"—it won't be so difficult—"

"Really. Haven't you noticed," (Again Katin) "how the whole social matrix is looked at as though it—"

"We don't know much about history." Lynceos scratched his silver wool. "I don't think—"

"—we could understand it now—"

"Of course you could!" (Katin encore) "I can explain it very—"

"—Maybe later—"

"—in the future—"

"—it'll be easier."

Dark and white smiles bobbed at him suddenly. The twins turned and walked away.

"Hey," Katin said. "Don't you ... ? I mean, I can ex ..." Then, "Oh."

He frowned and put his hands on his hips, watching the twins amble down the corridor. Idas' black back was a screen for fragmented constellations. After a moment Katin lifted his recorder, flicked the ruby pips and spoke softly:

"Note to myself number twelve thousand eight hundred and ten: Intelligence creates alienation and unhappiness in ..." He stopped the recorder. Blinking, he looked after the twins.

"Captain?"

At the top of the steps Lorq dropped his hand from the door and looked down.

The Mouse hooked his thumb through a tear in the side of his pants and scratched his thigh. "Eh . . . Captain?" Then he took the card out of the sack. "Here's your sun."

Rusty brows twisted in shadow.

Yellow eyes dropped their lights at the Mouse.

"I, eh, borrowed it from Tyÿ. I'll give it back——"

"Come up here, Mouse."

"Yes, sir." He started up the coiled steps. Ripples lapped the pool edge. His image, rising, glittered behind the philodendrons on the wall. Bare sole and boot heel gave his gait syncopation.

Lorq opened the door. They stepped into the captain's chamber.

The Mouse's first thought: His room isn't any bigger than mine.

His second: There's a lot more in it.

Besides the computers, there were projection screens on the walls, floor, and ceiling. Among the mechanical clutter, nothing personalized the cabin—not even graffiti.

"Let's see the card." Lorq sat on the cables coiled over the couch and examined the diorama.

Not having been invited to sit on the couch, the Mouse pushed aside a tool box and dropped cross-legged to the floor.

Suddenly Lorq's knees fell wide; he stretched his fists; his shoulders shook; the muscles of his face creased. The spasm passed, and he sat up again. He drew a breath that pulled the laces tight on his stomach. "Come sit here." He patted the edge of the couch. But the Mouse just swung around on the floor so that he sat by Lorq's knee.

Lorq leaned forward and placed the card on the floor.

"This is the card you stole?" The expression that was his frown wrinkled down his face. (But the Mouse was looking at the card.) "If this were the first expedition I pulled together to plumb this star . . ." He laughed. "Six trained and crackling men, who had studied the operation hypnotically, knew the timing of the whole business like they knew the beating of their own hearts, functioned closely as the layers in a bimetal strip. Stealing among the crew . . . ?" He laughed again, shaking his head slowly. "I was so sure of them. And the one I was surest of was Dan." He caught the Mouse's hair, gently shook the boy's head. "I like this crew better." He pointed to the card. "What do you see there, Mouse?"

"Well. I guess . . . two boys playing under a—"

"Playing?" Lorq asked. "They look as if they're playing?"

The Mouse sat back and hugged his sack. "What do you see, Captain?"

"Two boys with hands locked for a fight. You see how one is light and the other is dark? I see love against death, light against darkness, chaos against order. I see the clash of all opposites under . . . the sun. I see Prince and myself."

"Which is which?"

"I don't know, Mouse."

"What sort of person is Prince Red, Captain?"

Lorq's left fist flopped in the hammock of his right palm. "You saw him on the viewing screen in color and tri-D. You have to ask? Rich as Croesus, a spoiled psychopath; he has one arm and a sister so beautiful I . . ." Weight and hammock came apart. "You're from Earth, Mouse. The same world Prince comes from. I've visited it many times, but I've never lived there. Perhaps you know. Why should someone from Earth who's had every advantage that could be distilled from the wealth of Draco, boy, youth, and man be . . ." The voice caught. Weight and hammock again. "Never mind. Take out your hell-harp and play me something. Go on. I want to see and hear."

The Mouse scrabbled in his sack. One hand on the wooden neck, one sliding beneath curve and polish; he closed his fingers and his mouth and his eyes. Concentration became a frown; then a release. "You say he's one-armed?"

"Underneath that black glove he so dramatically smashed up the viewer with, there's nothing but clock-works."

"That means he's missing a socket," the Mouse went on in his rough whisper. "I don't know how it is where you come from; on Earth that's about the worst thing that can happen to you. Captain, my people didn't have any, and Katin back there just got finished explaining how that made me so mean." The syrynx came out of the sack. "What do you want me to play?" He hazarded a few notes, a few lights.

But Lorq was staring at the card again. "Just play. We'll have to plug up soon to come in to the Alkane. Go on. Quick now. Play, I told you."

The Mouse's hand fell toward the—

"Mouse?"

—and moved away without striking.

"Why did you steal *this* card?"

The Mouse shrugged. "It was just there. It fell out on the rug near me."

"But if it had been some other card, the Two of Cups, the Nine of Wands—would you have picked it up?"

"I guess so."

"Are you sure there isn't something in this card that's special? If any other had been there, you would have let it lie or handed it back ... ?"

Where it came from the Mouse didn't know. But it was fear again. To battle it, he whirled and caught Lorq's knee. "Look, Captain! Don't mind what the cards say, I'm going to *help* you get to that star, see? I'm going right with you, and you'll win your race. Don't let some crazy-woman tell you different!"

In their conversation, Lorq had been self-absorbed. Now he looked seriously at the dark frown. "You just remember to give the crazy-woman her card back when you leave here. We'll be at Vorpis soon."

The intensity could maintain itself no longer. Rough laughter broke the dark lips. "I still think they're playing, Captain." The Mouse turned back in front of the couch. Planting his bare foot on top of Lorq's sandaled one, for all the world like a puppy by its master, he struck.

The lights flickered over the machines, copper and ruby, to arpeggios recalling harpsichords; Lorq looked at the boy by his knee. Something happened to him. He did not know the cause. But for the first time in a long time, he was watching someone else for reasons having nothing to do with his star. He did not know what he saw. Still, he sat back and looked at what the Mouse made:

Nearly filling the cabin, the gypsy moved a myriad of flame-colored lights about a great sphere, in time to the crumbling figures of a grave and dissonant fugue.

Chapter Five

The world?

Vorpis.

A world has so much in it, on it—

"Welcome, travelers . . ."

—while a moon, Katin thought as they left the spacefield by dawn-blazed gates, a moon holds its gray glories miniatured in rock and dust.

". . . Vorpis has a day of thirty-three hours, a gravity just high enough to increase the pulse rate by point three of Earth normal over an acclimating period of six hours . . ."

They passed the hundred-meter column. Scales, burnished under the dawn, bled the mists scarfing the plateau: the Serpent, animated and mechanical, symbol of this whole sequined sector of night, writhed on his post. As the crew stepped onto the moving roadway, an oblate sun rouged away night's bruises.

". . . with four cities of over five million inhabitants. Vorpis produces fifteen per cent of all the dynaplasts for Draco. In the equatorial lavid zones, more than three dozen minerals are quarried from the liquid rock. Here, in the tropic polar regions, both the arolat and the aqualat are hunted by netriders along the inter-plateau cañons. Vorpis is famous throughout the galaxy for the Alkane Institute which is located in the capital city of its Northern Hemisphere, Phoenix . . ."

They passed the limit of the info-service voice, into silence. As the road buoyed them from the steps, Lorq, among the crew, gazed on the plaza.

"Captain, where we now go?" Sebastian had brought only

121

one of his pets from the ship. It swayed and stepped on his ridged shoulder.

"We take a fog crawler into the city and then go to the Alkane. Anyone can come with me who wants, wander around the museum, or take a few hours leave in the city. If anybody wants to stay back on the ship—"

"—and miss a chance to see the Alkane?—"

"—doesn't it cost a lot to get in?—"

"—but the captain's got an aunt working there—"

"—so we can get in free then," Idas finished.

"Don't worry about it," Lorq said as they jogged down the ramp to the slips where the fog crawlers moored.

Polar Vorpis was set with rocky mesas, many of them several square miles in area. Between, heavy fogs rilled and slopped, immiscible with the nitrogen/oxygen atmosphere above. Powdered aluminum oxide, and arsenic sulfate in vaporized hydrocarbons expelled from the violent floor, filled the space between mesas. Just beyond the table that held the spacefield was another with cultivated plants, indigenous to a more southern latitude of Vorpis but kept here as a natural park (maroon, rust, scarlet); on the largest mesa was Phoenix.

The fog crawlers, inertial-drive planes powered by the static charges built up between the positively ionized atmosphere and the negatively ionized oxide, plowed the surface of the mist like boats.

On the concourse, the departure times drifted beneath the transparent bricks, followed by arrows directing the crowds to the loading slip:

ANDROMEDA PARK — PHOENIX — MONTCLAIR

and a great bird dripping fire followed through the multi-chrome beneath boots, bare feet, and sandals.

On the crawler deck Katin leaned on the rail, looking through the plastic wall as white waves crackled and uncoiled over the sun to shatter by the hull.

"Have you ever thought," Katin said as the Mouse came up to him sucking on a piece of rock candy, "what a difficult time a man from the past would have understanding the present. Suppose someone who died in, let's say, the twenty-sixth century woke up here. Do you realize how totally horrified and confused he'd be just walking around this crawler?"

"Yeah?" The Mouse took the candy out of his mouth: "Want to finish this? I'm through with it."

"Thanks. Just take the matter of"—Katin's jaw staggered as his teeth crushed crystalline sugar from the linen thread.— "cleanliness. There was a thousand-year period from about fifteen hundred to twenty-five hundred, when people spent an incredible amount of time and energy keeping things *clean*. It ended when the last communicable disease finally became not only curable, but impossible. There used to be an incredibility called 'the common cold' that even in the twenty-fifth century you could be fairly sure of having at least once a year. I suppose back then there was some excuse for the fetish: there seemed to have been some correlation between dirt and disease. But after contagion became an obsolescent concern, sanitation became equally obsolescent. If our man from five hundred years ago, however, saw you walking around this deck with one shoe off and one shoe on, then saw you sit down to eat with that same foot, without bothering to wash it—do you have any *idea* how upset he'd be?"

"No kidding?"

Katin nodded.

Fog broke at a shaft of rock, sparking.

"The idea of paying a visit to the Alkane has inspired me, Mouse. I'm developing an entire theory of history. It's in conjunction with my novel. You don't mind indulging me with a few moments? I'll explain. It has occurred to me that if one considers—" He stopped.

Enough time passed for a handful of expressions to subsume the Mouse's face. "What is it?" he asked when he decided nothing in the moiling gray had Katin's attention. "What about your theory?"

"Cyana Von Ray Morgan!"

"What?"

"*Who*, Mouse. Cyana Von Ray Morgan. I've had a perfectly oblique thought: It just came to me who the captain's aunt is, the curator at the Alkane. When Tyÿ gave her Tarot reading, the captain mentioned an uncle who was killed when he was a child."

The Mouse frowned. "Yeah . . ."

Katin shook his head, mocking disbelief.

"Who *what?*" the Mouse asked.

"Morgan and Underwood?"

The Mouse looked down, sideways, and in the other directions people search for mislaid associations.

"I guess it happened before you were born," Katin said at last. "But you must have heard about it, seen it someplace. The whole business was being sent out across the galaxy on psychoramics while it happened. I was only three, but—"

"Morgan assassinated Underwood!" the Mouse exclaimed.

"Underwood," Katin said, "assassinated Morgan. But that's the idea."

"In Ark," the Mouse said. "In the Pleiades."

"With billions of people experiencing the whole business throughout the galaxy on psychoramics. I couldn't have been more than three at the time. I was at home on Luna watching the inauguration with my parents when that incredible character in the blue vest broke out of the crowd and sprinted across Chronaiki Plaza with that wire in his hand."

"He was strangled!" the Mouse exclaimed. "Morgan was strangled! I did see a psychorama of that! One time in Mars City, last year when I was doing the triangle run, I experienced it as a short subject. It was part of a documentary about something else, though."

"Underwood nearly severed Morgan's head," Katin elucidated. "Whenever I've experienced a re-run, they've cut out the actual death. But five billion-odd were subjected to all the emotions of a man, about to be sworn in for his second term as Secretary of the Pleiades, suddenly attacked by a madman and killed. All of us, we felt Underwood land on our backs; we heard Cyana Morgan scream and felt her try to pull him off; we heard Representative Kol-syn yell out about the third bodyguard—that's the part that caused all the confusion in the subsequent investigation—and we felt Underwood lock that wire around our necks, felt it cut into us; we struck out with our right hands, and our left hands were grabbed by Mrs. Tai; and we died." Katin shook his head. "Then the stupid projector operator—his name was Naibn'n and thanks to his idiocy he nearly had his brain burned out by a bunch of lunatics who thought he was involved in the plot— swung his psychomat on Cyana—instead of the assassin so we could have learned who he was and where he was going—and for the next thirty seconds we were all a hysterical woman crouching on the plaza, clutching our husband's streaming corpse amid a confusion of equally hysterical diplomats, representatives, and patrolmen, watching Underwood dodge and twist through the crowd and finally disappear."

"They didn't show that part in Mars City. But I remember Morgan's wife. That's the captain's aunt?"

"She must be his father's sister."

"How do you know?"

"Well, first of all, the name, Von Ray Morgan. I remember reading once, about seven or eight years back, that she had something to do with the Alkane. She was supposed to be quite a brilliant and sensitive woman. For the first dozen years or so after the assassination, she was the focus for that terribly sophisticated part of society always back and forth between Draco and the Pleiades; being seen at the Flame Beach on Chobe's World, or putting in an appearance with her two little daughters at some space regatta. She spent a lot of time with her cousin, Laile Selvin, who was Secretary of the Pleiades Federation herself for a term. The news-tapes were always torn between the desire to keep her at the edge of scandal and their respect for that whole horror with Morgan. Today if she appears at an art opening or a social event, it's still covered, though the last few years they've let go of her a little. If she is a curator of the Alkane, perhaps she's gotten too involved in it to bother with publicity."

"I've heard of her." The Mouse nodded, looking up at last.

"There was a period when she was probably the best known woman in the galaxy."

"Do you think we'll get to meet her?"

"Hey," Katin said, holding the rail and leaning back, "that would be something! Maybe I could do my novel on the Morgan assassination, a sort of modern historical."

"Oh yeah," the Mouse said. "Your book."

"The thing that's been holding me up is that I can't find a subject. I wonder what Mrs. Morgan's reaction would be to the idea. Oh, I wouldn't do anything like those sensational reports that kept coming out in the psychoramas right afterwards. I want to attempt a measured, studied work of art, treating the subject as one that traumatized an entire generation's faith in the ordered and rational world of man's—"

"Who killed who again?"

"Underwood—you know, it just occurred to me, he was my age now when he did it—strangled Secretary Morgan."

"Because I wouldn't want to make a mistake if I met her. They caught him, didn't they?"

"He stayed free for two days, gave himself up twice and was turned away twice with the other twelve hundred-odd people who confessed in the first forty-eight hours; he got as far as the spacefield where he had planned to join his two wives on one of the mining stations in the Outer Colonies, when he was apprehended at the emigrations office. There's enough material there for a dozen novels! I wanted a subject that was historically significant. If nothing else, it will be a chance to air my theory. Which, as I was about to say—"

"Katin?"

"Eh ... yes?" His eyes, before on copper clouds, came back to the Mouse.

"What is that?"

"Huh?"

"There."

In broken hills of fog, metal flashed. Then a black net rose rippling from the waves. Some thirty feet across, the net flung from the mist. Clinging to the center by hands and feet, vest flying, dark hair whipping from his masked face, a man rode the web into the trough; fog covered him.

"I believe," Katin said, "that is a net-rider hunting the inter-plateau cañons for the indigenous arolat—or possibly the aqualat."

"Yeah? You've been here before ..."

"No. At the university I experienced dozens of the Alkane's exhibits. Just about every big school is iso-sensory with them. But I've never been here in person; I was just listening to the info-voice back at the field."

"Oh."

Two more riders surfaced in their nets. Fog sparkled. As they descended, a fourth and fifth emerged, a sixth.

"Looks like a whole herd."

The riders swept the mists, doffing, electric, disappearing to emerge further on.

"Nets," Katin mused. He leaned forward on the rail. "A great net, spreading among the stars, through time—" He spoke slowly, softly. The riders disappeared. "*My* theory: if you conceive of society as a ..." Then he glanced down at a sound beside him like wind:

The Mouse had taken out his syrynx. From beneath dark and shaking fingers gray lights swiveled and wove.

Through the imitations of mist, gold webs glittered and doffed to a hexatonic melody. The air was tang and cool; there was the smell of wind; but no pressure of wind.

Three, five, a dozen passengers gathered to watch. Beyond the rail, the net-riders appeared once more, and someone, realizing the boy's inspiration, went, "Ohhhh, I see what he's ..." and stopped because so did everyone else.

It ended.

"That lovely was!"

The Mouse looked up. Tyÿ stood half behind Sebastian.

"Thanks." He grinned and started to put the instrument back into the bag. "Oh." He saw something and looked up again. "I have something for you." He reached into the sack. "I found this on the floor back in the *Roc*. I guess you ... dropped it?"

He glanced at Katin and caught the frown vanishing. Then he looked at Tyÿ and felt his smile open in the light of hers.

"I you thank." She put the card in the pouch pocket of her jacket. "You the card did enjoy?"

"Huh?"

"You on each card to gain must meditate."

"You did meditate?" Sebastian asked.

"Oh, yeah. I looked at it a whole lot. Me and the captain."

"That good is." She smiled.

But the Mouse was fiddling with his strap.

At Phoenix Katin asked, "You really don't want to go?"

The Mouse was fiddling with his strap again. "Naw."

Katin shrugged. "I think you'd enjoy it."

"I've seen museums before. I just want to walk around some."

"Well," Katin said. "Okay. We'll see you when we get back to the port." He turned and ran up the stone steps behind the captain and the rest of the crew. They reached the auto-ramp that carried them up through the crags toward gleaming Phoenix.

The Mouse looked down at the fog slopping along the

slate. The larger crawlers—they had just disembarked from one—were anchored down the docks to the left; the little ones bobbed to the right. Bridges arched from the rocks, crossing the crevices that cut here and there into the mesa.

The Mouse dug carefully in his ear with his little finger-nail, and went left.

The young gypsy had tried to live most of his life only with eyes, ears, nose, toes, and fingers. Most of his life he had succeeded. But occasionally, as on the *Roc* during Tyÿ's Tarot reading, or during the interviews with Katin and the captain afterwards, he was forced to accept that what had happened in his past affected present action. Then a time of introspection followed. Introspecting, he found the old fear. By now, he knew it had two irritant surfaces. One he could soothe by stroking the responsive plates of his syrynx. To ease the other required long, private sessions of self-definition. He defined:

Eighteen, nineteen?

Maybe. Anyway, a good four years past the age of reason, they call it. And I can vote in Draco. Never did, though. Again picking my way down the rocks and docks of another port. Where you going, Mouse? Where you been, and what you going to do when you get there? Sit down and play awhile. Only it's got to mean more than that. Yeah. It means something for Captain. Wish I could get that riled up over a light in the sky. Almost can when I hear him talk about it. Who else could fire my harp to ape the sun? A pretty big light it'd be, too. Blind Dan ... and I wonder what it looked like. Don't you want to make the next five fifths of your life with hands and eyes intact? Bind myself to a rock, get girls and make babies? Naw. Wonder if Katin's happy with his theories and notes and notes and theories? What would happen if I tried to play my syrynx the same way he's trying on this book, thinking, measuring? One thing, I wouldn't have time to ask myself these bad questions. Like: what does the captain think of me? He trips over me, laughs, and picks the Mouse up and puts him in his pocket. But it does mean more than that! Captain's got his crazy star. Katin makes his word-webs that no one listens to. Me, Mouse? A gypsy with a syrynx instead of a larynx. But for me, it isn't enough. Captain, where are you taking me? Come on. Sure I'll go.

There's no place else I'm supposed to be. Think I'll find out who I am when I get there? Or does a dying star really give that much light so as I can see . . .

The Mouse walked off the next bridge, thumbs in his pants, eyes down.

The sound of chains.

He looked up.

Chains crawled over a ten-foot drum, hauling a shape from the mists. On the rock before a warehouse, men and women lounged at giant machinery. In his cabin, the winch operator was still in his mask. Covered in nets, the beast rose from the fog, wing-fin whipping. Nets rattled.

The arolat (or it might have been an aqualat) was twenty meters long. Smaller winches lowered hooks. The net-riders holding to the flank of the beast caught at them.

As the Mouse walked down among the men to watch at the precipice, someone called: "Alex's hurt!"

Lowered on a pulley, a scaffold took down a crew of five.

The beast had stilled. Crawling the nets as though they were an easy ladder, they loosed one section of links. The rider hung centered and limp.

One nearly dropped his section; the injured rider swung against the blue flank.

"Hold it there, Bo!"

"That all right is! I it have!"

"Bring him up slow."

The Mouse gazed down into the fog. The first rider gained the rock, links clattering on the stone ten feet away. He came up dragging his net. He released the straps from his wrist, unplugged the connections from his arms, kneeled, and unplugged the lower sockets from his wet ankles. Now he dragged the net over his shoulder across the wide dock. The fog-floats at the net's edge still took the major weight of the web, buoying it through the air. Without them, the Mouse judged, not taking into account the slightly heavier gravity, the sprawling entrapment mechanism would probably weigh several hundred pounds.

Three more riders came up over the edge, their damp hair lank along their masks—standing out curly and red on one man's head—dragging their nets. Alex limped between two companions.

Four more riders followed. A blond, chunky man had just unplugged his net from his left wrist, when he looked up at the Mouse. Red eye-plates flittered in the black mask as he cocked his head. "Hey"—it was a guttural grunt—"that on your hip. What is?" His free hand pushed back his thick hair.

The Mouse looked down and up. "Huh?"

The man kicked the net loose from his left boot. His right foot was bare. "A sensory-syrynx is, hey?"

The Mouse grinned. "Yeah."

The man nodded. "A kid once who really the devil could play I knew—" He stopped, the head uncocked. He pried his thumb beneath the jaw of his mask. Mouth-guard and eye-plates came away.

When it hit him, the Mouse felt the tickly thing happen in his throat which was another aspect of his speech defect. He clamped his jaws and opened his lips; then he closed his lips and opened his teeth. You can't speak that way either. So he tried to let it out with a tentative question mark; it rasped in uncontrolled exclamation: "Leo!"

The squinting features broke. "You, Mouse, it is!"

"Leo, what are you . . . ? But . . . !"

Leo dropped the net from his other wrist, kicked the plug loose from his other ankle, then scooped up a handful of links. "You with me to the net-house come! Five years, a dozen . . . but more . . ."

The Mouse still grinned because that was all that was left to do. He scooped up links himself, and they dragged the net —with the help of the fog-floats—across the rock. "Hey, Caro, Bolsum, this the Mouse is!"

Two of the men turned around.

"You a kid I talked about remember? This him is. Hey, Mouse, you a half a foot taller even aren't! How many years, seven, eight, it is? And you still the syrynx have?" Leo looked around at the sack. "You good are, I bet. But you good were."

"Did you ever get hold of a syrynx for yourself, Leo? We could play together . . ."

Leo shook his head with an embarrassed grin. "Istanbul the last time a syrynx I held. Not since. By now I it all have forgotten."

"Oh," the Mouse said and sensed loss.

"Hey, that the sensory-syrynx you in Istanbul stole is?"

"I've had it with me ever since."

Leo broke out laughing and dropped his arm around the Mouse's sharp shoulders. The laughter (did the Mouse sense Leo's gain?) rolled through the fisherman's words. "And you the syrynx all that time have been playing? You for me now play. Sure! You for me the smells and sounds and colors will strike." Big fingers bruised the dark scapula beneath the Mouse's work vest. "Hey, Bo, Caro, you a real syrynx player now will see."

The two riders hung back:

"You really play that thing?"

"There was a guy through here about six months ago who could tinkle out some pretty ..." He made two curves in the air with his scarred hands, then elbowed the Mouse. "You know what I mean?"

"The Mouse better than that plays!" Leo insisted.

"Leo couldn't stop talking about this kid he used to know on Earth. He said he'd taught this kid to play himself, but when we gave Leo the syrynx ..." He shook his head, laughing.

"But this the kid is!" Leo exclaimed, pounding the Mouse's shoulder.

"Huh?"

"Oh!"

"The Mouse this is!"

They walked into the double-storied door of the net house. From high racks, swaying nets curtained labyrinths. The riders hung their nets on tenterhook arrangements that lowered from the ceiling by pullies. Once stretched, a rider could repair broken links, readjust the response couplers which caused the net to move and shape itself to the nerve impulses from the plugs.

Two riders were wheeling out a great machine with a lot of teeth.

"What's that?"

"With that they will the arolat butcher."

"Arolat?" The Mouse nodded.

"That's what we here hunt. Aqualats down around Black Table they hunt."

"Oh."

"But Mouse, what here you are doing?" They walked

through jingling links. "You in the nets will a while stay? You for a while with us will work? I a crew that a new man needs know—"

"I'm just on leave from a ship that's stopping over here awhile. It's the *Roc*, Captain Von Ray."

"Von Ray? A Pleiades ship is?"

"That's right."

Leo hauled down the hooking mechanism from the high beams and began to spread his net. "What it in Draco doing is?"

"The captain has to stop at the Alkane Institute for some technical information."

Leo gave a yank on the pulley chain and the hooks clattered up another ten feet. He began to spread out the next layer.

"Von Ray, yes. That a good ship must be. When I first into Draco came"—He strained black links across the next hook—"no one from the Pleiades ever into Draco came. One or two, maybe. I alone was." The links snapped in place; Leo hauled the chain again. The top of the net rose into the light from the upper windows. "Nowadays many people from the Federation I meet. Ten on this shore work. And ships back and forth all the time go." He shook his head unhappily.

Somebody called from across the work area. "Hey, where's the doc?" Her voice echoed in the webs. "Alex's been waiting here five minutes now."

Leo rattled his web to make sure it was firm. They looked back toward the door. "Don't worry! He'll here come!" he hollered out. He caught the Mouse's shoulder. "You with me go!"

They walked through the hangings. Other riders were still hooking.

"Hey, you gonna play that?"

They looked up.

The rider climbed halfway down the links, then jumped to the floor. "This I want to see."

"Sure he is," Leo exclaimed.

"You know, really I . . ." the Mouse began. As glad as he was to see Leo, he had been enjoying his private musings.

"Good! Cause Leo ain't been talking about nothing else."

As they continued through the webs, other riders joined them.

Alex sat at the bottom of the steps up to the observation balcony. He held his shoulder, and leaned his head against the spokes. Occasionally he sucked in his unshaven cheeks.

"Look," the Mouse said to Leo, "why don't we just go someplace and get something to drink? We can talk some, maybe. I'll play for you before we go . . ."

"Now you play!" Leo insisted. "Later we talk."

Alex opened his eyes. "Is this the guy you"—he grimaced—"were telling us about, Leo?"

"See, Mouse. After a dozen years, a reputation you have." Leo pulled over an upside-down lubricant drum that rasped on the cement. "Now you sit."

"Come on, Leo." The Mouse switched to Greek. "I don't really feel like it. Your friend is sick, and doesn't want to be bothered—"

"Malakas!" Alex said, then spat bloody froth between his frayed knees. "Play something. You'll take my mind off the hurt. Damn it, when is the medico going to get here?"

"Something for Alex you play."

"It's just . . ." The Mouse looked at the injured net-rider, then at the other men and women standing along the wall.

A grin mixed into the pain on Alex's face. "Give us a number, Mouse."

He didn't want to play:

"All right."

He took his syrynx from the sack and ducked his head through the strap. "The doc will probably get here right in the middle," the Mouse commented.

"I hope they get here soon," Alex grunted. "I know I've got at least a broken arm. I can't feel anything in the leg, and something's bleeding inside—" He spat red again. "I've got to go out on a run again in two hours. He better get me patched up quick. If I can't make that run this afternoon, I'll sue 'im. I paid my damned health insurance."

"He'll get you back together," one of the riders assured. "They ain't let a policy lapse yet. Shut up and let the kid play . . ." He stopped because the Mouse had already started.

Light struck glass and turned it copper. Thousands on thousands of round panes formed the concaved façade of the Alkane.

Katin strolled the path by the river that wound the museum garden. The river—the same heavy mists that oceaned polar Vorpis—steamed at the bank. Ahead, it flowed beneath the arched and blazing wall.

The captain was just far enough in front of Katin so that their shadows were the same length over the polished stones. Among the fountains, the elevated stage was continually bringing up another platform full of visitors, a few hundred at a time. But within seconds they dispersed on the variegated paths that wound down rocks licked through with quartz. On a bronze drum, at the focus of the reflecting panes, some hundred yards before the museum, her marble, armless grace vivid in the ruddy morning, was the Venus de Milo.

Lynceos squinted his pink eyes and averted his face from the glare. Idas, beside him, looked back and forth and up and down.

Tyÿ, her hand in Sebastian's, hung behind him, her hair lifting with the beating of the beast on his gleaming shoulder.

Now the light, thought Katin, as they passed beneath the arch into the lens-shaped lobby, goes blue. True, no moon has natural atmosphere enough to cause such dramatic diffraction. Still, I miss a lunar solitude. This cool structure of plastics, metal, and stone was once the largest building made by man. How far we've come since the twenty-seventh century. Are there a dozen buildings larger than this today through the galaxy? Two dozen? Odd position for an academic rebel here: conflict between the tradition thus embodied and the absurdity of its dated architecture. Cyana Morgan nests in this tomb of man's history. Fitting: the white hawk broods on bones.

From the ceiling hung an octagonal screen where public announcements were broadcast. A serial light-fantasia played now.

"Would you get me extension 739-E-6," Captain Von Ray asked a girl at the information desk.

She turned her hand up and punched the buttons on the little com-kit plugged on her wrist. "Certainly."

"Hello, Bunny?" Lorq said.

"Lorq Von Ray!" the girl at the desk exclaimed in a voice not hers. "You've come to see Cyana?"

"That's right, Bunny. If she isn't busy, I'd like to come up and talk to her."

"Just a moment and I'll see."

Bunny, wherever Bunny was in the hive around them, released control of the girl long enough for her to raise her eyebrows in surprise. "You're here to see Cyana Morgan?" she said in her own voice.

"That's right." Lorq smiled.

At which point Bunny came back. "Fine, Lorq. She'll meet you in South West 12. It's less crowded there."

Lorq turned to the crew. "Why don't you wander around the museum a while? I'll have what I want in an hour."

"Should he carry that"—The girl frowned at Sebastian— "*thing* around with him in the museum. We don't have facilities for pets." To which Bunny answered, "'The man's in your crew, Lorq, isn't he? It looks housebroken." She turned to Sebastian. "Will it behave itself?"

"Certainly it itself will behave." He petted the claw flexing on his shoulder.

"You can take it around," Bunny said through the girl. "Cyana is already on her way to meet you."

Lorq turned to Katin. "Why don't you come with me?"

Katin tried to keep surprise off his face. "All right, Captain."

"South West 12," the girl said. "You just take that lift up one level. Will that be all?"

"That's it." Lorq turned to the crew. "We'll see you later." Katin followed him.

Mounted on marble blocks beside the spiral lift was a ten-foot dragon's head. Katin gazed up at the ridges on the roof of the stone mouth.

"My father donated that to the museum," Lorq said as they stepped on the lift.

"Oh?"

"It comes from New Brazillia." As they rose about the central pole, the jaw fell. "When I was a kid I used to play inside one of its first cousins." Diminishing tourists swarmed the floor.

The gold roof received them.

Then they stepped from the lift.

Pictures were set at various distances from the gallery's central light source. The multilensed lamp projected on each suspended frame the closest approximation (as agreed on by the Alkane's several scholars) to the light under which each picture had originally been painted: artificial or natural, red sun, white sun, yellow or blue.

Katin looked at the dozen or so people wandering the exhibit.

"She won't be here for another minute or so," the captain said. "She's quite a ways away."

"Oh." Katin read the exhibit title.

Images of My People

Overhead was an announcement screen, smaller than the one in the lobby.

Right now it was stating that the paintings and photographs were all by artists of the last three hundred years and showed men and women at work or play on their various worlds. Glancing down the list of artists, Katin was chagrined to discover he recognized only two names.

"I wanted you with me because I needed to talk to somebody who can understand what's involved."

Katin, surprised, looked up.

"My sun—my nova. In my mind I've almost accustomed myself to its glare. Yet I'm still a man under all that light. All my life people around me have usually done what I wanted them to do. When they didn't—"

"You made them?"

Lorq narrowed yellow eyes. "When they didn't, I figured out what they *could* do and used them for that instead. Someone else always comes along to fill the other jobs. I want to talk to someone who will understand. But talking won't convey it. I wish I could do something to show you what this all means."

"I . . . I don't think I understand."

"You will."

Portrait of a Woman (Bellatrix IV): her clothing was twenty years dated. She sat by a window, smiling in the gold light of a sun not painted.

Go With Ashton Clark (no location): he was an old man. His work coveralls were two hundred years out of style. He was about to unplug himself from some great machine. But it was so big you couldn't see what it was.

"It's makes me wonder, Katin. My family—at least my father's part—is from the Pleiades. Still, I grew up speaking like a Draconian in my own home. My father belonged to that encysted nucleus of old-guard Pleiades citizens who still held over so many ideas from their Earth and Draconian ancestors; only it was an Earth that had been dead for fifty years by the time the earliest of these painters lifted a brush. When I settle on a permanent family, my children will probably speak the same way. Does it seem strange to you that you and I are probably closer than I and, say, Tyÿ and Sebastian?"

"I'm from Luna," Katin reminded him. "I only know Earth through extended visit. It's not my world."

Lorq ignored that. "There are ways Tyÿ, Sebastian, and myself are much alike. In those basic defining sensibilities we are closer than you and I."

Again it took Katin an uncomfortable second to interpret the wrecked face's agony.

"Some of our reactions to given situations will be more predictable to each other than to you; yes, I know it goes no further." He paused. "You're not from Earth, Katin. But the Mouse is. So is Prince. One's a guttersnipe; the other is ... Prince Red. Does the same relation exist between them as between Sebastian and me? The gypsy fascinates me. I do not understand him. Not in the way I think I understand you. I don't understand Prince either."

Portrait of a Net-rider. Katin looked at the date: the particular net-rider, with his pensive Negroid features, had sieved the mist two hundred and eighty years ago.

Portrait of a Young Man: contemporary, yes. He was standing in front of a forest of ... trees? No. Whatever they were, they weren't trees.

"In the middle of the twentieth century, 1950 to be exact,"—Katin looked back at the captain—"there was a small country on Earth called Great Britain that had by survey some fifty-seven mutually incomprehensible dialects of English. There was also a large country called the United States with almost four times the population of Great Britain spread out over six times the area. There were accent variants, but only two tiny enclaves composing less than twenty thousand people spoke in a way that could be called mutually incomprehensible with the standard tongue; I use these two to make my point because both countries spoke essentially the same language."

Portrait of a Child Crying (A.D. 2852 Vega IV)
Portrait of a Child Crying (A.D. 3052 New Brazillia II)

"What is your point?"

"The United States was a product of that whole communication explosion, movements of people, movements of information, the development of movies, radio, and television that standardized speech and the framework of thought—not thought itself, however—which meant that person A could understand not only person B, but person W, X, and Y as well. People, information, and ideas move over the galaxy much faster today then they moved across the United States in 1950. The potential of understanding is comparatively greater. You and I were born a third of a galaxy apart. Except for an occasional college weekend to Draco University at Centauri, this is the first time I've ever been outside the Solar System. Still, you and I are much closer in information structure than a Cornishman and Welshman a thousand years ago. Remember that when you try to judge the Mouse—or Prince Red. Though the Great Snake coils his column on a hundred worlds, people in the Pleiades and the Outer Colonies recognize it; Vega Republic furniture implies the same things about its owners here or there; Ashton Clark has the same significance for you as for me. Morgan assassinated Underwood and it became part of both our experiences—" He stopped; because Lorq had frowned.

"You mean Underwood assassinated Morgan."

"Oh, of course ... I meant ..." Embarrassment broiled beneath his cheeks. "Yes ... but I didn't mean ..."

Coming between the paintings was a woman in white. Her hair was high-coifed and silver.

She was thin.

She was old.

"Lorq!" She held out her hands. "Bunny said you were here. I thought we'd go up to my office."

Of course! Katin thought. Most of the pictures he would have seen of her would have been taken fifteen, twenty years ago.

"Cyana, thank you. We could have gotten up ourselves. I didn't want to disturb you if you were busy. It won't take much time."

"Nonsense. The two of you come along. I've been considering bids for half a ton of Vegan light sculptures."

"From the Republic period?" Katin asked.

"Alas, no. Then we might be able to get them off our

hands. But they're a hundred years too early to be worth anything. Come." As she led them among the mounted canvases, she glanced down at the wide metal bracelet that covered her wrist socket. One of the micro-dials was blinking.

"Excuse me, young man." She turned to Katin. "You have a . . . recorder of some sort with you?"

"Why . . . yes, I do."

"I have to ask you not to use it here."

"Oh. I wasn't—"

"Not so much recently, but often I have had problems maintaining privacy." She laid her wrinkled hand on his arm. "You will understand? There's an automatic erasing field that will completely clear the machine should it go on."

"Katin's on my crew, Cyana. But it's a very different crew from the last one. There's no secrecy any more."

"So I gathered." She took her hand away. Katin watched it fall back to the white brocade.

She said—and both Katin and Lorq looked up when she said it—"When I arrived at the museum this morning there was a message for you from Prince."

They reached the galley's end.

She turned briefly to Lorq. "I'm taking you at your word about secrecy." Her eyebrows made a bright metallic stroke on her face.

Lorq's brows were metal rusted; the stroke was broken by his scar. Still, Katin thought, that must be part of the family's marking.

"Is he on Vorpis?"

"I have no idea." The door dilated and they passed through. "But he knows you're here. Isn't that what's important?"

"I just arrived at the spacefield an hour and a half ago. I leave tonight."

"The message arrived about an hour and twenty-five minutes ago. Its origin was conveniently garbled so the operators couldn't have it traced without a lot of difficulty. They're going through that difficulty now—"

"Don't bother." He said to Katin: "What will he have to say this time?"

"We shall all see fairly soon," Cyana said. "You say no secrecy. I would still prefer to talk in my office."

This gallery was confusion: a storage room, or material for an exhibit not yet sorted.

Katin was going to, but Lorq asked first: "Cyana, what is this junk?"

"I believe"—she looked at the date in gold decalcomania on the ancient wooden case—"1923: the Aeolian Corporation. Yes, they're a collection of twentieth-century musical instruments. That's an Ondes Martinot, invented by a French composer of the same name in 1942. Over here we have"—she bent to read the tag—"a Duo Arts Player Piano made in 1931. And this thing is ... Mill's Violano Virtuoso, built in 1916."

Katin peered through the glass door in the front of the violano.

Strings and hammers, stops, fobs, and plectra hung in shadow.

"What did it do?"

"It stood in bars and amusement parks. People would put a coin in the slot and it would automatically play a violin that's on the stand in there with a player-piano accompaniment, programmed on a perforated paper roll." She moved her silver nail to a list of titles. " 'The Darktown Strutters' Ball' ..." The moved on through the clutter of theremins, encore banjoes, and hurdy-gurdies. "Some of the newer academics question the institute's preoccupation with the twentieth century. Nearly one out of four of our galleries is devoted to it." She folded her hands on brocade. "Perhaps they resent that it has been the traditional concern of scholars for eight hundred years; they refuse to see the obvious. At the beginning of that amazing century, mankind was many societies living on one world; at its end, it was basically what we are now: an informatively unified society that lived on several worlds. Since then, the number of worlds has increased; our informative unity has changed its nature several times, suffered a few catastrophic eruptions, but essentially it has remained. Until man becomes something much, much different, that time must be the focus of scholarly interest: that was the century in which we became."

"I have no sympathy with the past," Lorq announced. "I have no time for it."

"It intrigues me," Katin offered. "I want to write a book; perhaps it will deal with that."

Cyana looked up. "You do? What sort of book?"

"A novel, I think."

"A novel?" They passed beneath the gallery's announcement screen: gray. "You're going to write a novel. How fascinating. I had an antiquarian friend some years ago who attempted to write a novel. He only finished the first chapter. But he claimed it was a terribly illuminating experience and gave him a great deal of insight into just exactly how the process took place."

"I've been working on it for quite some time, actually," Katin volunteered.

"Marvelous. Perhaps, if you finish, you'll allow the institute to take a psychic recording under hypnosis of your creative experience. We have an operable twenty-second-century printing press. Perhaps we'll print up a few million and distribute them with a documentary psychoramic survey to libraries and other educational institutions. I'm sure I could raise some interest in the idea among the board."

"I hadn't even thought about getting it printed . . ." They reached the next gallery.

"Through the Alkane is the only way you might. Do keep it in mind."

"I . . . will."

"When is *this* mess going to be straightened out, Cyana?"

"Dear nephew, we have much more material than we can possibly display. It has to go somewhere. There are over twelve hundred public and seven hundred private galleries in the museum. As well as three thousand five hundred storage rooms. I'm fairly acquainted with the contents of most of them. But not all."

They ambled beneath high ribs. Vertebrae arched toward the roofing. Cold ceiling lights cast the shadow of teeth and socket on the brass pedestal of a skull the size of an elephant's hip.

"It looks like a comparative exhibit of reptilian osteology between Earth and . . ." Katin gazed through bone cages. "I couldn't tell you where *that* thing comes from."

Blade of scapula, pelvic saddle, clavicle bow . . .

"Just how far away is your office, Cyana?"

"About eight hundred yards as the arolat flies. We take the next lift."

They walked through the archway into the lift-well.

The spiral carrier took them up some dozens of floors.

A corridor of plush and brass.

Another corridor, with a glass wall . . .

Katin gasped: all Phoenix patterned below them, from central towers to fog-lapped wharf. Though the Alkane was no longer the tallest building in the galaxy, it was by far the tallest in Phoenix.

A ramp curved into the building's heart. Along the marbled wall hung the seventeen canvases in the Dehay sequence, *Under Sirius.*

"Are these the . . . ?"

"Nyles Selvin's molecular-reproduction forgeries, done in twenty-eight hundred at Vega. For a long time they were more famous than the originals—which are downstairs on display in the South Green Chamber—but there's so much history connected with the forgeries Bunny decided to hang them here."

And a door.

"Here we are."

It opened on darkness.

"Now, nephew of mine,"—As they stepped inside, three shafts of light fell from someplace high to circle them on the black carpet—"would you be so good as to explain to me why you are back? And what is all this business with Prince?" She turned to face Lorq.

"Cyana, I want another nova."

"You *what?*"

"You know the first expedition had to be abandoned. I'm going to try again. No special ship is needed. We learned that last time. It's a new crew; and new tactics." The spotlights followed them across the carpet.

"But Lorq—"

"Before, there was meticulous planning, movements oiled, meshed, propelled by confidence in our own precision. Now we're a desperate bunch of dock-rats, with a Mouse among us; and the only thing that propels us is my outrage. But that's a terrible thing to flee, Cyana."

"Lorq, you just can't go off and repeat—"

"The captain is different too, Cyana. Before, the *Roc* flew under half a man, a man who'd only known victory. Now I'm a whole man. I know defeat as well."

"But what do you want me—"

"There was another star under study by the Alkane that was near the point of nova. I want the name and when it's likely to go off."

"You're just going to go like that? And what about Prince? Does he know why you're going to the nova?"

"I couldn't care less. Name my star, Cyana."

Uncertainly troubled her gauntness. She touched something on her silver bracelet.

New light:

Rising from the floor was a bank of instruments. She sat on the bench that rose too and looked over the indicator lights. "I don't know if I'm doing right, Lorq. Outrage? If the decision did not so much affect my life as well as yours, it would be easier for me to give it in the spirit you demand. Aaron was responsible for my curatorship."

She touched the board, and above them appeared—

"Till now I have always been as welcome in Aaron Red's home as I was in my own brother's. But the machine has worked round to a point where this may no longer be. You have placed me in this position: of having to make a decision that ends a time of great comfort for me."

—appeared the stars.

Katin suddenly realized the chamber's size. Some fifty feet across, massed from points of light, hung a hologramic projection of the galaxy, turning.

"We have several study expeditions out now. The nova that you missed was there." She touched a button and one star among the billions flared—so brightly Katin's eyes narrowed. It faded, and again the whole domed astrarium was ghosted with starlight. "At present we have an expedition attending a build-up—"

She stopped.

She reached out; and opened a small drawer.

"Lorq, I really am troubled by this whole business—"

"Go on, Cyana. I want the star's name. I want a tape of its galactic co-ordinates. I want my sun."

"And I'll do all I can to give it to you. But you must indulge the old woman first." From the drawer she took— Katin formed a small surprise-sound in the back of his mouth, then swallowed it—a deck of cards. "I want to see what guidance the Tarot gives."

"I've already had my cards read for this undertaking. If

they can tell me a set of galactic co-ordinates, fine. Otherwise, I have no time for them."

"Your mother was from Earth and always harbored the Earthman's vague distrust of mysticism, even though she admitted its efficacy intellectually. I hope you take after your father."

"Cyana, I've already had one complete reading. There's nothing that a second one can tell me."

She fanned the cards face down. "Perhaps there's something it can tell me. Besides, I don't want to do a complete reading. Just pick one."

Katin watched the captain draw, and wondered if the cards had prepared her for that bloody noon on Chronaiki Plaza a quarter of a century ago.

The deck was not the common three-D dioramic type that Tyÿ owned. The figures were drawn. The cards were yellow. It could easily have dated from the seventeenth century or before.

On Lorq's card a nude corpse hung from a tree by a rope tied to the ankle.

"The *Hanged-man*." She closed the deck. "Reversed. Well, I can't say I'm surprised."

"Doesn't the *Hanged-man* imply a great spiritual wisdom is coming, Cyana?"

"Reversed," she reminded him. "It will be achieved at great price." She took the card and put it, with the rest of the deck, back in the drawer. "These are the co-ordinates of the star you want." She pressed another button.

A ribbon of paper fed into her palm. Tiny metal teeth chomped it. She held it up to read. "The co-ordinates are all there. We've had it under observation two years. You're in luck. The blowup date has been predicted at between ten and fifteen days off."

"Fine." Lorq took the tape. "Come on, Katin."

"What about Prince, Captain?"

Cyana rose from the bench. "Don't you want to see your message?"

Lorq paused. "Go on. Play it." And Katin saw something come alive in Lorq's face. He walked over to the console as Cyana Morgan searched the message index.

"Here it is." She pressed a button.

Across the room Prince turned to face them. "Just what the hell"—His black-gloved hand struck a crystal beaker, as well as its embossed dish, from the table—"do you think you're doing, Lorq?" The hand came back; the dagger and the carved wooden stick clattered to the floor from the other side. "Cyana, you're helping too, aren't you? You are a traitorous bitch. I *am* angry. I *am* furious! I am Prince Red—I am Draco! I am a crippled Serpent; but I'll strangle you!" The damask table cloth crumpled in black fingers; and the sound of the wood beneath, splintering.

Katin swallowed his shock a second time.

The message was a 3-D projection. An out-of-focus window behind Prince threw light from some sun's morning—probably Sol's—across a smashed breakfast.

"I can do anything, anything I want. You're trying to stop that." He leaned across the table.

Katin looked at Lorq, at Cyana Morgan.

Her hand, pale and veined, clamped brocade.

Lorq's, ridged and knot-knuckled, lay on the instrument bank; two fingers held a toggle.

"You've insulted me; I can be very vicious, simply out of caprice. Do you remember that party where I was forced to break your head to teach you manners? Your existence is an insult to me, Lorq Von Ray. I am going to devote myself to gaining reparation for that insult."

Cyana Morgan suddenly looked at her nephew, saw his hand on the toggle. "Lorq! What are you doing—?" She seized his wrist; but he seized hers and pushed her hand from his.

"I know a lot more about you than I did the last time I sent a message to you," Prince said from the table.

"Lorq, take your hand off that switch!" Cyana insisted. "Lorq . . ." Frustration cracked her voice.

"The last time I spoke to you, I told you I was going to stop you. Now, I tell you that if I have to kill you to stop you, I will. The next time I speak to you . . ." His gloved hand pointed. His forefinger quivered . . .

As Prince flickered out, Cyana struck Lorq's hand away. The toggle clicked 'off.' "Just what do you call yourself doing?"

"Captain . . . ?"

Under wheeling stars Lorq's laughter answered.

Cyana spoke angrily: "You sent Prince's message through the public announcement system! That blasphemous madman was just seen on every screen throughout the institute!" In anger she struck the response plate.

Indicator lights dimmed.

Bank and bench fell into the floor.

"Thank you, Cyana. I've got what I came for."

A museum guard burst into the office. A shaft of light lit him as he came through the door. "Excuse me, I'm terribly sorry, but there was—oh, just a moment." He punched his wrist com-kit. "Cyana, have you gone and flipped your silver wig?"

"Oh, for heaven's sake, Bunny. It was an accident!"

"An accident! That was Prince Red, wasn't it?"

"Of course it was. Look, Bunny—"

Lorq clasped Katin's shoulder. "Come on."

They left the guard/Bunny arguing with Cyana.

"Why . . . ?" Katin tried to ask around the captain's shoulder.

Lorq stopped.

Under Sirius #11 (Selvin forgery) flared in purple cascade behind his shoulder. "I said I couldn't tell you what I meant. Perhaps this shows you a little. We'll get the others now."

"How will you find them? They're still wandering around the museum."

"You think so?" Lorq started again.

The lower galleries were chaos.

"Captain . . ." Katin tried to picture the thousands of tourists confronted with Prince's vehemence; he remembered his initial confrontation on the *Roc*.

Visitors swarmed the onyx floor of the FitzGerald Salon. The iridescent allegories of the twentieth-century genius glazed the vaulted walls with light. Children chattered to their parents. Students pattered to one another. Lorq strode between them with Katin close after.

They spiraled out into the lobby above the dragon's head.

A black thing flapped over the crowd, was jerked back. "The others must be with him," Katin cried, pointing to Sebastian.

Katin swung around the stone jaw. Lorq overtook him on the blue tile.

"Captain, we just saw—"

"—Prince Red, like on the ship—"

"—on the announcement screens, it was—"

"—was all over the museum. We got back—"

"—here so we wouldn't miss you—"

"—when you came down. Captain, what—"

"Let's go." Lorq stopped the twins with a hand on each of their shoulders. "Sebastian! Tyÿ! We have to get back to the wharf and get the Mouse."

"And get off this world and to your nova!"

"Let's just get to the wharf first. Then we'll talk about where we're going next."

They pushed their way toward the archway.

"I guess we've got to hurry up before Prince gets here," Katin said.

"Why?"

That was Lorq.

Katin tried to translate his visage.

It was indecipherable.

"I have a third message coming. I am going to wait for it."

Then the garden: boisterous and golden.

"Thanks, doc!" Alex called. He kneaded his arm: a fist, a flex, a swing. "Hey, kid." He turned to the Mouse. "You know, you really can play that syrynx. Sorry about the medico-unit coming in right in the middle of things. But thanks anyway." He grinned, then looked at the wall clock. "Guess I'll make my run after all. Malakas!" He strode down among the clinking veils.

Leo asked sadly, "Now you it away put?"

The Mouse pulled the sack's draw string and shrugged. "Maybe I'll play some more later." He started to stick his arm through the strap. Then his fingers fell in the leather folds. "What's the matter, Leo?"

The fisherman stuck his left hand beneath the tarnished links of his belt. "You just me very nostalgic make, boy." The right hand now. "Because so much time passed has, that you no longer a boy are." Leo sat down on the steps. Humor brushed his mouth. "I not here happy am, I think. Maybe time again to move is. Yeah?" He nodded. "Yeah."

"You think so?" The Mouse turned around on his drum to face him. "Why now?"

Leo pressed his lips. The expression said about the same as a shrug. "When I the old see, I know how much the new I need. Besides, leaving for a long time I have been thinking of."

"Where're you going?"

"To this Pleiades I go."

"But you're from the Pleiades, Leo. I thought you said you want to see someplace new?"

"There a hundred-odd worlds in the Pleiades are. I maybe a dozen have fished. I something new want, yes; but also, after these twenty-five years, home."

The Mouse watched the thick features, the pale hair: familiarity? You adjust it like you would a mist-mask, the Mouse thought; then fit it on the face that must wear it. Leo has changed so much. The Mouse, who had had so little childhood, lost some more of it now. "I just want the new, Leo. I wouldn't want to go home . . . even if I had one."

"Some day as I the Pleiades, you Earth or Draco will want."

"Yeah." He shrugged his sack onto his shoulder. "Maybe I will. Why shouldn't I, in twenty-five years?"

An echo:

"Mouse!"

And:

"Hey, Mouse?"

And again:

"Mouse are you in there?"

"Hey!" The Mouse stood and cupped his hands to his mouth. "Katin?" His shout was even uglier than his speech.

Long and curious, Katin came between the nets. "Surprise, surprise. I didn't think I'd find you. I've been going down the wharf asking people if they'd seen you. Some guy said you'd been playing in here."

"Is the captain through at the Alkane? Did he get what he wanted?"

"And then some. There was a message from Prince waiting for him at the institute. So he played it over the public announcement system." Katin whistled. "Vicious!"

"He's got his nova?"

"He does. Only he's waiting around here for something else. I don't understand it."

"Then we're off to the star?"

"Nope. Then he wants to go to the Pleiades. We have a couple of weeks' wait. But don't ask me what he wants to do there."

"The Pleiades?" the Mouse asked. "Is that where the nova will be?"

Katin turned up his palms. "I don't think so. Maybe he thinks it'll be safer to pass the time in home territory."

"Wait a minute!" The Mouse swung around to Leo again. "Leo, maybe Captain will give you a lift back to the Pleiades with us."

"Huh?" Leo's chin came off his hands.

"Katin, Captain Von Ray wouldn't mind giving Leo a ride out to the Pleiades, would he?"

Katin tried to look reservedly doubtful. The expression was too complicated and came out blank.

"Leo's an old friend of mine. From back on Earth. He taught me how to play the syrynx, when I was a kid."

"Captain's got a lot on his mind—"

"Yeah, but he wouldn't care if—"

"But much better than me now he plays," Leo interjected.

"I bet Captain would do it if I asked him."

"I no trouble with your captain want to make—"

"We can ask him." The Mouse tucked his sack behind him. "Come on, Leo. Where is the captain, Katin?"

Katin and Leo exchanged the look of unintroduced adults put in league by youth's enthusiasms.

"Well? Come on!"

Leo stood up and followed the Mouse and Katin toward the door.

Seven hundred years ago the first colonists on Vorpis carved the Esclaros des Nuages into the mesa rock-rim of Phoenix. Between the moorings for the smaller fog crawlers and the wharfs where the net-riders docked, the stairs descended into the white fog. They were chipped and worn today.

Finding the steps deserted at the Phoenix mid-day siesta, Lorq strolled down between the quartz-shot walls. Mist lapped the bottom steps; wave on white wave rolled from the horizon, each blued with shadow on the left, gilded with sun on the right, like rampant lambs.

"Hey, Captain!"

Lorq looked back up the steps.

"Hey, Captain, can I talk to you a minute?" the Mouse came crabwise down the stairway. His syrynx jogged on his hip. "Katin told me you were going to go to the Pleiades after we leave here. I just ran into a guy I used to know back on Earth, an old friend. Taught me how to play the syrynx." He shook his sack. "I thought maybe since we were going in that direction we could sort of drop him off home. He was really a good friend of—"

"All right."

The Mouse cocked his head. "Huh?"

"It's only five hours to the Pleiades. If he's at the ship when we leave and stays in your projection chamber, it's fine with me."

The Mouse's head went back the other way; he decided to scratch it. "Oh. Gee. Well." Then he laughed. "Thanks, Captain!" He turned and ran up the steps. "Hey, Leo!" He took the last ones double. "Katin, Leo! Captain says it's all right." And called back, "Thanks again!"

Lorq walked a few steps down.

After a while he sat against the rough wall.

He counted waves.

When the number got to four figures, he stopped.

The polar sun circled the horizon; less gilt, more blue.

When he saw the net, his hands slid his thighs, stopped on the bone knots of his knees.

Links clinked on the bottom steps. Then the rider stood up, waist-high in the rolling white. Fog-floats carried the nets up. Quartz caught blue sparks.

Lorq had been leaning against the wall. He raised his head.

The dark-haired rider walked up the steps, webs of metal waving above and behind. Nets struck the walls and rattled. A half dozen steps below him, she pulled off her mist-mask. "Lorq?"

His hands unclasped. "How did you find me, Ruby? I knew you would. Tell me how?"

She breathed hard, unused to the weight she wielded.

Laces tightened, loosened, tightened between her breasts. "When Prince found that you'd left Triton, he sent tapes to six dozen places that you might have gone. Cyana was only one. Then he left it to me to get the report on which one was received. I was on Chobe's World; so when you played that tape at the Alkane, I came running." Nets folded on the steps. "Once I found out you were on Vorpis, in Phoenix . . . well, it took a lot of work. Believe me, I wouldn't do it again." She rested her hand on the rock. Nets rustled.

"I'm taking chances this game, Ruby. I tried to play it through once with a computer plotting the moves." He shook his head. "Now I'm playing by hand, eye, and ear. So far I've come out no worse. And it's moving a lot faster. I've always liked speed. That's perhaps the one thing that makes me the same person I was when we first met."

"Prince said something very much like that to me, once." She looked up. "Your face." Pain flickered in hers. She was close enough to him to touch the scar. Her hand moved, then fell back. "Why didn't you ever have it . . . ?" She didn't finish.

"It's useful. It allows each polished surface in all these brave, new worlds to serve me."

"What sort of service is that?"

"It reminds me what I'm here for."

"Lorq"—and exasperation grew in her voice—"what are you doing? What do you, or your family, think they can accomplish?"

"I hope that neither you nor Prince knows yet. I haven't tried to hide it. But I'm getting my message to you by a rather archaic method. How long do you think it will take a rumor to bridge the space between you and me?" He sat back. "At least a thousand people know what Prince is trying to do. I played them his message this morning. No secrecy any more, Ruby. There are many places to hide; there is one where I can stand in the light."

"We know you're trying to do something that will destroy the Reds. That's the only thing that you would have put so much time and effort into."

"I wish I could say you were wrong." He meshed his fingers. "But you still don't know what it is."

"We know it has something to do with a star."

He nodded.

"Lorq, I want to shout at you, scream—who do you think you are?"

"Who am I to defy Prince, and the beautiful Ruby Red? You are beautiful, Ruby, and I stand before your beauty very much alone, suddenly cursed with a purpose. You and I, Ruby, the worlds we've been through haven't really fit us for meanings. If I survive, then a world, a hundred worlds, a way of life survives. If Prince survives ..." He shrugged. "Still, perhaps it is a game. They keep telling us we live in a meaningless society, that there is no solidity to our lives. Worlds are tottering about us now, and *still* I only want to play. The one thing I have been prepared to do is play, play hard, hard as I can; and with style."

"You mystify me, Lorq. Prince is so predictable—" She raised her eyebrows. "That surprises you? Prince and I have grown up together. But you present me with an unknown. At that party, years ago, when you wanted me, was that part of the game too?"

"No—yes—I know I hadn't learned the rules."

"Now?"

"I know the way through is to make your own. Ruby, I want what Prince has—no. I want to *win* what Prince has. Once I have it, I might turn around and throw it away. But I want to gain it. We battle, and the course of how many lives and how many worlds swings? Yes, I do know all that. You said it then: we are special people, if only by power. But if I tried to keep that knowledge forward in my mind, I'd be paralyzed. Here I am, at this moment, in this situation, with all this to do. What I've learned, Ruby, is how *I* can play. Whatever I do—I, the person I am and have been made—I have to do it that way to win. Remember that. You've done me another favor now. I owe it to you to warn you. It's why I waited."

"What is it you want to do that you have to give such an inflated apology for?"

"I don't know, yet," Lorq laughed. "It does sound pretty stuffy, doesn't it. But it's true."

She breathed in deeply. Her high forehead wrinkled as the wind pushed her hair forward across her shoulder. Her eyes were in shadow. "I suppose I owe you the same warning." He nodded. "Consider it given." She stood up from the wall.

"I do."

"Good." Then she drew back her arm; flung it forward!

And three hundred square feet of chain webbing swung over her head and rattled down on him.

The links caught on his raised hands and bruised them. He staggered under their weight.

"Ruby . . . !"

She flung her other arm; another layer fell.

She leaned back, and the nets pulled, striking his ankles so that he slipped.

"No! Let me . . ."

Through shifting links he saw she was masked again: glittering glass, her eyes; her mouth and nostrils, grilled. All expression was in her slim shoulders, the small muscles suddenly defined. She bent; her stomach creased. The adapter circuits magnified the strength in her arms some five hundred to one. Lorq was wrenched forward down the steps. He fell, caught at the wall. Rock and metal hurt his arms and knees.

What the links gave in strength, they sacrificed in precision of movement. A swell swept the web, but he was able to duck beneath and gain two steps. But Ruby kicked back; he was yanked down four more. He took two on his back, then one on his hip. She was reeling him down. Fog lapped her calves; she backed further into the suffocating mists, stooped till her black mask was at the fog's surface.

He threw himself away from her, and fell five more steps. Lying on his side, he caught at the links and heaved. Ruby staggered, but he felt another stone edge scrape his shoulder.

Lorq let go—of the nets, of his held breath. Again he tried to duck what fell at him.

But he heard a gasp from Ruby.

He beat links from his face and opened his eyes. Something outside . . .

It darted, dark and flapping, between the walls.

Ruby flung up an arm to ward it off. And a sheet of netting exploded up from Lorq. It rose, avoiding the links.

Fifty pounds of metal fell back into the fog. Ruby staggered, disappeared.

Lorq went down more steps. The mist lapped his thighs. The astringent arsenic fog clogged his head. He coughed and clutched rock.

The dark thing flapped about him now. The weight lifted a moment; he scrambled up the stones on his belly. Sucking fresher air, gasping and dizzy, he looked back.

The net hovered above him, grappling with the beast. He pulled himself up another step as the shape flapped free. Links fell heavy on his leg; pulled from his leg; dragged down the steps; vanished.

Lorq sat up and forced himself to follow the thing's flight between the stones. It cleared the walls, gyred twice, then returned to Sebastian's shoulder:

The squat cyborg stud looked down from the wall.

Lorq swayed to his feet, squeezed his eyes closed, shook his head, then lurched up the Esclaros des Nuages.

Sebastian was fastening the steel band about the creature's flexing claw when Lorq reached him at the head of the steps.

"Again, I"—Lorq took another breath and dropped his hand on Sebastian's gold-matted shoulder—"you thank."

They looked from the rocks out where no rider broke the mist.

"You in much danger are?"

"I am."

Tyÿ came quickly across the wharf to Sebastian's side. "What it was?" Her eyes, alive like metal, flashed between the men. "I the black gilly saw released!"

"It all right is," Lorq told her. "Now, anyway. I a run-in with the Queen of Swords just had. But your pet me saved."

Sebastian took Tyÿ's hand. As her fingers felt the familiar shapes of his, she calmed.

Sebastian asked, seriously: "It time to go is?"

And Tyÿ: "Your sun to follow?"

"No. Yours."

Sebastian frowned.

"To the Dim, Dead Sister now we go," Lorq told them.

Shadow and shadow; shadow and light: the twins were coming across the wharf. You could see the puzzled expression on Lynceos' face. Not on Idas'.

"But . . . ?" Sebastian began. Then Tyÿ's hand moved in his and he stopped.

Lorq volunteered no answer to the unfinished question. "The others we get now. I what I waited for have. Yes; time to go it is."

Katin fell forward to clutch the links. The rattle echoed in the net house.

Leo laughed. "Hey, Mouse. In that last bar your big friend too much to drink had, I think."

Katin regained his balance. "I'm not drunk." He raised his head and looked up the curtained metal. "It'd take twice as much as that to get me drunk."

"Funny. I am." The Mouse opened his sack. "Leo, you said you wanted me to play some more. What do you want to see?"

"Anything, Mouse. Anything you like, play."

Katin shook the nets again. "From star to star, Mouse; imagine, a great web that spreads across the galaxy, as far as man. That's the matrix in which history happens today. Don't you see? That's it. That's my theory. Each individual is a junction in that net, and the strands between are the cultural, the economic, the psychological threads that hold individual to individual. Any historical event is like a ripple in the net." He rattled the links again. "It passes over and through the web, stretching or shrinking those cultural bonds that involve each man with each man. If the event is catastrophic enough, the bonds break. The net is torn a while. De Eiling and 34-Alvin are only arguing where the ripples start and how fast they travel. But their overall view is the same, you see. I want to catch the throw and scope of this web in my ... my novel, Mouse. I want it to spread about the whole web. But I have to find that central subject, that great event which shakes history and makes the links strike and glitter for me. A moon, Mouse; to retire to some beautiful rock, my art perfected, to contemplate the flow and shift of the net; that's what I want, Mouse. But the subject won't come!"

The Mouse was sitting on the floor, looking in the bottom of the sack for a control knob that had come off the syrynx. "Why don't you write about yourself?"

"Oh, that's a fine idea! Who would read it? You?"

The Mouse found the knob and pushed it back on its stem. "I don't think I could read anything as long as a novel."

"But if the subject were, say, the clash between two great families like Prince's and the captain's, wouldn't you at least want to?"

"How many notes have you made on this book?" The Mouse chanced a tentative light through the hangar.

"Not a tenth as many as I need. Even though it's doomed as an obsolete museum reliquary, it will be jeweled"—he swung back on the nets—"crafted"—the links roared; his voice rose—"a meticulous work; perfect!"

"I was born," the Mouse said. "I must die. I am suffering. Help me. There, I just wrote your book for you."

Katin looked at his big, weak fingers against the mail. After a while he said, "Mouse, sometimes you make me want to cry."

The smell of cumin.

The smell of almonds.

The smell of cardamon.

Falling melodies meshed.

Bitten nails, enlarged knuckles; the backs of Katin's hands flickered with autumn colors; across the cement floor his shadow danced in the web.

"Hey, there you go," Leo laughed. "You play, yeah, Mouse! You play!"

And the shadows danced on till voices:

"Hey, are you guys still—"

"—in here? Captain told us to—"

"—said to hunt you up. It's—"

"—it's time to get going. Come on—"

"—we're going!"

Chapter Six

"The Page of Wands."

"*Justice.*"

"*Judgement.* My trick. The Queen of Cups."

"Ace of Cups."

"The *Star.* My trick. The *Hermit.*"

"With trumps she leads!" Leo laughed. "*Death.*"

"The *Fool.* My trick is. Now: the Knight of Coins."

"Trey of Coins."

"King of Coins. My trick it is. Five of Swords."

"The Deuce."

"The *Magus;* my trick."

Katin watched the darkened chess table where Sebastian, Tyÿ, and Leo, after the hour of reminiscence, played three-handed Tarot-whist.

He did not know the game well; but they did not know this, and he ruminated that they had not asked him to play. He had observed the game for fifteen minutes over Sebastian's shoulder (the dark thing huddled by his foot), while hairy hands dealt and fanned the cards. From his small knowledge Katin tried to construct a cutting brilliance to toss into the play.

They played so fast ...

He gave up.

But as he walked to where the Mouse and Idas sat on the ramp with their feet hanging over the pool, he smiled; in his pocket he thumbed the pips on the end of his recorder, wording another note.

Idas was saying: "Hey, Mouse, what if I were to turn this knob ... ?"

"Watch it!" The Mouse pushed Idas' hand from the syrynx. "You'll blind everybody in the room!"

Idas frowned. "The one I had, back when I fooled around with it, didn't have—" His voice trailed, waiting for an absent completion.

The Mouse's hand slipped from wood to steel to plastic. His fingers brushed the strings and snagged unamplified notes. "You can really hurt somebody if you don't use this thing properly. It's highly directional, and the amount of light and sound you can get out of it could detach somebody's retina or rupture an eardrum. To get opacity in the hologram images, you know, this thing uses a laser."

Idas shook his head. "I never played around with one long enough to find how it worked inside all the—"

He reached out to touch the safer strings.

"It sure is a nice-looking—"

"Hello," Katin said.

The Mouse grunted and went on tuning drones.

Katin sat down on the other side of the Mouse and watched for a few moments. "I just had a thought," he said. "Nine times out of ten, when I just say 'hello' to someone in passing, or when the person I speak to is going off to do something else, I spend the next fifteen minutes or so rehearsing the incident, wondering whether my smile was taken for undue familiarity, or my sober expression improperly construed as coldness. I repeat the exchange to myself a dozen times, varying my tone of voice and trying to extrapolate the change this might cause in the other person's reaction—"

"Hey." The Mouse looked up from his syrynx. "It's all right. I like you. I was just busy is all."

"Oh." Katin smiled; the the smile was worn away by a frown. "You know, Mouse, I envy the captain. He's got a mission. And his obsession precludes all that wondering about what other people think of him."

"I don't go through all that like you described," the Mouse said. "Much."

"I do." Idas looked around. "Whenever I'm by myself, I do it all the—" and dropped his dark head to examine his knuckles.

"It's pretty fair of him to let us all have this time off and fly the ship with Lynceos," Katin said.

"Yeah," said Idas. "I guess it—" and turned his hands over to follow the dark scribings on his palms.

"Captain's got too many things to worry about," the

Mouse said. "And he doesn't want them. It doesn't take anything to get across this part of the trip, so he'd just as soon have something to occupy his mind. That's what I think."

"You think the captain has bad dreams?"

"Maybe." The Mouse struck cinnamon from his harp, but so strongly their noses and the backs of their mouths burned.

Katin's eyes teared.

The Mouse shook his head and turned down the knob Idas had touched. "Sorry."

"Knight of . . ." Across the room Sebastian looked up from the game and wrinkled his nose. ". . . Swords."

Katin, the only one with legs long enough, tipped the water below the ramp with the toe of his sandal. Colored gravel shook; Katin took out his recorder and flipped the recording pip:

"Novels were primarily about relationships." He gazed at the distortions in the mosaic wall behind the leaves as he spoke. "Their popularity lay in that they belied the loneliness of the people who read them, people essentially hypnotized by the machinations of their own consciousness. The captain and Prince, for example, through their obsessions are totally related—"

The Mouse leaned over and spoke into the jeweled box: "The captain and Prince probably haven't even seen each other face to face for ten years!"

Katin, annoyed, clicked the recorder off. He considered a retort; found none. So he flipped it on again: "Remember that the society which allows this to happen is the society that has allowed the novel to become extinct. Bear in mind as you write that the subject of the novel is what happens between people's faces when they talk to one another." Off again.

"*Why* are you writing this book?" the Mouse asked. "I mean what do you want to do with it?"

"Why do you play your syrynx? I'm sure it's for essentially the same reason."

"Only if I spent all that time just getting ready, I'd never play a thing; and that's a hint."

"I begin to understand, Mouse. It's not my aim, but my methods of achieving it which bug you, as it were."

"Katin, I *do* understand what you're doing. You want to

make something beautiful. But it don't work that way. Sure, I had to practice a long time to be able to play this thing. But if you're going to make something like that, it's got to make people feel and thrill to the life around them, even if it's only that one guy who goes looking for it in the Alkane's cellar. It won't make it if you don't understand some of that feeling yourself."

"Mouse, you're a fine, good, and beautiful person. You just happen to be wrong is all. Those beautiful forms you wield from your harp, I've looked at your face closely enough to know how much they're impelled by terror."

The Mouse looked up and wrinkles scored his forehead.

"I could sit and watch you play for hours. But they're only momentary joys, Mouse. It's only when all one knows of life is abstracted and used as an underlining statement of significant patterning that you have what is both beautiful and permanent. Yes, there is an area of myself I haven't been able to tap for this work, one that flows and fountains in you, gushes from your fingers. But there's a large part of you that's playing to drown the sound of someone screaming in there." He nodded to the Mouse's scowl.

The Mouse made his sound again.

Katin shrugged.

"I'd read your book," Idas said.

The Mouse and Katin looked up.

"I've read a ... well, some books—" He looked back at his hands.

"You would?"

Idas nodded. "In the Outer Colonies, people read books, even novels sometimes. Only there aren't very ... well, only old—" He looked up at the frame against the wall: Lynceos lay like an unborn ghost; the captain was in the other. He looked back with loss in his face. "It's very different in the Outer Colonies than it is—" He gestured around the ship, indicating all of Draco. "Say, do you know the place we're going well?"

"Never been there," Katin said.

The Mouse shook his head.

"I was wondering if you knew whether we could get hold of some ..." He looked back down. "Never mind ..."

"You'd have to ask them," Katin said, pointing to the cardplayers across the room. "It's their home."

"Oh," Idas said. "Yeah. I guess—" Then he pushed himself off the ramp, splashed into the water, waded onto the gravel, and walked, dripping, across the rug.

Katin looked at the Mouse and shook his head.

But the trail of water was completely absorbed in the blue piling.

"Six of Swords."

"Five of Swords."

"Excuse me, do any of you know—"

"Ten of Swords. My trick. Page of Cups."

"—on this world we're going. Do you know if—"

"The *Tower*."

("I wish that card hadn't come up reversed in the captain's reading," Katin whispered to the Mouse. "Believe me, it portends no good.")

"The Four of Cups."

"My trick. Nine of Wands."

"—we can get hold of—"

"Seven of Wands."

"—any bliss?"

"The *Wheel of Fortune*. My trick is." Sebastian looked up. "Bliss?"

The explorer who decided to name the outermost of the Dim, Dead Sister's planets Elysium had indulged a poor joke. With all the planoforming devices available, it was still a frozen cinder ellipsing at trans-Plutonian distances from Her ghost-light, barren and uninhabited.

Someone had once proposed the doubtful theory that all three of the remaining worlds were really moons that had been in the shadow of a gigantic planet when the catastrophe occurred, and thus escaped the fury that had annihilated their protector. Poor moon if moon you are, Katin thought as they swept by. You've done no better as a world. A lesson there in pretension.

Once the explorer explored further, he regained his sense of proportion. His grin faltered at the middle world; he called it Dis.

His fate suggests the agenbite of inwit come too late; flaunting the gods even once reaped a classical reward. His ship crashed on the innermost planet. It remained unnamed, and to this day was referred to as the other world, without pomp, circumstance, or capitals. It was not till a second explorer came that the other world suddenly disclosed a secret. Those great plains, which from a distance had been judged solidified slag, turned out to be oceans—of water, frozen. True, the top ten to a hundred feet was mixed with every sort of rubble and refuse. It was finally decided that the other world had once been entirely under two to twenty-five miles of water. Perhaps nineteen twentieths had steamed into space when the Dim, Dead Sister went nova. This left a percentage of dry land just a little higher than Earth's. The unbreathable atmosphere, the total lack of organic life, the sub-sub temperatures? Minor problems, compared to the gift of seas; easily corrected. So humanity, in the early days of the Pleiades, encroached on the charred and frozen land. The other world's oldest city—though not its biggest, for the commercial and economic shift over the past three hundred years had shifted the population—had been very carefully named: the City of Dreadful Night.

And the *Roc* put down by the black blister of the City tipping the Devil's Claw.

"... of eighteen hours." And that was the end of the info-voice.

"Is this home enough for you?" the Mouse asked.

Leo gazed across the field. "I never this world walked," the fisherman sighed. Beyond, the sea of broken ice stretched toward the horizon. "But great segmented and six-flippered nhars in schools across that sea move. The fishermen for them with harpoons long as five tall men together hunt. The Pleiades it is; home enough it is." He smiled, and his frosted breath rose to dim his blue eyes.

"This is your world, isn't it, Sebastian?" Katin asked. "You must feel good coming home."

Sebastian pushed a dark wing away that beat before his eyes. "Still mine, but ..." He looked around, shrugged. "I from Thule come. It a bigger city is; a quarter of the way around the other world it lies. From here very far is; and very different." He looked up at the twilight sky. Sister was high, a bleary pearl behind a gun-colored sheath of cloud. "Very different." He shook his head.

"Our world, yes," Tyÿ said. "But not our home at all."

The captain, a few steps before them, looked back when they spoke. "Look." He pointed to the gate. Beneath the scar his face was fixed. "No dragon on his column coils. This home is. For you and you and you and me, this home is!"

"Home enough," Leo repeated. But his voice was guarded.

They followed the captain out through the serpentless gates.

The landscape held all the colors of burning:

Copper: it oxidizes to a mottled, yellow-shot green.

Iron: black and red ash.

Sulfur: its oxide is an oozy, purplish brown.

The colors smeared in from the dusty horizon, and were repeated in the walls and towers of the City. Once Lynceos shaded the silver fringe of his lashes to look at the sky where a swarm of shadows like mad, black leaves winked on the exhausted sun, capable of no more than evening, even at noon. He looked back at the creature on Sebastian's shoulder that spread its wings now and rattled its leash. "And how does the gilly feel to be home?" He reached out to chuck the perched thing, only to jerk his white hand back from a dark claw. The twins looked at one another and laughed.

They descended into the City of Dreadful Night.

Halfway down, the Mouse began to walk backwards up the escalator. "It's . . . it's not Earth."

"Huh?" Katin glided by, saw the Mouse, and began back-tracking himself.

"Look at it all down there, Katin. It isn't the Solar System. It isn't Draco."

"This trip is your first time away from Sol, isn't it?"

The Mouse nodded.

"It won't be too different."

"But just look at it, Katin."

"The City of Dreadful Night," Katin mused. "All those lights. They're probably afraid of the dark."

They stick-legged a moment more, gazing across the checkerboard: ornate gaming pieces, a huddle of kings, queens, and rooks towered knights and pawns.

"Come on," the Mouse said.

The twenty-meter blades of metal that made up the giant stair swept them down.

"We better catch up with Captain."

The streets near the field were crowded with cheap rooming houses. Marquees arched the walkways, advertising dance halls and psychoramas. The Mouse looked through the transparent wall at people swimming in a recreation club. "It isn't that different from Triton. Sixpence @sg? Prices are sure a hell of a lot lower, though."

Half the people on the streets were obviously crew or officers. The streets were crowded. The Mouse heard music. Some of it was from the open doors of bars.

"Hey, Tyÿ." The Mouse pointed to an awning. "Did you ever work in a place like that?"

"In Thule, yes."

Expert Readings: the letters glittered, shrank, and expanded on the sign.

"We stay in the City—"

They turned to the Captain.

"—five days."

"Are we going to put up on the ship?" the Mouse asked. "Or here in town where we can have some fun?"

Take that scar. Cut it with three close lines near the top: the captain's forehead creased. "You all suspect the danger we're in." He swept his eyes over the buildings. "No. We're not staying either here or on the ship." He stepped into the wings of a communications booth. Not bothering to swing the panels shut, he passed his hand before the inductance plates. "This Lorq Von Ray is. Yorgos Setsumi?"

"I if his advisory meeting over is will see."

"An android of him will do," Lorq said. "Just a minor favor I want."

"He always to you in person, Mr. Von Ray, likes to talk. Just a moment, I he available is think."

A figure materialized in the viewing column. "Lorq, so long now you I have not seen. What for you can I do?"

"Is anybody using Taafite on Gold for the next ten days?"

"No. I'm in Thule now, and will be for the next month. I gather you're in the City and need a place to stay?"

Katin had already noted the captain's slide between dialects.

There were unrecordable similarities between the captain's

voice and this Setsumi's that illuminated both. Katin recognized common eccentricities that began to define for him an upper-class Pleiades accent. He looked at Tyÿ and Sebastian to see if they responded to it. Only a small movement in the muscles around the eyes, but there. Katin looked back at the viewing column.

"I have a party with me, Yorgy."

"Lorq, my houses are your houses. I hope you and your guests enjoy your stay."

"Thanks, Yorgy." Lorq stepped from the booth.

The crew looked among themselves.

"There's a possibility," Lorq said, "that the next five days I spend on the other world will be the last I spend anywhere." He searched intently for their reactions. As intently, they tried to hide them. "We might as well pass the time pleasantly. We go this way."

The mono crawled up the rail and flung them out across the City. "That Gold is?" Tyÿ asked Sebastian.

The Mouse, beside them, pressed his face against the glass. "Where?"

"There." Sebastian pointed across the squares. Among the blocks, a molten river faulted the City.

"Hey, just like on Triton," the Mouse said. "Is the core of this planet melted by Illyrion too?"

Sebastian shook his head. "The whole planet too big for that is. Only the space under each city. That crack Gold is called."

The Mouse watched the brittle, igneous outcroppings fall back along the lavid fissure.

"Mouse?"

"Huh?" He looked up as Katin pulled out his recorder. "What do you want?"

"Do something."

"What?"

"I'm trying an experiment. Do something."

"What do you want me to do?"

"Anything that comes into your head. Go on."

"Well . . ." The Mouse frowned. "All right."

The Mouse did.

The twins, from the other end of the car, turned to stare.

Tyÿ and Sebastian looked at the Mouse, then at one another, then back at the Mouse.

"Characters," said Katin into his recorder, "are fixed most vividly by their actions. The Mouse stepped back from the window, then swung his arm around and around. From his expression, I could tell he was both amused by my surprise at the violence of his action, at the same time curious if I were satisfied. He dropped his hands back on the window, breathing a little hard, and flexed his knuckles on the sill—"

"Hey," the Mouse said. "I just swung my arm. The panting, my knuckles—that wasn't part—"

" 'Hey,' the Mouse said, hooking his thumb in the hole at the thigh of his pants. 'I just swung my arm. The panting, my knuckles—that wasn't part—' "

"God damn!"

"The Mouse unhooked his thumb, made a nervous fist, ejaculated, 'God damn!' then turned away in frustration. There are three types of actions: purposeful, habitual, and gratuitous. Characters, to be immediate and apprehensible, must be presented by all three." Katin looked toward the front of the car.

The captain gazed through the curving plate that lapped the roof. His yellow eyes fixed Her consumptive light that pulsed like fire-spots in a giant cinder. The light was so weak he did not squint at all.

"I am confounded," Katin admitted to his jeweled box, "nevertheless. The mirror of my observation turns and what first seemed gratuitous I see enough times to realize it is a habit. What I suspected as habit now seems part of a great design. While what I originally took as purpose explodes into gratuitousness. The mirror turns again, and the character I thought obsessed by purpose reveals his obsession is only a habit; his habits are gratuitously meaningless; while those actions I construed as gratuitous reveal a most demonic purpose."

The yellow eyes had fallen from the tired star. Lorq's face erupted about the scar at some antic from the Mouse that Katin had missed.

Rage, Katin pondered. Rage, Yes, he is laughing. But how is anyone supposed to distinguish between laughter and rage in that face.

But the others were laughing too.

"What's the smoke?" the Mouse asked, stepping around the steaming grate in the cobbles.

"It just the sewer grating is, I think," Leo said. The fisherman looked at the fog winding up the pole that supported the brilliant, induced-fluorescence streetlight. At the ground the steam ballooned and sagged; before the light it danced and quivered.

"Taafite is just at the end of this street," Lorq said.

They walked up the hill past a half dozen other gratings that steamed through the perpetual evening.

"I guess Gold is right—"

"—right behind that embankment there?"

Lorq nodded to the twins.

"What sort of a place is the Taafite?" the Mouse demanded.

"A place where I can be comfortable." Subtle agony played the captain's features. "And where I won't have to be bothered with you." Lorq made to cuff him, but the Mouse ducked. "We're here."

The twelve-foot gate, with chunks of colored glass set in wrought iron, fell back when Lorq laid his hand to the plate.

"It remembers me."

"Taafite isn't yours?" Katin asked.

"It belongs to an old school friend, Yorgos Setsumi who owns Pleiades Mining. A dozen years ago I used it often. That's when the lock was keyed to my hand. I've done the same for him with some of my houses. We don't see each other much now but we used to be very close."

They entered Taafite's garden.

The flowers here were never meant to be seen in full light. The blossoms were purple, maroon, violet—colors of the evening. The mica-like scales of the spidery tilda glistened over the leafless branches. There was much low shrubbery, but all the taller plants were slim and sparse, to make as little shadow as possible.

The front wall of Taafite itself was a curving shape of glass. For a long stretch there wasn't any wall at all and house and garden merged. A sort of path led to a sort of flight of steps cut into the rock below what probably was the front door.

When Lorq put his hand on the door plate, lights began to flicker all through the house, above them in windows, far at the ends of corridors, reflected around corners, or shifting through a translucent wall, veined like violet jade, or panes of black-shot amber. Even under: a section of the floor was transparent and they could see lights coming on in rooms stories down.

"Come in."

They followed the captain across the beige carpeting. Katin stepped ahead to examine a shelf of bronze statuettes. "Benin?" he asked the captain.

"I believe so. Yorgos has a passion for thirteenth-century Nigeria."

When Katin turned to the opposite wall his eyes widened. "Now those can't be the originals." Then narrowed. "The Van Meegeren forgeries?"

"No. I'm afraid those are just plain old copies."

Katin chuckled. "I've still got Dehay's *Under Sirius* on the brain."

They continued down the hall.

"I think there's a bar in here." Lorq turned into a doorway.

The lights only came halfway up because of what was beyond the forty feet of glass opposite.

Inside the room yellow lamps played on a pool of opalescent sand filled by siftings from the rock wall. Refreshments were already moving into the room on the rotary stage. On floating glass shelves sat pale statuettes. Benin bronzes in the hall; here were early Cycladics, lucent and featureless.

Outside the room was Gold.

Down among brackish crags, lava flamed like day.

The river of rock flowed by, swinging the crags' shadows between the wooden beams of the ceiling.

The Mouse stepped forward and said something without sound.

Tyÿ and Sebastian narrowed their eyes.

"Now isn't that—"

"—that something to look at!"

The Mouse ran around the sand-pool, leaned against the glass with his hands by his face. Then he grinned back over his shoulder. "It's like being right down in the middle of some Hell on Triton!"

The thing on Sebastian's shoulder dropped, flapping, to the

floor and cowered behind its master as something in Gold exploded. Falling fire dropped light down their faces.

"Which brew of the other world do you want to try first?" Lorq asked the twins as he surveyed bottles on the stage.

"The one in the red bottle—"

"—in the green bottle looks pretty good—"

"—not as good as some of the stuff we got on Tubman—"

"—I bet. On Tubman we got some stuff called bliss—"

"—you know what it is bliss, Captain?"

"No bliss." Lorq held up the bottles, one in each hand. "Red or green. They're both good."

"I could sure use some—"

"—me too. But I guess he doesn't have—"

"—guess he doesn't. So I'll take—"

"—red—"

"—green."

"One of each. Coming up."

Tyÿ touched Sebastian's arm.

"What is?" Sebastian frowned.

She pointed to the wall as one of the shelves floated away from a long painting.

"The view from Thule down Ravine Dank is!" Sebastian seized Leo's shoulder. "Look. That home is!"

The fisherman looked up.

"You out the back window of the house where I was born look," Sebastian said. "All that you see."

"Hey." The Mouse reached up to tap Katin's shoulder.

Katin looked down from the sculpture he was examining at the Mouse's dark face. "Huh?"

"That stool over there. You remember that Vega Republic stuff you were talking about back on the ship?"

"Yes."

"Is that stool one?"

Katin smiled. "No. Everything here is all patterned on pre-star-flight designs. This whole room is a pretty faithful replica of some elegant American mansion of the twenty-first or second century."

The Mouse nodded. "Oh."

"The rich are always enamored of the ancient."

"I never been in a place like this before." The Mouse looked about the room. "It's something, huh?"

"Yes. It is."

"Come get your poison," Lorq called from the stage.

"Mouse! Now you your syrynx play?" Leo brought over two mugs, pushed one into the Mouse's hands, the other into Katin's. "You play. Soon I down to the ice docks will go. Mouse, play for me."

"Play something that we can dance—"

"—dance with us, Tyÿ. Sebastian—"

"—Sebastian will you dance with us too?"

The Mouse shucked his sack.

Leo went over to get a mug for himself, came back, and sat down on the stool. The Mouse's images were paled by Gold. But the music was ornamented with sharp, insistent quarter tones. It smelled like a party.

On the floor, the Mouse balanced the body of the syrynx against his blackened, horny foot, tapped time with the toe of his boot, and rocked. His fingers flew. Light from Gold, from the fixtures about the room, from the Mouse's syrynx, lashed the captain's face to fury. Twenty minutes later he said, "Mouse, I'm going to steal you for a while."

He stopped playing. "What you want, Captain?"

"Company. I'm going out."

The dancers' faces fell.

Lorq turned a dial on the stage. "I've had the sensory recorder running." The music began again. And the ghostly visions of the Mouse's syrynx cavorted once more, along with images of Tyÿ, Sebastian, and the twins dancing, the sound of their laughter—

"Where are we going, Captain?" the Mouse asked. He put his syrynx down on the case.

"I've been thinking. We need something here. I'm going to get some bliss."

"You mean you know—"

"—where to get hold of some?"

"The Pleiades is my home," the Captain said. "We'll be gone maybe an hour. Come on, Mouse."

"Hey, Mouse, will you leave your—"

"—syrynx here with us—"

"—now? It'll be okay. We won't—"

"—won't let anything happen to it."

With lips pulled thin, the Mouse looked from the twins to

his instrument. "All right. You can play it. But watch out, huh?"

He walked over to where Lorq stood at the door.

Leo joined them. "Now it too time for me to go is."

Inside the Mouse, surprise opened like a wound over the inevitable. He blinked.

"For the lift, Captain, I you thank."

They walked down the hall and through Taafite's garden. Outside the gate, they stopped by the smoking grate. "For the ice docks down there you go." Lorq pointed down the hill. "You the mono to the end of the line take."

Leo nodded. His blue eyes caught the Mouse's dark ones, and puzzlement passed on his face. "Well, Mouse. Maybe some day again we'll see, huh?"

"Yeah," the Mouse said. "Maybe."

Leo turned and walked down the fuming street, boot heel clicking.

"Hey," the Mouse called after a moment.

Leo looked back.

"Ashton Clark."

Leo grinned, then started again.

"You know," the Mouse said to Lorq, "I'll probably never see him again in my life. Come on, Captain."

"Are we anywhere near the spacefield?" the Mouse asked. They came down the crowded steps of the monorail station.

"Within walking distance. We're about five miles down Gold from Taafite."

The spray trucks had recently been by. The wandering people were reflected on the wet pavement. A group of youngsters—two of the boys with bells around their necks—ran by an old man, laughing. He turned, followed them a few steps, hand out. Now he turned back and came toward the Mouse and Lorq.

"An old guy with something, you help? Tomorrow, tomorrow into a job I plug. But tonight . . ."

The Mouse looked back after the panhandler, but Lorq kept on.

"What's in there?" The Mouse pointed to a high arcade of lights. People clustered before the door on the shining street.

"No bliss there."

They turned the corner.

On the far side of the street, couples had stopped by a fence. Lorq crossed the street. "That's the other end of Gold down there."

Below the ragged slope, bright rock wound into the night. One couple turned away hand in hand, with burnished faces.

Flashing from his hair, hands, and shoulders, a man came up the walkway in a lamé vest. A tray of jewels hung around his neck. The couple stopped him. She bought a jewel from the vendor and, laughing, placed it on her boyfriend's forehead. The sequined streamers from the central cluster of stones ran back and wound themselves in his long hair. They laughed up the wet street.

Lorq and the Mouse reached the end of the fence. A crowd of uniformed Pleiades patrolmen came up the stone steps; three girls ran up behind them, screaming. Five boys overtook them, and the screams turned to laughter. The Mouse looked back to see them cluster about the jewelry man.

Lorq started down the steps.

"What's down there?" The Mouse hurried on behind.

On the side of the broad steps, people drank at tables set beside the cafés cut into the rock wall.

"You look like you know where you're going, Captain." The Mouse caught up with Lorq's elbow. "Who is *that?*" He gazed after one stroller. Among the lightly clad people, she wore a heavy parka rimmed with fur.

"She's one of your ice-fishermen," the captain told him. "Leo will be wearing one of them soon. They spend most of their time away from the heated part of the City."

"Where are we going?"

"I think it was down this way." They turned along a dim ledge; there were a few windows in the rock. Blue light leaked from the shades. "These places change owners every couple of months, and I haven't been in the City for five years. If we don't find the place I'm looking for, we'll find one that'll do."

"What sort of place is it?"

A woman shrieked. A door swung open; she staggered out. Another suddenly reached from the darkness, caught her by the arm, slapped her twice, and yanked her back. The door slammed on a second shriek. An old man—probably another ice-fisherman—supported a younger man on his shoulder. "We you back to the room you take. Your head up hold. All right it will be. To the room we you take."

The Mouse watched them stagger by. A couple had stopped back near the stone stairway. She was shaking her head. Finally he nodded, and they turned back.

"The place I was thinking of, among other things, used to have a thriving business conning people to work in the mines in the Outer Colonies, then collecting a commission on each recruit. It was perfectly legal; there're a lot of stupid people in the universe. I've been a foreman in one of those mines and seen it from the other end. It's not very pretty." Lorq looked over a doorway. "Different name. Same place."

He started down the steps. The Mouse looked quickly behind him, then followed. They entered a long room with a plank bar by one wall. A few panels of multichrome gave out feeble color. "Same people too."

A man older than the Mouse, younger than Lorq, with stringy hair and dirty nails came up. "What can I do for you boys?"

"What have you got to make us feel good?"

He closed an eye. "Have a seat."

Dim figures passed and paused before the bar.

Lorq and the Mouse slipped into a booth. The man pulled up a chair, reversed it, straddled it, and sat at the table's head. "How good do you want to feel?"

Lorq turned his hands palms up on the table.

"Downstairs we have a . . ." The man glanced toward a doorway in the back where people moved in and out. ". . . pathobath?"

"What's that?" the Mouse asked.

"A place with crystal walls that reflect the color of your thoughts," Lorq told him. "You leave your clothes at the door and float among columns of light on currents of glycerin. They heat it to body temperature, mask out all your senses. After a little while, deprived of contact with sensory reality, you go insane. Your own psychotic fantasies provide the floor show." He looked back at the man. "I want something we can take with us."

Behind thin lips the man's teeth came together sharply.

On the stage at the end of the bar a naked girl stepped into the coral spotlight and began to chant a poem. Those sitting at the bar clapped in time.

The man looked quickly back and forth between the captain and the Mouse.

Lorq folded his hands. "Bliss."

The man's eyebrows raised under the matted hair that fell down his forehead. "That's what I thought." His own hands came together. "Bliss."

The Mouse looked at the girl. Her skin was unnaturally shiny. Glycerin, the Mouse thought. Yeah, glycerin. He leaned against the stone wall, then quickly pulled away. Drops of water ran the cold rock. The Mouse rubbed his shoulder and looked back at the captain.

"We'll wait for it."

The man nodded. After a moment he said to the Mouse, "What do you and pretty-man do for a living?"

"Crew on a . . . freighter." The captain nodded just enough to communicate approval.

"You know, there's good work in the Outer Colonies. You ever thought about doing a hitch in the mines?"

"I worked the mines for three years," Lorq said.

"Oh." The man fell silent.

After a moment, Lorq asked, "Are you going to send for the bliss?"

"I already did." A limp grin washed his lips.

At the bar the rhythmic clapping broke into applause as the girl finished her poem. She leaped from the stage, and ran across the floor toward them. The Mouse saw her take something quickly from one of the men at the bar. She hugged the man at the table with them. Their hands joined, and as she ran into the shadow, the Mouse saw the man's hand fall on the table, the knuckles high with something underneath. Lorq placed his hand over the man's, completely masking them.

"Three pounds," the man said, "@sg."

With his other hand Lorq put three bills on the table.

The man pulled his hand away and picked them up.

"Come on, Mouse, we've got what we want." Lorq rose from the table and started across the room.

The Mouse ran after him. "Hey, Captain. That man didn't speak the Pleiades way!"

"In a place like this, they always speak your language, no matter what it is. That's where their business comes from."

Just as they reached the door, the man suddenly hailed them once more. He nodded at Lorq. "Just wanted to remind you to come on back when you want some more. So long, beautiful."

"See you around, ugly." Lorq went out the door. In the cool night, he paused at the top of the steps, bent his head over his cupped hands and breathed deeply. "Here you go, Mouse." He held his hands out. "Have a whiff on me."

"What am I supposed to do?"

"Take a deep breath, hold it for a while, then let it go."

As the Mouse leaned down, a shadow fell that was not his own. The Mouse jumped.

"All right. What you got?"

The Mouse looked up at, and Lorq looked down at the patrolman.

Lorq narrowed his eyes and opened his hands.

The patrolman decided to ignore the Mouse and looked at Lorq. "Oh." He moved his lower lip over his upper teeth. "Something dangerous it could have been. Something illegal, understand?"

Lorq nodded. "It could have been."

"These places around here, you got to watch out."

Lorq nodded again.

So did the patrolman. "Say, how about the law swinging out a little, you let?"

The Mouse saw the smile the captain had not yet allowed out on his face. Lorq raised his hands to the patrolman. "Out yourself knock."

The patrolman bent, sucked a breath, stood. "Thanks," and he turned into the dark.

The Mouse watched him a moment, shook his head, shrugged, then gave the captain a cynical frown.

He put his hands around Lorq's, leaned over, emptied his lungs, then filled them. After he held his breath for nearly a minute, he exploded, *"Now* what's supposed to happen?"

"Don't worry about it," Lorq said. "It is."

They started back along the ledge past the blue windows.

The Mouse looked at the river of bright rock. "You know," he said after a while, "I wish I had my syrynx. I want to play." They had almost reached the steps with the open

cafés under the lights. There was the tinkling of amplified
music. Someone at a table dropped a glass that broke on the
stone, and the sound disappeared under an onslaught of
applause. The Mouse looked at his hands. "This stuff makes
my fingers itchy." They started up the steps. "When I was a
kid back on Earth, in Athens, there was a street like this.
Odós Mnisicléous, it ran right up through the Plaka. I
worked at a couple of places in the Plaka, you know? The
Golden Prison, the *'O kai 'H*. And you climb the stairs up
from Adrianou and way above is the back porch of the
Erechtheum in a spotlight over the Acropolis wall at the top
of the hill. And people at the tables on the sides of the
street, they break their plates, see, and laugh. You ever been
in the Plaka in Athens, Captain?"

"Once, a long time ago," Lorq said. "I was just about your
age now. It was only for an evening though."

"Then you don't know the little neighborhood above it.
Not if you were just there one evening." The Mouse's hoarse
whisper gained momentum. "You keep going up that street of
stone steps till all the night clubs give out and there's nothing
but dirt and grass and gravel, but you keep going, with the
ruins still poking over that wall. Then you come to this place
called Anaphiotika. That means 'Little Anaphi,' see? Anaphi
was an island that was almost destroyed by an earthquake, a
long time ago. And they got little stone houses, right in the
side of the mountain, and streets eighteen inches wide with
steps so steep it's like climbing a ladder. I knew a guy who
had a house there. And after I got finished work, I'd get
some girls. And some wine. Even when I was a kid, I could
get girls—" The Mouse snapped his fingers. "You climb up to
his roof by a rusty spiral stair outside the front door, chase
the cats off. Then we'd play and drink wine and watch the
city spread all down the mountain like a carpet of lights, and
then up the mountain with the little monastery like a splinter
of bone at the top. Once we played too loud and the old lady
in the house above us threw a pitcher at us. But we laughed
at her and yelled back and made her get up and come down
for a glass of wine. And already the sky was getting gray
behind the mountains, behind the monastery. I liked that,
Captain. And I like this too. I can play much better than I
could back then. That's because I play a lot. I want to play
the things I can see around me. But there's so much around

me I can see that you can't. And I have to play that too. Just
because you can't touch it, doesn't mean you can't smell and
see and hear it. I walk down one world and up another and I
like what I see in all of them. You know the curve of your
hand in the hand of someone more important to you than
anybody? That's the spirals of the galaxy locked in one another. You know the curve of your hand when the other hand is
gone and you're trying to remember how it felt? There is no
other curve like that. I want to play them against each other.
Katin says I'm scared. I am, Captain. Of everything around
me. So whatever I see, I press against my eyeballs, stick my
fingers and tongue in it. I like today; that means I have to
live scared. Because today is scary. And at least I'm not
afraid of being frightened. Katin, he's all mixed up with the
past. Sure, the past is what makes now like now makes
tomorrow; Captain, there's a river crashing by us. But we
can only go down to drink one place and it's called 'now.' I
play my syrynx, see, and it's like an invitation for everybody
to come down and drink. When I play I want everybody to
applaud. Cause when I play I'm up there, see, with the
tightrope walkers, balancing on that blazing rim of crazy
where my mind still works. I dance in the fire. When I play, I
lead all the other dancers where you, and you"——the Mouse
pointed at people passing—"and him and her, can't get without my help. Captain, back three years ago, when I was
fifteen in Athens, I remember one morning up on that roof. I
was leaning on the frame of the grape arbor with shiny grape
leaves on my cheek and the lights of the city going out under
the dawn, and the dancing had stopped, and two of the girls
were making out in a red blanket back under the iron table.
And suddenly I asked myself, 'What am I doing here?' Then
I asked it again: 'What am I doing here?' Then it got like a
tune caught in my head, playing through again and again. I
was scared, Captain. I was excited and happy and scared to
death, and I bet I was grinning wide as I'm grinning now.
That's how I run, Captain. I haven't got the voice to sing or
shout it. But I play my harp, don't I? And what am I doing
now, Captain? Climbing another street of stone steps worlds
away, dawn then, night now, happy and scared as the devil.
What am I doing here? Yeah! What am I doing?"

  "You're rapping, Mouse." Lorq let go of the post at the
top of the steps. "Let's get back to Taafite."

"Oh, yeah. Sure, Captain." The Mouse suddenly looked into the ruined face. The captain looked down at him. Deep among the broken lines and lights, the Mouse saw humor and compassion. He laughed. "I wish I had my syrynx now. I'd play your eyes out of your head. I'd turn your nose inside out from both nostrils, and you'd be twice as ugly as you are now, Captain!" Then he looked across the street: at once wet pavement and people and lights and reflections kaleidoscoped behind amazing tears. "I wish I had my syrynx," the Mouse whispered again, "had it with me . . . now."

They headed back to the monorail station.

"Eating, sleeping, current wages: how would I explain the present concept of these three to somebody from, say, the twenty-third century?"

Katin sat at the edge of the party watching the dancers, himself among them, laughing before Gold. Now and then he bent over his recorder.

"The way we handle these processes would be totally beyond the comprehension of someone from seven hundred years ago, even though he understood intravenous feeding and nutrition concentrates. Still he would have nowhere near the informational equipment to understand how everyone in this society, except the very, very rich, or the very, very poor, take their daily nourishment. Half the process would seem completely incomprehensible; the other half, disgusting. Odd that drinking has remained the same. At the same period of time these changes took place—bless Ashton Clark—the novel more or less died. I wonder if there's a connection. Since I have chosen this archaic art form, must I consider my audience the people who will read it tomorrow, or should I address it to yesterday? Past or future, if I left those elements out of the narrative, it might serve to give the work more momentum."

The sensory recorder had been left on to record and re-record so that the room was crowded with multiple dancers and the ghosts of dancers. Idas played a counterpoint of sounds and images on the Mouse's syrynx. Conversations, real and recorded, filled the room.

"Though all these dance around me now, I make my art for a mythological audience of one. Under what other circumstances can I hope to communicate?"

Tyÿ stepped from among Tyÿs and Sebastians. "Katin, the door-light flashing is."

Katin flipped off his recorder. "The Mouse and Captain must be back. Don't bother, Tyÿ. I'll let them in." Katin stepped out of the room and hurried down the hall.

"Hey, Captain"—Katin swung the door back—"the party's going—" He dropped his hand from the knob. His heart pounded twice in his throat, and then might as well have stopped. He stepped back from the door.

"I gather you recognize myself and my sister? I won't bother with introductions then. May we come in?"

Katin's mouth started working toward some word.

"We know he's not here. We'll wait."

The iron gate with its chunk-glass ornamentation closed on a scarf of steam. Lorq looked about the plants in silhouette against Taafite's amber.

"Hope they still have a party going," the Mouse said. "To go all this way and find them curled up in the corner asleep!"

"Bliss'll wake them up." As Lorq mounted the rocks, he took his hands from his pockets. A breeze pushed beneath the flaps of his vest, cooled the spaces between his fingers. He palmed the circle of the door plate. The door swung in. Lorq stepped inside. "Doesn't sound like they've passed out."

The Mouse grinned and hopped toward the living room.

The party had been recorded, re-recorded, and re-recorded again. Multiple melodies flailed a dozen dancing Tyÿs to different rhythms. Twins before were duodecuplets now. Sebastian, Sebastian, and Sebastian, at various stages of inebriation, poured drinks of red, blue, green.

Lorq stepped in behind the Mouse. "Lynceos, Idas! We got your—I can't tell which is which. Quiet a minute!" He slapped at the wall switch of the sensory recorder—

From the edge of the sand-pool the twins looked up; white hands fell apart; black came together.

Tyÿ sat at Sebastian's feet, hugging her knees: gray eyes flashed under beating lids.

Katin's Adam's apple bounded in his long neck.

And Prince and Ruby turned from contemplating Gold. "We seem to have put a damper on the gathering. Ruby suggested they just go on and forget us, but—" He shrugged. "I'm glad we meet here. Yorgy was reluctant to tell me where you were. He's a good friend to you. But not so good as I am an enemy." The black vinyl vest hung loose on his bone-white chest. Ridged ribs scored it sharply. Black pants, black boots. Around his upper arm at the top of his glove: white fur.

A hand slapped Lorq's sternum, slapped it again, again. The hand was inside. "You've threatened me a great deal, and interestingly. How are you going to carry it out?" Bearing Lorq's fear was a net of exaltation.

As Prince stepped forward, a wing of Sebastian's pet brushed his calf. "Please ..." Prince glanced down at the creature. At the sand-pool he stopped, stooped between the twins, scooped his false hand into the sand, and made a fist. "Ahhhh ..." His breath, even with parted lips, hissed. He stood now, opened his fingers.

Dull glass fell smoking to the rug. Idas pulled his feet back sharply. Lynceos just blinked faster.

"How does that answer my question?"

"Consider it a demonstration of my love of strength and beauty. Do you see?" He kicked the shards of hot glass across the rug. "Bah! Too many impurities to rival Murano. I came here—"

"To kill me?"

"To reason."

"What did you bring beside reasons?"

"My right hand. I know you have no weapons. I trust my own. We are both playing this one by ear, Lorq. Ashton Clark has set the rules."

"Prince, what are you trying to do?"

"Keep things as they are."

"Stasis is death."

"But less destructive than your insane movements."

"I am a pirate, remember?"

"You're fast on your way to becoming the greatest criminal of the millennium."

"Are you about to tell me something I don't know?"

"I sincerely hope not. For our sake here, for the sake of worlds around us ..." Then Prince laughed. "By every logical extension of argument, Lorq, I'm *right* as far as this battle goes. Has that occurred to you?"

Lorq narrowed his eyes.

"I know you want Illyrion," Prince continued. "The only reason you want it is to upset the balance of power; otherwise, it wouldn't be worth it to you. Do you know what will happen?"

Lorq set his mouth. "I'll tell you: it will ruin the economy of the Outer Colonies. There will be a whole wave of workers to relocate. They'll swarm in. The empire will come as close to war as it's been since the suppression of Vega. When a company like Red-shift Limited reaches stasis in this culture, that's tantamount to destruction. That should kill as much work for as many people in Draco as the destruction of my companies would mean in the Pleiades. Does that begin your argument well?"

"Lorq, you are incorrigible!"

"Are you relieved that I've thought it through?"

"I'm appalled."

"Here's another argument you can use, Prince: you're fighting not only for Draco, but for the economic stability of the Outer Colonies as well. If I win, a third of the galaxy moves forward and two thirds fall behind. If you win, two thirds of the galaxy maintains its present standard and one third falls."

Prince nodded. "Now, demolish me with *your* logic."

"I must survive."

Prince waited. He frowned. The frown parted with puzzled laughter. "That's all you can say?"

"Why should I bother to tell you that the workers can be relocated in spite of the difficulty? That there will be no war because there are enough worlds and food for them—if it is properly distributed, Prince? That the increase in Illyrion will create enough new projects to absorb these people?"

Prince's black brows arched. "That much Illyrion?"

Lorq nodded. "That much."

By the great window, Ruby picked up the ugly lumps of glass. She examined them, seeming unconscious of the conversation. But Prince held out his hand. Immediately, she placed them on his palm. She was following their words closely.

"I wonder," Prince said, looking at the fragments, "if this will work." His fingers closed. "Do you insist on reopening this feud between us?"

"You're a fool, Prince. The forces that have pried up the old hostilities were moving about us when we were children. Why pretend here that these parameters mark our field?"

Prince's fist began to quiver. His hand opened. Bright crystals were shot with internal blue light. "Heptodyne quartz. Are you familiar with it? Mild pressure on impure glass will often produce—I say 'mild.' That's a geologically relative term, of course."

"You're threatening again. Go away—now. Or you'll have to kill me."

"You don't want me to go. We're trying to maneuver a single combat here to decide which worlds fall where." Prince hefted the crystals. "I could put one of these quite accurately through your skull." He turned his hand over; again shards fell on the floor. "I'm not a fool, Lorq. I'm a juggler. I want to keep all our worlds spinning about my ears." He bowed and stepped back. Again his foot brushed the beast.

Sebastian's pet yanked at its chain. Sails cracked the air, jerked its master's arm back and forth—

"Down! Down, now you go . . . !"

—the chain pulled from Sebastian's hand. It rose, swept back and forth beneath the ceiling. Then it dove at Ruby.

She whirled her arms around her head. Prince dodged at her, ducked beneath the wings. His gloved hand struck up.

It squealed, flapped back. Prince whipped his hand again at the black body. It shook in the air, collapsed.

Tyÿ cried out, ran to the beast, which flapped weakly on its back, and pulled it away. Sebastian rose from his stool with knotted fists. Then he dropped to his knees to minister to his injured pet.

Prince turned his black hand over. Wet purple blotched the nap. "That was the creature that attacked you on the Esclaros, wasn't it?"

Ruby stood up, still silent, and pushed dark hair from her shoulder. Her dress was white, rimmed at hem, collar, and sleeve with black. She touched her satin bodice where bangles of blood had dropped.

Prince regarded the mewing thing between Tyÿ and Sebastian. "That almost settles the score, Ruby?" He rubbed his hands: flesh and bloody black.

He frowned at his smeared fingers. "Lorq, you asked me a question: when am I going to make good my threats? Some time within the next sixty seconds. But we have a sun to settle between us. Those rumors you mentioned to Ruby have reached us. The protective gauze the Great White Bitch of the North, your Aunt Cyana, drapes about herself, is most effective. It fell the moment you left her office. But we've listened at other keyholes; and we heard news of a sun, about to go nova. It, or suns like it, have apparently been the center of your interest for some time." His blue eyes rose from his stained palm. "Illyrion. I don't see the connection. No matter. Aaron's men are working on it."

Tension rode like pain between Lorq's hips and in the small of his back. "You are preparing for something. Go on. Do it."

"I must figure out how. With my bare hand, I think ... no." His brows arched; he held up his dark fist. "No, this one. I respect your attempt to justify yourself to me. But how do you justify yourself to them?" With bloody fingers he gestured at the crew.

"Ashton Clark would side with you, Prince. So would justice. I'm not here because I willed a situation. I'm only struggling to solve it. The reason I must fight you is I think I can win. There's only that one. You're for stasis. I'm for movement. Things move. There's no ethic there." Lorq looked at the twins. "Lynceos? Idas?"

The black face looked up; the white, down.

"Do you know what you risk in this contest?"

One looking at him, one looking away, they nodded.

"Do you want to sign off the *Roc?*"

"No, Captain, we—"

"—I mean, even if it all—"

"—all changes, on Tubman—"

"—in the Outer Colonies, maybe—"

"—maybe Tobias will leave there—"

"—and join us here."

Lorq laughed. "I think Prince would take you with him—if you wanted."

"Tarred and feathered," Prince said. "Etiolated and denigrated. You've lived out your own myths. Damn you, Lorq."

Ruby stepped forward. "You!" she said to the twins. Both looked at her. "Do you really know what happens if you help Captain Von Ray and he succeeds?"

"He may win—" Lynceos finally looked away, silver lashes quivering.

Idas moved closer to shield his brother. "—or he may not."

"What do they say about our cultural solidarity?" from Lorq. "It's not the world you thought it was, Prince."

Ruby turned sharply. "Does the evidence say it's yours?" Without waiting for answer, she turned to Gold. "Look at it, Lorq."

"I'm looking. What do you see, Ruby?"

"You—you and Prince—want to control the internal flames that run worlds against the night. There, the fire has broken out. It's scarred this world, this city, the way Prince scarred you."

"To bear such a scar," Prince (Lorq felt his jaw stiffen; muscles bunched at temple and forehead) said slowly, "you may have to be greater than I."

"To bear it I have to hate you."

Prince smiled.

The Mouse, Lorq saw from the corner of his eye, had backed against the doorjamb, both hands behind him. Slack lips had fallen from white teeth; white encircled both pupils.

"Hate is a habit. We have hated each other a long time, Lorq. I think I'll finish it now." Prince's fingers flexed. "Do you remember how it started?"

"On São Orini? I remember you were as spoiled and vicious then as you—"

"Us?" Prince's eyebrows arched again. "Vicious? Ah, but you were blatantly cruel. And I've never forgiven you for it."

"For making fun of your hand—"

"Did you? Odd, I don't remember. Insults of that nature I rarely forget. But no. I'm talking about that barbaric exhibition you took us to in the jungle. Beasts; and we couldn't even see the ones in the pit. All of them, hanging over the edge, sweating, shouting, drunk, and—bestial. And Aaron was one of them. I remember him to this day, his forehead glistening, his hair straggling, face contorted in a grisly shout, shaking his fist." Prince closed his velvet fingers. "Yes, his fist. That was the first time I saw my father like that. It terrified me. We've seen him like that many times since, haven't we, Ruby?" He glanced at his sister. "There was the

De Targo merger when he came out of the board room that evening ... or the Anti-Flamina scandal seven years ago ... Aaron is a charming, cultured, and utterly vicious man. You were the first person to show me that viciousness naked in his face. I could never forgive you for that, Lorq. This scheme of yours, whatever it is, with this ridiculous sun: I have to stop it. I have to stop the Von Ray madness." Prince stepped forward. "If the Pleiades Federation crashes when you crash, it is only so that Draco live—"

Sebastian rushed him.

It came that suddenly, surprised all equally.

Prince dropped to one knee. His hand fell on the quartz lumps; they shattered with blue fire. As Sebastian struck at him, Prince whipped one of the fragments through the air: *thwik*. It sank in the cyborg stud's hairy arm. Sebastian roared, staggered backward. Prince's hand swept again over the bright, broken crystals.

... *thwik, thwik,* and *thwik.*

Blood dribbled from two spots on Sebastian's stomach, one on his thigh. Lynceos lunged from the pool edge. "Hey, you can't—"

"—yes he can!" Idas grappled his brother; white fingers tried and failed to tear the black bar from his chest. Sebastian fell.

Thwik ...

Tyÿ shrieked and dropped to his side, grabbing his bleeding face and rocking above him.

... *thwik, thwik.*

He arched his back, gasping. The wounds on his thigh and cheek, and two on his chest flickered.

Prince stood. "Now, I'm going to kill you." He stepped over Sebastian's feet as the stud's heels gouged the carpet. "Does that answer your question?"

It came up from somewhere deep below Lorq's gut, moored among yesterdays. Bliss made his awareness of its shape and outline precise and luminous. Something inside him shook. From the hammock of his pelvis it clawed into his belly, vaulted his chest and wove wildly, erupted from his face; Lorq bellowed. In the sharp peripheral awareness of the drug, he saw the Mouse's syrynx where it had been left on the stage. He snatched it up—

"No, Captain!"

—as Prince lunged. Lorq ducked with the instrument against his chest. He twisted the intensity knob.

The edge of Prince's hand shattered the doorjamb (where a moment before the Mouse had leaned). Splinters split four and five feet up the shaft.

"Captain, that's my . . . !"

The Mouse leaped, and Lorq struck him with his flat hand. The Mouse staggered backward and fell in the sand-pool.

Lorq dodged sideways and whirled to face the door as Prince, still smiling, stepped away.

Then Lorq struck the tuning haft.

A flash.

It was reflection from Prince's vest; the beam was tight. Prince flung his hand up to his eyes. Then he shook his head, blinking.

Lorq struck the syrynx again.

Prince clutched his eyes, stepped back, and screeched.

Lorq's fingers tore at the sound-projection strings. Though the beam was directional, the echo roared about the room, drowning the scream. Lorq's head jarred under the sound. But he beat the sounding board again. And again. With each sweep of his hand, Prince reeled back. He tripped on Sebastian's feet, but did not fall. And again. Lorq's own head ached. That part of his mind still aloof from the rage thought: his middle ear *must* have ruptured. . . . Then the rage climbed higher in his brain. There was no part of him separate from it.

And again.

Prince's arms flailed about his head. His ungloved hand struck one of the suspended shelves. The statuette fell.

Furious, Lorq smashed at the olfactory plate.

An acrid stench burned his own nostrils, seared the roof of his nasal cavity so that his eyes teared.

Prince screamed, staggered; his gloved fist hit the plate glass. It cracked from floor to ceiling.

With blurred and burning eyes, Lorq stalked him.

Now Prince struck both fists against the glass; glass exploded. Fragments rang on the floor and the rock.

"*No!*" from Ruby. Her hands were over her face.

Prince lurched outside.

Heat slapped at Lorq's face. But he followed.

Prince wove and stumbled down toward the glow of Gold. Lorq crab-walked the jagged slope.

And struck.

Light whipped Prince. He must have regained some of his vision, because he clawed at his eyes again. He went down on one knee.

Lorq staggered. His shoulder scraped hot rock. He was already slicked with sweat. It trickled his forehead, banked in his eyebrows, poured through at the scar. He took six steps. With each he struck light brighter than Gold, sound louder than the lava's roar, odor sharper than the sulfur fumes that rasped his throat. His rage was real and red and brighter than Gold. "Vermin . . . Devil . . . Dirt!"

Prince fell just as Lorq reached him. His bare hand leaped about the scalding stone. His head came up. His arms and face had been cut by falling glass. His mouth was opening and closing like a fish. His blind eyes blinked and wrinkled and opened again.

Lorq swung his foot back, smashed at the gasping face. . . .

And it was spent.

He sucked hot gas. His eyes raged with heat. He turned, arms slipping against his sides. The ground tilted suddenly. The black crust opened and heat struck him back. He staggered up between the pitted crags. The lights of Taafite quivered behind shaking veils. He shook his head. His thoughts reeled about the burning cage of bone. He was coughing; the sound was a distant bellow. And he had dropped the syrynx . . .

. . . she cleared between the jagged edges.

Cool touched his face, seeped into his lungs. Lorq pulled himself erect. She stared at him. Her lips fluttered before no word. Lorq stepped toward her.

She raised her hand (he thought she was going to strike him. And he did not care) and touched his corded neck.

Her throat quivered.

Lorq looked over her face, her hair, twisted about a silver comb. In the flicker of Gold her skin was the color of a velvet nut-hull; her eyes were kohled wide over prominent cheekbones. But her magnificence was in the slight tilt of her chin, the expression on her copper mouth, caught between a terrifying smile and resignation to something ineffably sad; in the curve of her fingers against her throat.

Her face loomed against his. Warm lips struck his own, became moist. On the back of his neck, still the warmth of her fingers, the cool of her ring. Her hand slid.

Then, behind them, Prince screamed.

Ruby jerked away, snarling. Her nails raked his shoulder. She fled past him down the rock.

Lorq did not even watch her. Exhaustion held him in the flow. He stalked through the fragments of glass. He glared about at the crew. "Come on, God damn it! Get out of here!"

Beneath the knotted cable of flesh, the muscles rode like chains. Red hair jerked up and down over his gleaming belly with each breath.

"Go on now!"

"Captain, what happened to my . . . ?"

But Lorq had started toward the door.

The Mouse looked wildly from the captain to flaming Gold. He dashed across the room and ducked out the broken glass.

In the garden, Lorq was about to close the gate when the Mouse slipped through behind the twins, syrynx clutched under one arm, sack under the other.

"Back to the *Roc*," Lorq was saying. "We get off this world!"

Tyÿ supported the injured pet on one shoulder and Sebastian on the other. Katin tried to help her, but Sebastian was too short for Katin really to assist the weak, glittering stud. At last Katin stuck his hands under his belt.

Mist twisted beneath the streetlights as they hurried along the cobbles through the City of Dreadful Night.

"Page of Cups."

"Queen of Cups."

"The *Chariot*. My trick is. Nine of Wands."

"Knight of Wands."

"Ace of Wands. The trick to the dummy-hand goes."

Take-off had gone smoothly. Now Lorq and Idas flew the ship; the rest of the crew sat around the commons.

From the ramp Katin watched Tyÿ and Sebastian play a two-handed game of cards. "*Parsifal*—the pitied fool—

having forsaken the Minor Arcana, must work his way through the remaining twenty-one cards of the Major. He is shown at the edge of a cliff. A white cat tears the seat of his pants. One is unable to tell if he will fall or fly away. But later in the series, we have an indication in the card called the *Hermit:* an old man with a staff and a lantern on that same cliff looks sadly down the rocks—"

"What the hell are you talking about?" the Mouse asked. He kept running his finger over a scar on the polished rosewood. "Don't tell me. Those damned Tarot cards—"

"I'm talking about quests, Mouse. I'm beginning to think my novel might be some sort of quest story." He raised his recorder again. "Consider the archetype of the Grail. Oddly unsettling that no writer who has attacked the Grail legend in its naked entirety has lived to complete the work. Malory, Tennyson, and Wagner, responsible for the most popular versions, distorted the basic material so greatly that the mythical structure of their versions is either unrecognizable or useless—perhaps the reason they escaped the jinx. But all true Grail tellings, Chrétien de Troyes' *Conte del Graal* in the twelfth century, Robert de Boron's Grail cycle in the thirteenth century, Wolfram von Eschenbach's *Parzival,* or Spenser's *Faerie Queene* in the sixteenth, were all incomplete at their authors' deaths. In the late nineteenth century I believe an American, Richard Hovey, began a cycle of eleven Grail plays and died before number five was finished. Similarly, Lewis Carroll's friend George MacDonald left incomplete his *Origins of the Legend of the Holy Grail.* The same with Charles William's cycle of poems *Taliessin through Logres.* And a century later—"

"Will you shut up! I swear, Katin, if I did all the brain-hacking you did, I'd go nuts!"

Katin sighed, and flipped off his recorder. "Ah, Mouse, I'd go nuts if I did as little as you."

The Mouse put the instrument back in his sack, crossed his arms on the top, and leaned his chin on the back of his hands.

"Oh, come on, Mouse. See, I've stopped babbling. Don't be glum. What are you so down about?"

"My syrynx . . ."

"So you got a scratch on it. But you've been over it a dozen times and you said it won't hurt the way it plays."

"Not the instrument." The Mouse's forehead wrinkled. "What the captain did with . . ." He shook his head at the memory.

"Oh."

"And not even that." The Mouse sat up.

"What then?"

Again the Mouse shook his head. "When I ran out through the cracked glass to get it . . ."

Katin nodded.

"The heat was incredible out there. Three steps and I didn't think I was going to make it. Then I saw where Captain had dropped it, halfway down the slope. So I squinched my eyes and kept going. I thought my foot would burn off, and I must have got halfway there hopping. Anyway, when I got it, I picked it up, and . . . I saw them."

"Prince and Ruby?"

"She was trying to drag him back up the rocks. She stopped when she saw me. And I was scared." He looked up from his hands. His fingers were clenched; nails cut the dark palms. "I turned the syrynx on her, light, sound, and smell all at once, hard. Captain doesn't know how to make a syrynx do what he wants. I do. She was blind, Katin. And I probably busted both her eardrums. The laser was on such a tight beam her hair caught fire, then her dress—"

"Oh, Mouse . . ."

"I was scared, Katin! After all that with Captain and them. But, Katin . . ." The whisper snagged on all sorts of junk in the Mouse's throat. "It's no good to be that scared . . ."

"Queen of Swords."

"King of Swords."

"The *Lovers*. My trick is. Ace of Swords—"

"Tyÿ, come in and relieve Idas for a while," Von Ray's voice came through the loud speaker.

"Yes, sir. Three of Swords from the dummy comes. The *Empress* from me. My trick is." She closed the cards and left the table for her projection chamber.

Sebastian stretched. "Hey, Mouse?"

Chapter Seven

"What?"

Sebastian walked across the blue rug, kneading his forearm. The ship's medico-unit had fixed his broken elbow in forty-five seconds, having taken somewhat less time over the smaller, brighter wounds. (It had blinked a few odd-colored lights when the dark thing with a collapsed lung and three torn rib cartilages was presented to it. But Tyÿ had fiddled with the programming till the unit hummed efficiently over the beast.) The creature waddled now behind its master, ominous and happy. "Mouse, why you not the ship's med your throat let fix?" He swung his arm. "It a good job would do."

"Can't. Couple of times they tried when I was a kid. Back when I got my plugs they gave it a go." The Mouse shrugged.

Sebastian frowned. "Not very serious now it sounds."

"It isn't," the Mouse said. "It doesn't bother me. They just can't fix it. Something about neurological con-something-or-other."

"What that is?"

The Mouse turned up his palms and looked blank.

"Neurological congruency," Katin said. "Your unattached vocal cords must be a neurologically congruent birth defect."

"Yeah, that's what they said."

"Two types of birth defects," Katin explained. "In both, some part of the body, internal or external, is deformed, atrophied, or just put together wrong."

"My vocal cords are all there."

191

"But at the base of the brain there's a small nerve cluster which, if you see it in cross section, looks more or less like a template of a human being. If this template is complete, then the brain has the nervous equipment to handle a complete body. Very rarely the template contains the same deformity as the body, as in the Mouse's case. Even if the physical difficulty is corrected, there are no nerve connections within the brain to manipulate the physically corrected part."

"That must be what's wrong with Prince's arm," the Mouse said. "If it had been torn off in an accident or something, they could graft a new one on, connect up the veins and nerves and everything and have it just like new."

"Oh," Sebastian said.

Lynceos came down the ramp. White fingers massaged the ivory clubs of his wrists. "Captain's really doing some fancy flying—"

Idas came to the rim of the pool. "This star he's going to, where is—?"

"—its co-ordinates put it at the tip of the inner arm—"

"—in the Outer Colonies then—"

"—beyond even the Far Out Colonies."

"That a lot of flying is," Sebastian said. "And Captain all the way himself will fly."

"The captain has a lot of things to think about," Katin suggested.

The Mouse slipped his strap over his shoulder. "A lot of things he doesn't want to think about too. Hey, Katin, how about that game of chess?"

"Spot you a rook," Katin said. "Let's keep it fair."

They settled to the gaming board.

Three games later Von Ray's voice came through the commons. "Everyone report to his projection chamber. There's some tricky crosscurrents coming up."

The Mouse and Katin pushed up from their bubble chairs. Katin loped toward the little door behind the serpentine staircase. The Mouse hurried across the rug, up the three steps. The mirrored panel slid into the wall. He stepped over a tool box, a coil of cable, three discarded frozen-coil memory bars—melting, they had stained the plates with salt where the puddle had dried—and sat on the couch. He shook out the cables and plugged them in.

Olga winked solicitously above, around, beneath him.

Crosscurrents: red and silver sequins flung in handfuls. The captain wielded them against the stream.

"You must have been quite a racer, Captain," commented Katin. "What kind of yacht did you fly? We had a racing club at school that leased three yachts. I thought of going out for it one term."

"Shut up and hold your vane steady."

Here, down the galaxy's spiral, there were fewer stars. Gravimetric shifts gentled here. Flight at galactic center, with its more condensed flux, yielded a dozen conflicting frequencies to work with. Here, a captain had to pick at the trail wisps of ionic inflections.

"Where are we going, anyway?" the Mouse asked.

Lorq pointed co-ordinates on the static matrix and the Mouse read them against matrix moveable.

Where was the star?

Take concepts like "distant," "isolate," "faint," and give them precise mathematical expression. They'll vanish under such articulation.

But just before they do, that's where it lay.

"My star." Lorq swept vanes aside so they could see. "That's my sun. That's my nova, with eight-hundred-year-old light. Look sharp, Mouse, and swing her down hard. If your slapdash vaning keeps me a second from this sun—"

"Come on, Captain!"

"—I'll ram Tyÿ's deck down your gullet, sideways. Swing her back."

And the Mouse swung as all night rushed about his head.

"Captains from out here," Lorq mused when the currents cleared, "when they come into the inflected confusion of the central hub, they can't ride the flux in a complicated cluster like the Pleiades to save themselves. They go off beams, take spins, and go headlong into all kinds of mess. Half the accidents you've heard about were with eccentric captains. I talked to some of them once. They told me that here on the rim, it was us who were always piling up ships in gravity spin. 'You always fall asleep on your strings,' they told me." He laughed.

"You know you've been flying a long time, Captain," Katin said. "It looks pretty clear. Why don't you turn off for a while?"

"I feel like diddling my fingers in the ether for another

watch. You and Mouse stay tied up. The rest of you puppets cut strings."

Vanes deflated and folded till each was a single pencil of light. And the light turned off.

"Oh, Captain Von Ray, something—"

"—something we meant to ask you—"

"—before. Do you have any more—"

"—could you tell us where you put—"

"—I mean if it's okay, Captain—"

"—the bliss?"

Night grew easy about their eyes. The vanes swept them toward the pinhole in the velvet masking.

"They must have a pretty high time of it in the mines on Tubman," the Mouse commented after a while. "I've been thinking about that, Katin. When the captain and me moseyed down Gold for bliss, there were some characters who tried to get us to sign up for work out there. I started thinking, you know: a plug is a plug and a socket is a socket, and if I'm on one end, it shouldn't make too much difference to me if there's a star-ship vane, aqualat net, or an ore cutter on the other. I think I might go out there for a time."

"May the shade of Ashton Clark hover over your right shoulder and guard your left."

"Thanks." After another while he asked, "Katin, why do people always say Ashton Clark whenever you're going to change jobs? They told us back at Cooper that the guy who invented plugs was named Socket or something."

"Souquet," Katin said. "Still, he must have considered it an unfortunate coincidence. Ashton Clark was a twenty-third-century philosopher *cum* psychologist whose work enabled Vladimeer Souquet to develop his neural plugs. I guess the answer has to do with work. Work as mankind knew it up until Clark and Souquet was a very different thing from today, Mouse. A man might go to an office and run a computer that would correlate great masses of figures that came from sales reports on how well, let's say, buttons—or something equally archaic—were selling over certain areas of the country. This man's job was vital to the button industry: they had to have this information to decide how many buttons to make next year. But though this man held an essential job in the button industry, was hired, paid, or fired by the button industry, week in and week out he might not see a button. He was given a certain amount of money for running his computer; with that money his wife bought food and clothes for him and his family. But there was no *direct* connection between where he worked and how he ate and lived the rest of his time. He wasn't paid with buttons. As farming, hunting, and fishing became occupations of a smaller and smaller per cent of the population, this separation between man's work and the way he lived—what he ate, what he wore, where he slept—became greater and greater for more people. Ashton Clark pointed out how psychologically damaging this was to humanity. The entire sense of self-control and self-responsibility that man acquired during the Neolithic Revolution when he first learned to plant grain and domesticate animals and live in one spot of his own choosing was seriously threatened. The threat had been coming since the Industrial Revolution and many people had pointed it out before Ashton Clark. But Ashton Clark went one step further. If the situation of a technological society was such that there could be no direct relation between a man's work and his *modus vivendi*, other than money, at least he must feel that he is directly changing things by his work, shaping things, making things that weren't there before, moving things from one place to another. He must exert energy in his work and see these changes occur with his own eyes. Otherwise he would feel his life was futile.

"Had he lived another hundred years either way, probably nobody would have heard of Ashton Clark today. But technology had reached the point where it could do something about what Ashton Clark was saying. Souquet invented his plugs and sockets, and neural-response circuits, and the whole basic technology by which a machine could be controlled by direct nervous impulse, the same impulses that cause your hand or foot to move. And there was a revolution in the concept of work. All major industrial work began to be broken down into jobs that could be machined 'directly' by man. There had been factories run by a single man before, an uninvolved character who turned a switch on in the morning, slept half the day, checked a few dials at lunchtime, then turned things off before he left in the evening. Now a man went to a factory, plugged himself in, and he could push the raw materials into the factory with his left foot, shape thousands on thousands of precise parts with one hand, assemble them with the other, and shove out a line of finished products with his right foot, having inspected them all with his own eyes. And he was a much more satisfied worker. Because of its nature, most work could be converted into plug-in jobs and done much more efficiently than it had been before. In the rare cases where production was slightly less efficient, Clark pointed out the psychological benefits to the society. Ashton Clark, it has been said, was the philosopher who returned humanity to the working man. Under this system, much of the endemic mental illness caused by feelings of alienation left society. The transformation turned war from a rarity to an impossibility, and—after the initial upset—stabilized the economic web of worlds for the last eight hundred years. Ashton Clark became the workers' prophet. That's why even today, when a person is going to change jobs, you send Ashton Clark, or his spirit along with him."

The Mouse gazed across the stars. "I remember that sometimes the gypsies used to curse by him." He thought a moment. "Without plugs, I guess we would."

"There were factions who resisted Clark's ideas, especially on Earth, which has always been a bit reactionary. But they didn't hold out very long."

"Yeah," the Mouse said. "Only eight hundred years. Not all gypsies are traitors like me." But he laughed into the winds.

"The Ashton Clark system has only had one serious drawback that I can see. And it's taken it a long time to materialize."

"Yeah? What's that?"

"Something professors have been telling their students for years, it seems. You'll hear it said at every intellectual gathering you go to, at least once. There seems to be a certain lack of cultural solidity today. That's what the Vega Republic was trying to establish back in 2800. Because of the ease and satisfaction with which people can work now, anywhere they want, there have been such movements of peoples from world to world in the past dozen generations that society has fragmented around itself. There is only a gaudy, meretricious interplanetary society which has no real tradition behind it—" Katin paused. "I got hold of some of

Captain's bliss before I plugged up. And while I was talking I just counted in my mind how many people I've heard say that between Harvard and Hell⁶. And you know something? I think they're wrong."

"They are?"

"They are. They're all just looking for our social traditions in the wrong place. There *are* cultural traditions that have matured over the centuries, yet culminate now in something vital and solely of today. And you know who embodies that tradition more than anyone I've met?"

"The captain?"

"You, Mouse."

"Huh?"

"You've collected the ornamentations a dozen societies have left us over the ages and made them inchoately yours. You're the product of those tensions that clashed in the time of Clark and you resolve them on your syrynx with patterns eminently of the present—"

"Aw, cut it out, Katin."

"I've been hunting a subject for my book with both historical import and humanity as well. You're it, Mouse. My book should be *your* biography! It should tell where you've been, what you've done, the things you've seen, and the things you've shown other people. There's my social significance, my historical sweep, the spark among the links that illuminates the breadth of the net—"

"Katin, you're crazy!"

"No I'm not. I've finally seen what I've—"

"Hey there, keep your vanes spread taut!"

"Sorry, Captain."

"Yes, Captain."

"Don't go chattering to the stars if you're going to do it with your eyes closed."

Ruefully the two cyborg studs turned their attention back to the night. The Mouse was pensive. Katin was belligerent.

"There's a star coming up bright and hot. It's the only thing in the sky. Remember that. Keep it smack in front of us and don't let her waver. You can babble about cultural solidity on your own time."

Without horizon, the star rose.

At twenty times the distance of Earth from the sun (or

Ark from its sun) there was not enough light from a medium G-type star to defract daytime through an Earth-type atmosphere. At such distances, the brightest object in the night would still look like a star, not a sun—a very bright star.

They were two billion miles, or a little over twenty solar distances, from it now.

It was the brightest star.

"A beauty, huh?"

"No, Mouse," Lorq said. "Just a star."

"How can you tell—"

"—it's going to go nova?"

"Because of the build-up of heavy materials on the surface," Lorq explained to the twins. "There's just the faintest reddening of the absolute color, corresponding to the faintest cooling in the surface temperature. There's also a slight speed-up of sunspot activity."

"From the surface of one of her planets, though, there would be no way to tell?"

"That's right. The reddening is far too faint to be detected with the naked eye. Fortunately this star has no planets. There's some moon-sized junk floating up a bit closer that may have been a failed attempt at a world."

Moons? "Moons!" Katin objected. "You can't have moons without planets. Planetoids, maybe, but not moons!"

Lorq laughed. "Moon-*sized* is all I said."

"Oh."

All vanes had been used to swing the *Roc* into its two-billion-mile-radius orbit about the star. Katin lay in his projection chamber, hesitant to release the view of the star for the lights of his chamber. "What about the study stations the Alkane has set up?"

"They're drifting as lonely as we are. We'll hear from them in due time. But for now we don't need them and they don't need us. Cyana has warned them we're coming. I'll point them on matrix moveable. There, you can follow their locations and their movements. That's the major manned station. It's fifty times as far out as we are."

"Are we within the danger zone when she goes?"

"When that nova starts, that star is going to eat up the sky and everything in it a long way out."

"When does it begin?"

"Days, Cyana predicted. But such predictions have been

known to be off by two weeks in either direction. We'll have a few minutes to clear if she goes. We're about two and a half light-hours from her now." All their views came in not by light, but by ethric disturbance, which gave them a synchronous view of the sun. "We'll see her start at exactly the instant she goes."

"And the Illyrion?" Sebastian asked. "How we that get?"

"That's my worry," Lorq told him. "We'll get it when the time comes to get it. You can all cut loose for a while now."

But no one hurried to release cables. Vanes diminished to single lines of light, but only after a while did two, and two wink off.

Katin and the Mouse lingered longest.

"Captain?" Katin asked after a few minutes. "I was just wondering. Did the patrol say anything special when you reported Dan's . . . accident?"

It was nearly a minute before Lorq said: "I didn't report it."

"Oh," Katin said. "I didn't really think you had."

The Mouse started to say "But" three times, and didn't.

"Prince has access to all official records coming through the Draco patrol. At least I assume he has; I've got a computer scanning all those that come through the Pleiades. His is certainly programmed to trace down thoroughly anything that comes in vaguely connected with me. If he traced down Dan, he'd find a nova. I don't want him to find it that way. I'd just as soon he didn't know Dan was dead. As far as I know, the only people who do know are on this ship. I like it that way."

"Captain!"

"What, Mouse?"

"There's something coming."

"A supply ship for the station?" Katin asked.

"It's in too far. They're sniffing along after our faery dust."

Lorq was silent while the strange ship moved across the co-ordinate matrix. "Cut loose and go into the commons. I'll join you."

"But, Captain—" The Mouse got it out.

"It's a seven-vaned cargo ship like this one, only its identification says Draco."

"What's it doing here?"

"Into the commons I said."

Katin read the name of the ship as its identification beam translated at the bottom of the grid: *"The Black Cockatoo? Come on, Mouse. Captain says cut loose."*

They unplugged, and joined the others at the pool's edge.

At the head of the winding steps, the door rolled up. Lorq stepped out on the shadowed stair.

The Mouse watched Von Ray come down and thought: Captain's tired.

Katin watched Von Ray and Von Ray's reflection on the mirrored mosaic and thought: he moves tired, but it's the tiredness of an athlete before his second wind.

When Lorq was halfway down, the light-fantasia in the gilt frame on the far wall cleared.

They started. The Mouse actually gasped.

"So," Ruby said. "Nearly a tie. Or is that fair? You are still ahead. We don't know where you intend to find the prize. This race goes by starts and stops." Her blue gaze washed the crew, lingered on the Mouse, returned to Lorq. "Till last night at Taafite, I'd never felt such pain. Perhaps I've lived a sheltered life. But whatever the rules are, handsome Captain," (contempt resonated now) "we too have been bred to play."

"Ruby, I want to talk to you ..." Lorq's voice faltered. "And Prince. In person."

"I'm not sure if Prince wants to talk to you. The time between your leaving us at the edge of Gold and our finally struggling to a medico is not one of my—*our* pleasantest memories."

"Tell Prince I'm shuttling over to *The Black Cockatoo*. I'm tired of this horror tale, Ruby. There are things you want to know from me. There are things I want to say to you."

Her hand moved nervously to the hair falling on her shoulder. Her dark cloak closed in a high collar. After a moment she said, "Very well." Then she was gone.

Lorq looked down at his crew. "You heard. Back on your vanes. Tyÿ, I've watched the way you swing on your strings. You've obviously had more experience flying than anyone else here. Take the captain's sockets. And if anything odd happens—*anything*, whether I'm back or not, take the *Roc* out of here, fast."

The Mouse and Katin looked at each other, then at Tyÿ.

Lorq crossed the carpet, mounted the ramp. Halfway over the white arc, he stopped and gazed at his reflection. Then he spat.

He disappeared before ripples touched the bank.

Exchanging puzzled looks, they broke from the pool.

On his couch, Katin plugged in and switched on his sensory input outside the ship to find the others were all there already.

He watched *The Black Cockatoo* drift closer to receive the shuttle.

"Mouse?"

"Yeah, Katin."

"I'm worried."

"About Captain?"

"About us."

The Black Cockatoo, beating vanes on the darkness, turned slowly beside them to match orbits.

"We were drifting, Mouse, you and I, the twins, Tyÿ and Sebastian, good people all of us—but aimless. Then an obsessed man snatches us up and carries us out here to the edge of everything. And we arrive to find his obsession has imposed order on our aimlessness; or perhaps a more meaningful chaos. What worries me is that I'm so thankful to him. I should be rebelling, trying to assert my own order. But I'm not. I want him to win his infernal race. I want him to win, and until he wins or loses, I can't seriously want anything else for myself."

The Black Cockatoo received the shuttle boat like a cannon shot in reverse. Without the necessity of maintaining matched orbits, she drifted a ways from them. Katin watched her dark rotations.

"Good morning."

"Good evening."

"By Greenwich time it's morning, Ruby."

"And I do you the politeness of greeting you by Ark time. Come this way." She held back her robe to let him pass into the black corridor.

"Ruby?"

"Yes?" Her voice was just behind his left shoulder.

"I've always wondered something, each time I've seen you. You've shown me so many hints of the magnificent person you are. But it gleams from under the shadow Prince throws. Years ago, when we talked at that party on the Seine, it struck me what a challenging person you would be to love."

"Paris is worlds and worlds away, Lorq."

"Prince controls you. It's petty of me, but that's what I can least forgive him. You've never shown your own will before him. Except at Taafite, that once beneath the exhausted sun on the other world. You thought Prince was dead. I know you remember it. I've thought of little else since. You kissed me. But he screamed, and you ran to him. Ruby, he's trying to destroy the Pleiades Federation. That's all the worlds that circle three hundred suns, and how many billions of people. They're my worlds. I can't let them die."

"You would topple the column of Draco and send the Serpent crawling off through the dust to save them? You would pull the economic support out from under Earth and let the fragments fall into the night? You would bowl the worlds to Draco into epochs of chaos, civil strife, and deprivation? The worlds of Draco are Prince's worlds. Are you really presumptuous enough to think he loves his less than you love yours?"

"What do you love, Ruby?"

"You are not the only one with secrets, Lorq. Prince and I have ours. When you came up out of the burning rocks, yes, I thought Prince was dead. There was a hollow tooth in my jaw filled with strychnine. I wanted to give you a victory kiss. I would have, if Prince had not screamed."

"Prince loves Draco?" He whirled, caught her upper arms, dragged her against him.

Her breath surged against his chest. With eyes opened their faces struck. He mashed her thin mouth with his full one till her lips drew back, and his tongue ground teeth.

Her fingers grappled his rough hair. She made ugly sounds.

The moment his grip relaxed, she was away, eyes wide; then her lids veiled the blue light till fury widened them again.

"Well?" He was breathing hard.

She drew her cloak around her. "When a weapon fails me

once"—her voice was hoarse as the Mouse's—"I throw it away. Otherwise, handsome pirate, you ..." Did the harshness lessen? *"We* would be ... But I have other weapons now."

The *Cockatoo's* commons was small and stark. Two cyborg studs sat on the benches. Another stood on the steps beside the door to his projection chamber.

Sharp-featured men in white uniforms, they reminded Lorq of another crew he had worked. On their shoulders they wore the scarlet emblem of Red-shift, Ltd. They glanced at Lorq and Ruby. The one standing stepped back into his chamber and the plate door clanged in the high room. The other two got up to go.

"Will Prince come down?"

Ruby nodded toward the iron stair. "He'll see you in the captain's cabin."

Lorq began to climb. His sandals clacked on the perforated steps. Ruby followed him.

He knocked on the studded door.

It swung in, Lorq stepped inside, and a metal and plastic gauntlet on a jointed arm telescoped from the ceiling and struck him across the face, twice.

Lorq reeled against the door—it was covered in leather on the inside and set with brass heads—so that it slammed.

"That," the corpse announced, "is for manhandling my sister."

Lorq rubbed his cheek and looked at Ruby. She stood by the jade wall. The draping valences were the same deep wine as her cloak.

"Do you think I don't watch everything that goes on on the ship?" asked the corpse. "You Pleiades barbarians are as uncouth as Aaron always said you were."

Bubbles rose in the tank, caressed the stripped and naked foot, caught and clustered on the shriveled groin, rolled up the chest—ribs scored between blackened flaps of skin—and fanned about the burned, bald head. The lipless mouth gaped on broken teeth. No nose. Tubes and wires snaked the rotten sockets. Tubes pierced at belly, hip, and shoulder. Fluids swirled in the tank and the single arm drifted back and forth, charred fingers locked with rigor mortis in a claw.

"Weren't you ever told it was impolite to stare? You are staring, you know."

The voice came from a speaker in the glass wall.

"I'm afraid I sustained a bit more damage than Ruby back on the other world."

Above the tank two mobile cameras shifted as Lorq stepped from the door.

"For someone who owns Red-shift Limited, your turn to match orbits wasn't very ..." The banality did not mask Lorq's astonishment.

Cables for running the ship were plugged into sockets set on the tank's glass face. The glass itself was part of the wall. The cables coiled over black and gold tiles to disappear into the coppery grill covering the computer face.

On walls, floor, and ceiling, in opulent frames, ethric-disturbance screens all showed the same face of night:

At the edge of each was the gray shape of the *Roc*.

Centered on each was the star.

"Alas," the corpse said, "I was never the sportsman you were. Still, you wanted to speak to me. What do you have to say?"

Again Lorq looked at Ruby. "I've said most of it to Ruby, Prince. You heard it."

"Somehow I doubt you'd drag us both out here to the brink of a stellar catastrophe just to tell us that. Illyrion, Lorq Von Ray. Neither you nor I have forgotten your major purpose for coming here. You will not leave without telling where you intend to get—"

The star went nova.

The inevitable is that unprepared for.

In the first second the images about them changed from points to floodlights. And the floodlights got brighter.

Ruby backed against the wall, arm across her eyes.

"It's early!" the corpse shouted. "It's days early ... !"

Lorq took three steps across the room, yanked two plugs from the tank, and fixed them in his wrists. The third plug he twisted into his spinal socket. The play of the ship surged through him. Sensory input came in. His vision of the room was overlaid with the night. And night was catching fire.

Wresting control from the studs, he swung the *Cockatoo* around to point her toward the node of light. The ship plunged forward.

Twin cameras swiveled to focus him.

"Lorq, what are you *doing?*" Ruby cried.

"Stop him!" from the corpse. "He's flying us into the sun!"

Ruby leaped at Lorq, caught him. They turned together, staggered. The chamber and the sun outside fixed on his eyes like a double exposure. She caught up a loop of cable, flung it around his neck, twisted it, and began to strangle him. The cable housing chewed his neck. He locked his arm behind her, and pushed his other hand against her face. She grunted, and her head went back (his hand pushed at the center of the light). Her hair slipped, came loose; the wig fell from her burned scalp. She had only used the medico to return health. The cosmetic plasti-skin with which she had restored her face tore between his fingers. Rubbery film pulled from her blotched and hollowed cheek. Lorq suddenly jerked his hand away. As her ruined face screamed toward him through fire, he ripped her hands from his neck and pushed her away. Ruby went backwards, tripped on her cloak, fell. He turned just as the mechanical hand swung down at him from the ceiling.

He caught it.

And it had less than human strength.

Easily he held it at arm's length as the fingers grasped from the raging star. "Stop!" he bellowed. At the same time he willed the sensory input off all over the ship.

The screens went gray.

The sensory input had always been clamped off on all six of the ship's cyborg studs.

The fires went out in his eyes.

"What in heaven are you trying to *do*, Lorq?"

"Dive into hell and fish Illyrion out with my bare hands!"

"He's insane!" the corpse shrieked. "Ruby, he's insane! He's killing us, Ruby! That's all he wants to do, kill us!"

"Yes! I'm killing you!" Lorq tossed the hand away. It grasped at the cable hanging from his wrist to jerk the plug. Lorq caught the arm again; the ship lurched.

"For God's sake, pull us out, Lorq!" the corpse cried. "Pull us out of here!"

The ship jerked again. The artificial gravity slipped long enough for liquid to break on the tank face, then bead the glass as gravity righted.

"It's too late," Lorq whispered. "We're caught in gravity spin!"

"Why are you doing this?"

"Just to *kill* you, Prince." Lorq's face raged till laughter spilled it. "That's all, Prince! That's all I want to do now."

"I don't want to die again!" the corpse shrieked. "I don't want to flash out like an insect burning!"

"Flash?" Lorq's face twisted about the scar. "Oh no! It'll be slow, slower than before. Ten, twenty minutes at least. It's already getting warm, isn't it? But it won't be unbearable for another five." Below the gold blaze Lorq's face darkened. Spittle flecked his lips with each consonant. "You'll boil in your jar like a fish—" He stopped to rub his stomach beneath his vest. He looked around the chamber. "What can burn in here? The drapes? Is your desk real wood? And all those papers?"

The mechanical hand yanked from Lorq's. The arm swung across the room. The fingers seized Ruby's hand. "No, Ruby! Stop him! Don't let him kill us!"

"You're in liquid, Prince, so you'll see them afire before you go. Ruby, the places where you're already burned won't be able to sweat. So you'll die first. He'll be able to watch you a few moments before his own fluids begin to boil, the rubber runs, the plastic melts—"

"No!" The hand jerked from Ruby's, swung across the room, and smashed into the tank face. "Criminal! Thief! Pirate! Murderer! Murderer! No—!"

The hand was weaker than it had been at Taafite.

So was the glass.

The glass broke.

Nutrient fluids splashed Lorq as he danced back on flooded sandals. The corpse crumpled in the tank, netted in tubes and wires.

The cameras swung wildly out of focus.

The hand clattered to the wet tile.

As the fingers stilled, Ruby screamed, and screamed again. She flung herself across the floor, scrambled over the ragged hem of glass, caught up the corpse, hugged it to her, kissed it, and screamed, and kissed it again, rocking back and forth. Her cloak darkened in the puddle.

Then her scream choked. She dropped the body, hurled herself back against the tank wall, and clutched her neck. Her face flushed deeply beneath burns and wrecked makeup. She slid slowly down the wall. Her eyes were closed when she reached the bottom.

"Ruby ...?" Whether or not she had cut herself climbing over the glass, it didn't matter. The kiss would have done it. So soon after severe burns, even with what the medico could do, she must have been in a hyperallergic state. The alien proteins in Prince's nutrient fluid had entered her system, causing a massive histamine reaction. She had succumbed in seconds to anaphylactic shock.

And Lorq laughed.

It started like a rearrangement of boulders in his chest. Then it opened to a full sound, ringing on the high walls of the flooded chamber. Triumph was laughable and terrible and his.

He took a deep breath. The ship surged at his fingertips. Still blind, he urged *The Black Cockatoo* into the bursting sun.

Somewhere in the ship one of the cyborg studs was crying

. . .

"The star!" the Mouse cried. "She's blown nova!"

Tyÿ's voice shot through the master circuit: "Out of here we go! Now!"

"But the captain!" Katin shouted. "Look at *The Black Cockatoo!*"

"The *Cockatoo,* my God, it's—"

"—Lord, it's falling toward—"

"—falling into the—"

"—the sun!"

"All right, everybody, vanes spread. Katin, I your vanes spread said!"

"My God ..." Katin breathed. "Oh, no ..."

"It too bright is," Tyÿ decided. "Off sensory we go!"

The *Roc* began to pull away.

"Oh my God! They—they really are, they're really falling! It's so bright! They'll die! They'll burn up like—they're falling! Oh, Lord, stop them! Somebody do something! The captain's on there. You've got to do something!"

"Katin!" the Mouse shouted. "Get the hell off sensory! Are you crazy?"

"They're going down! No! It's like a bright hole in the

middle of everything! And they're falling into it. Oh, they're falling. They're falling—"

"Katin!" the Mouse shrieked. "Katin, don't look at it!"

"It's growing, it's so bright ... bright ... brighter! I can hardly see them!"

"Katin!" Suddenly it came to him, and the Mouse cried out: "Don't you remember Dan? Turn your sensory input off!"

"No! No, I've got to see it! It's roaring now. It's shaking the whole night apart! You can smell it burning, burning up the darkness. I can't see them any more—no, there they are!"

"Katin, stop it!" The Mouse twisted beneath Olga. "Tyÿ, cut off his input!"

"I can't. I this ship against gravity must fly. Katin! Off sensory, I you order!"

"Down ... down ... I've lost them again! I can't see them any more. The light's turning all red now ... I can't—"

The Mouse felt the ship lurch as Katin's vane suddenly flailed wild.

Then Katin screamed. "I can't see!" The scream became a sob. "I can't see *anything!*"

The Mouse balled up on the couch with his hands over his eyes, shaking.

"Mouse!" Tyÿ shouted. "Damn it, we one vane have lost. Down you sweep!"

The Mouse swept blindly down. Tears of terror squeezed between his lids as he listened to Katin's sobs.

The *Roc* rose from and *The Black Cockatoo* fell into it.

And it was nova.

Sprung from pirates, reeling blind in fire, I am called pirate, murderer, thief.

I bear it.

I will gather my prizes in a moment and become the man who pushed Draco over the edge of tomorrow. That it was to save the Pleiades does not diminish such a crime. Those with the greatest power must ultimately commit the greatest felonies. Here on *The Black Cockatoo* I am a flame away from forever. I told her once that we had not been fit for meaning. Neither for meaningful deaths. (There is a death whose only meaning is that it was died to defend chaos. And they are dead . . .) Such lives and deaths preclude significance, keep guilt from the murderer, elation from the socially beneficent hero. How do other criminals support their crimes? The hollow worlds cast up their hollow children, raised only to play or fight. Is that sufficient for winning? I have struck down one third the cosmos to raise up another and let one more go staggering; and I feel no sin on me. Then it must be that I am free and evil. Well, then, I am free, mourning her with my laughter. Mouse, Katin, you who can speak out of the net, which one of you is the blinder for not having watched me win under this sun? I can feel fire churn by me. Like you, dead Dan, I will grasp at dawn and evening, but I will win the noon.

Darkness.

Silence.

Nothing.

Then thought shivers:

I think . . . therefore I . . . I am Katin Crawford? He fought away from that. But the thought was him; he was the thought. There was no place in here to anchor.

A flicker.

A tinkle.

The scent of caraway.

It was beginning.

No! He clawed back down into darkness. The mind's ear recalled someone shrieking, "Remember Dan . . ." and the mind's eye pictured the staggering derelict.

Another sound, smell, flicker beyond his lids.

He fought for unconsciousness in terror of the torrent. But terror quickened his heart, and the increased pulse drove him upward, upward, where the magnificence of the dying star lay in wait for him.

Sleep was killed in him.

He held his breath and opened his eyes—

Pastels pearled before him. High chords rang softly on one another. Then caraway, mint, sesame, anise—

And behind the colors, a figure.

"Mouse?" Katin whispered, and was surprised how clearly he heard himself.

The Mouse took his hands from the syrynx.

Color, smell, and music ceased.

"You awake?" The Mouse sat on the window sill, shoulders and the left side of his face lit with copper. The sky behind him was purple.

Katin closed his eyes, pushed his head back into the pillow, and smiled. The smile got broader, and broader, split over his teeth, and suddenly verged against tears. "Yes." He relaxed, and opened his eyes again. "Yes. I'm awake." He pushed himself up. "Where are we? Is this the Alkane's manned station?" But there was landscape through the window.

The Mouse shoved down from the sill. "Moon of a planet called New Brazillia."

Katin got up from the hammock and went to the window. Beyond the atmosphere-trap, over the few low buildings, a black and gray rock-scape carpeted toward a lunar-close horizon. He pulled in a cool, ozone-tainted breath, then looked back at the Mouse. "What happened, Mouse? Oh, Mouse, I thought I was going to wake up like . . ."

"Dan caught his on the way into the sun. You caught yours while we were pulling out. All the frequencies were dopplering down the red shift. It's the ultraviolets that detach retinas and do things like happened to Dan. Tyÿ finally got a moment to shut your sensory input off from the master controls. You really were blind for a while, you know. We got you into the medico as soon as we were safe."

Katin frowned. "Then what are we doing here? What happened then?"

"We stayed out by the manned stations and watched the fireworks from a safe distance. It took a little over three hours to reach peak intensity. We were talking with the Alkane's crew when we got the captain's signal from *The Black Cockatoo.* So we scooted on around, picked him up, and let all the *Cockatoo's* cyborg studs loose."

"Picked him up! You mean he *did* get out?"

"Yeah. He's in another room. He wants to talk to you."

"He wasn't fooling us about ships going into a nova and coming out the other side?" They started toward the door.

Outside they passed down a corridor with a glass wall that looked across broken moon. Katin had lost himself in marvelous contemplation of the rubble when the Mouse said, "Here."

They opened the door.

A crack of light struck in across Lorq's face. "Who's there?"

Katin asked, "Captain?"

"What?"

"Captain Von Ray?"

". . . Katin?" His fingers clawed the chair arms. Yellow eyes stared, jumped; jumped, stared.

"Captain, what . . . ?" Katin's face furrowed. He fought down panic, forced his face to relax.

"I told Mouse to bring you to see me when you were up and around. You're . . . you're all right. Good." Agony spread the ruptured flesh, then faltered. And for a moment there was agony.

Katin stopped breathing.

"You tried to look too. I'm glad. I always thought you would be the one to understand."

"You . . . fell into the sun, Captain?"

Lorq nodded.

"But how did you get out?"

Lorq pressed his head against the back of the chair. Dark skin, red hair shot with yellow, his unfocused eyes, were the only colors in the room. "What? Got out, you say?" He barked a laugh. "It's an open secret now. How did I get out?" A muscle quivered on the wrack of his jaw. "A sun—" Lorq held up one hand, the fingers curved to support an imaginary sphere "—it rotates, like a world, like some moons. With something the mass of a star, rotation means incredible centripetal force pushing out at the equator. At the end of the build-up of heavy materials at the surface, when the star actually novas, it all falls inward toward the center." His fingers began to quiver. "Because of the rotation, the material at the poles falls faster than the material at the equator." He clutched the arm of the chair again. "Within seconds after the nova begins you don't have a sphere any more, but a . . ."

"A torus!"

Lines scored Lorq's face. And his head jerked to the side, as if trying to avoid a great light. Then the scarred lineaments came back to face them. "Did you say torus? A torus? Yes. That sun became a doughnut with a hole big enough for two Jupiters to fit through, side by side."

"But the Alkane's been studying novas up close for nearly a century! Why didn't *they* know?"

"The matter displacement is all toward the center of the sun. The energy displacement is all outwards. The gravity shift will funnel everything toward the hole; the energy displacement keeps the temperature as cool inside the hole as the surface of some red giant star—well under five hundred degrees."

Though the room was cool, Katin saw sweat starting in the ridges of Lorq's forehead.

"The topological extension of a torus of that dimension— the corona which is all the Alkane's stations can see—is almost identical to a sphere. Large as the hole is, compared to the size of the energy-ball, that hole would be pretty hard to find unless you knew where it was—or fell into it by accident." On the chair arm the fingers suddenly stretched, quivered. "The Illyrion—"

"You ... you got your Illyrion, Captain?"

Again Lorq raised his hand before his face, this time in a fist. He tried to focus on it. With his other hand he grabbed for it, half missed, grabbed again, missed completely, then again; opened fingers grappled the closed ones. The doubled fist shook as with palsy.

"Seven tons! The only materials dense enough to center in the hole are the trans-three-hundred elements. Illyrion! It floats free there, for whoever wants to go in and sweep it up. Fly your ship in, then look around to see where it is, and sweep it up with your projector vanes. It collects on the nodes of your projectors. Illyrion—nearly free of impurities." His hands came apart. "Just ... go on sensory input, and look around to see where it is." He lowered his face. "She lay there, her face ... her face an amazing ruin in the center of hell. And I swept my seven arms across the blinding day to catch the bits of hell that floated by—" He raised his head again. "There's an Illyrion mine down on New Brazillia ..." Outside the window a mottled planet hung huge in the sky. "They have equipment here for handling Illyrion shipments. But you should have seen their faces when we brought in our seven tons, hey, Mouse?" He laughed loudly again. "That's right, Mouse? You told me what they looked like, yes? ... Mouse?"

"That's right, Captain."

Lorq nodded, breathed deep. "Katin, Mouse, your job is over. You've got your walking papers. Ships leave here regularly. You shouldn't have any trouble getting on another one."

"Captain," Katin ventured, "what are you going to do?"

"On New Brazillia, there's a home where I spent much pleasant time when I was a boy. I'm going back there ... to wait."

"Isn't there something you could do, Captain? I looked and—"

"What? Speak louder."

"I said, I'm all right, and *I* looked!" Katin's voice broke.

"You looked going away. I looked searching the center. The neural distortion is all the way up into the brain. Neurocongruency." He shook his head. "Mouse, Katin, Ashton Clark to you."

"But Captain—"

"Ashton Clark."

Katin looked at the Mouse, then back at the captain. The Mouse fiddled with the strap of his sack. Then he looked up. After a moment they turned and left the lightless room.

Outside they once more gazed across the moonscape.

"So," Katin mused. "Von Ray has it and Prince and Ruby don't."

"They're dead," the Mouse told him. "Captain said he killed them."

"Oh." Katin looked out on the moonscape. After a while he said: "Seven tons of Illyrion, and the balance begins to shift. Draco is setting as the Pleiades rises. The Outer Colonies are going to go through some changes. Bless Ashton Clark that labor relocation isn't too difficult today. Still, there are going to be problems. Where're Lynceos and Idas?"

"They've already gone. They got a stellar-gram from their brother and they've gone to see him, since they were here in the Outer Colonies."

"Tobias?"

"That's right."

"Poor twins. Poor triplets. When this Illyrion gets out and the change begins ..." Katin snapped his fingers. "No more bliss." He looked up at the sky, nearly bare of stars. "We're at a moment of history, Mouse."

The Mouse scraped wax from his ear with his little finger-nail. His earring glittered. "Yeah. I was thinking that my-self."

"What are you going to do now?"

The Mouse shrugged. "I really don't know. So I asked Tyÿ to give me a Tarot reading."

Katin raised his eyebrows.

"She and Sebastian are downstairs now. Their pets got loose around the bar. Scared everybody half to death and almost broke up the place." He laughed harshly. "You should have seen it. Soon as they get finished calming down the owner, they're coming up to read my cards. I'll probably get another job studding. There's not much reason to think about the mines now." His fingers closed on the leather sack under his arm. "There's still a lot to see, a lot I have to play. Maybe you and me can stick together a while, get on the same ship. You're funny as hell sometimes. But I don't dislike you half as much as I dislike a lot of other people. What are your plans?"

"I haven't really had time to think about them." He slipped his hands beneath his belt and lowered his head.

"What are you doing?"

"Thinking."

"What?"

"That here I am on a perfectly good moon; I've just finished up a job, so I won't have any worries for a while. Why not sit down and get some serious work done on my novel?" He looked up. "But you know, Mouse? I don't really know if I want to write a book."

"Huh?"

"When I was looking at that nova ... no, after it, just before I woke and thought I'd have to spend the rest of my life in blinkers, ear and nose plugs, while I went noisily nuts, I realized how much I hadn't looked at, how much I hadn't listened to, smelled, tasted—how little I knew of those basics of life you have literally at your fingertips. And then Cap-tain—"

"Hell," the Mouse said. With his bare foot he toed dust from his boot. "You're not going to write it after all the work you've already done?"

"Mouse, I'd like to. But I still don't have a subject. And I've just gotten prepared to go out and find one. Right now

I'm just a bright guy with a lot to say and nothing to say it about."

"That's a fink-out," the Mouse grunted. "What about the captain and the *Roc?* And you said you wanted to write about me. Okay, go ahead. And write about you too. Write about the twins. You really think they'd sue you? They'd be tickled pink, both of them. *I* want you to write it, Katin. I might not be able to read it, but I'd sure listen if you read it to me."

"You would?"

"Sure. After all you've put into it this far, if you stopped now, you wouldn't be happy at all."

"Mouse, you tempt me. I've wanted to do nothing else for years." Then Katin laughed. "No, Mouse. I'm too much the thinker still. This last voyage of the *Roc?* I'm too aware of all the archetypical patterns it follows. I can see myself now, turning it into some allegorical Grail quest. That's the only way I could deal with it, hiding all sorts of mystic symbolism in it. Remember all those writers who died before they finished their Grail recountings?"

"Aw, Katin, that's a lot of nonsense. You've got to write it!"

"Nonsense like the Tarot? No, Mouse. I'd fear for my life with such an undertaking." Again he looked over the landscape. The moon, so known to him, for a moment put him at peace with all the unknown beyond. "I want to. I really do. But I'd be fighting a dozen jinxes from the start, Mouse. Maybe I could. But I don't think so. The only way to protect myself from the jinx, I guess, would be to abandon it before I finish the last

Athens, June '66—
New York, May '67

ABOUT THE AUTHOR

"Samuel R. Delany is the most interesting author of science fiction writing in English today," said *The New York Times Book Review*. He was born in New York City in 1942. His acclaimed science fiction novels include *Babel-17* and *The Einstein Intersection*, both winners of the Nebula Award for best science fiction novel. He has also written *Nova, Triton*, the bestselling *Dhalgren* and the Nevèrÿon fantasy series, *Tales of Nevèrÿon, Neveryóna* and *Flight from Nevèrÿon. Stars in My Pocket like Grains of Sand* is the first volume of a science fiction diptych which will conclude with *The Splendor and Misery of Bodies, of Cities,* to be published by Bantam Spectra Books in 1986. Also a critic of science fiction, he has published two essay collections on the field, *The Jewel-Hinged Jaw* and *Starboard Wine,* as well as *The American Shore,* a book-length semiotic study of the science fiction short story "Angouleme" by Thomas M. Disch.